Praise for

"Gorgeous . . . [A] haunting first novel."

—Kate Tuttle, *The Boston Globe*

"A book full of sentences so apt and well wrought, I sometimes had to read them twice . . . I found myself barreling on into the book, eager to find the answers to my questions . . . Whitehouse's prose is pure sparkle."

—Henry Alford, *San Francisco Chronicle*

"A charming debut . . . 'If this is life, then why get out of bed?' Beyond the obvious answer—so that your skin doesn't eventually merge with the linen—the reasons for every reader are blessedly personal."

—*The New York Times Book Review*

"Thoroughly inventive . . . the story courses with bone-dry verse. . . . Nothing here is sacred."

—*The Daily Beast*

"Surreal, farcical, *Bed* works because of Whitehouse's verve and fancy. He appears, right down to the dull thud of his protagonist's name—Mal—dedicated to the idea of being the next Martin Amis."

—*Maclean's*

"Brilliantly imagined and rings consistently true."

—*Daily Mail* (UK)

"The best new novel I've read in ages."

—Sam Delaney, *The Guardian* (UK)

"Sad and funny and pretty brilliant, too."

—*The Observer* (UK)

"Halfway through reading this, I wrote in my notes: 'Best debut novel of the year?' Later, I crossed out the word 'debut' and the question mark."

—*The Sun-Herald* (Australia)

Bed

A Novel

David Whitehouse

Scribner

New York London Toronto Sydney New Delhi

SCRIBNER
A Division of Simon & Schuster, Inc.
1230 Avenue of the Americas
New York, NY 10020

First Scribner trade paperback edition August 2012

For information about special discounts for bulk purchases,
please contact Simon & Schuster Special Sales at
1-866-506-1949 or business@simonandschuster.com.

The Simon & Schuster Speakers Bureau can bring authors to your live event.
For more information or to book an event contact the Simon & Schuster Speakers
Bureau at 1-866-248-3049 or visit our website at www.simonspeakers.com.

Designed by Carla Jayne Jones

Manufactured in the United States of America

1   3   5   7   9   10   8   6   4   2

Library of Congress Control Number: 2011017817

ISBN 978-1-4516-1422-0
ISBN 978-1-4516-1423-7 (pbk)
ISBN 978-1-4516-1424-4 (ebook)

For Mum and Dad. And Rebecca.

One

Asleep he sounds like a pig hunting truffles in soot. It isn't snoring, more of a death rattle. But for that it is a quiet morning, the morning of Day Seven Thousand Four Hundred and Eighty-Three, according to the display on the wall.

The peace is punctuated only by the crashing of a crow into the patio door. This almighty clatter doesn't wake Mal, who continues to produce great growls from deep within his chest. They echo in my ears like the sonar conversations between dolphins and submarines.

Mal weighs a hundred stone, they predicted. That's big. That's more than half a ton. Those photographs you see of whales that have beached and exploded, split by the buildup of gases inside, the thick coating of blubber that blankets the sand, that's what Mal looks like. He has grown and swelled across the bed, two king-size and a single tied together. He has spread out so far from the nucleus of his skeleton, he is an enormous meat duvet.

It has taken him twenty years to become this big. He isn't even the color of skin anymore. Peppered with burst capillaries, a truck-size block of sausage meat packed into a pair of cheap tights. The fat has claimed his toe- and fingernails, his nipples have stretched to the span of a female hand, and only something with the tenacity of a biscuit crumb could meander through the folds of his tummy. There must be enough for a full packet of biscuits in there by now. In twenty years Mal has become a planet with its own uncharted territories. We are the moons, caught in his orbit, Lou and Mum and Dad and me.

I lie in bed next to him, listening to the great honks his lungs make as they work their hardest to fart a little more air from his mouth. Just the dull, constant drone of it, like having your ears packed with wet bread.

Every rise of his chest triggers a seismic shudder through the room. The ripple of his flab sends waves across the puddle of his body. I ride them, nothing to do but stare out over Mal's fleshy expanse, the enormous blistered coffin that trapped my brother inside it, to the garden where I watch the bird coat the glass. Maybe it saw Mal as it flew by and mistook him for an enormous trifle.

Twenty years in bed. Mal's death is the only thing that can save this family because his life has destroyed it. And here I am, at the end, sharing this room with him. The room we began in. Or at least a fraction of it.

Dad told me once, "To love someone is to watch them die."

Two

In the tiny front room of a seaside bed-and-breakfast we were making a scene. The little old lady who had carried our bowls of cornflakes through from the kitchen had thin, yellow skin. She looked as though she were woven from cigarette smoke. Rather than meet Mum's eye, she shuffled cushions she'd already shuffled and pretended to have spilt a drop of ghostly weak tea on the doily that lay across the dresser.

That morning Mal had woken me as he argued with Mum in the doorway of the room that we were sharing. He was naked but not embarrassed by it like other boys his age. Sometimes he wouldn't get dressed for days. Dad would say, "Jesus Christ, Malcolm, will you put some fucking clothes on?" Mal wouldn't reply but Mum would say it didn't matter. Mum. Killing us with her kindness. On occasion Dad would grip Mal under his armpit and drag him to his room, our room. He'd hold him on the bed with one hand on his chest and fold Mal's reluctant little legs into tracksuit bottoms. Mal would resist and Dad would sweat, ordering him to stay there until he could stop acting like "a fucking baby." Mal would jig back in within minutes, his clothes cast across the floor. He looked like a bald baby chicken, skinny arms and corners.

"You're round the fucking hat rack, you," Dad would grumble.

"Please, love, leave him be," Mum would whisper. Mal could do nothing Mum wouldn't forgive. She'd stand between his eccentricities and the world, even as her face pinkened.

"This is why we don't go on bloody holiday, Malcolm!" she yelled. "This is why we're better off at home. Everything is much, much easier at home. Now put some bloody clothes on, we're going to the beach."

"I don't want to go to the beach" was the length of it.

"Then you'll have to have breakfast naked then, won't you?" Mum said.

So we were having breakfast. Not Dad, he'd "gone to put a bet on," he said, though it was probably a lie. And Mal was naked. And he was flicking cereal about the table. And Mum was staring at the old lady pretending to straighten the curtains. And the family at the table next to ours hadn't said a word over their crumpets and orange juice. I leaned over to Mal and whispered, "Why?"

He popped one of those little cartons of milk into his mouth and burst it with his teeth so that it dripped down his chest, and then he shivered because it was as cold as snowman-building fingers.

When Dad arrived back he was still an angry purple, the shade of a kick to the shins. He took one look at Mal, who was busy stirring his tea with a flower from the vase in the center of the table, caught him by the elbow and carried his limp, naked body outside to the car.

Mal went to sleep almost immediately. He slept more than anyone else I knew, but then, I didn't know many people. I didn't even know Mal very well. I listened to Mum and Dad have an argument in which both were fighting for the same thing but neither realized it. Apparently we had to pay for that bed-and-breakfast for the full week even though we'd been there for just two days.

Mal didn't put any clothes on for a fortnight. We never did go to the beach. I didn't mind, it was November.

Three

Dad didn't work, he toiled. That's what he said. Toiling seemed a bit like work except far harder and much less enjoyable. Even the sound was unpleasant. Toil.

He was big, like a robot, like a monster, but he was quiet like neither. His hands were whitened with hardened skin that had buckled and cracked, gloves of used tinfoil, and so when he'd take us fishing I wouldn't hold them except for when we crossed the road. When I did they had the power in them to crush mine like you'd grip and smash the head of a frozen rose.

Mal, on the other side, would embed his hand in Dad's rough palm and be guided down the path by it, chirping and fidgeting, a Mexican jumping bean boy.

Dad would shout "hurry up" and I'd follow their meshed shadow all the way to the canal. He'd slip a maggot into his mouth, loll it under his tongue and grin, the one trick of an old dog, and amaze Mal over and over again. I'd seen it once, it was enough. Then they would talk, Dad filling Mal's head with infinite possibilities. Suggestions, things to make and do. He'd tell us all about the world, promote it and intrigue us. The controller and the fantasist, harmonious fact and fiction on the slippery bank. I hated fishing, it was just waiting in mud. I couldn't wait to go home to Mum. None of us could, really.

Four

Mal liked to be the first person to do things. Not just the first person in the house, or the first person in his class, but the first person in the entire world. There is a limit to the things you can be first to do when you are a child. He used to ask, "Has anyone ever . . . ?" Mum would say yes, if only to stop him trying to walk across the bottom of the sea. She learned this lesson on a rare occasion when she chose not to listen to him. Five hours after she had palmed him off with an absentminded "no," the policeman that came to placate her worst fears spotted Mal naked on the roof, clinging to the television aerial. It was the middle of the summer. The fire brigade came and carried him down, much against his will. I'd hoped they'd have to shoot him with a tranquilizer dart like a bear that needed urgent medical attention, and that he might roll all the way off and land in a dustbin.

Soon, to limit the chances of him presenting himself to danger, Mum hit upon the idea of speech. She told Mal that there were almost infinite combinations of words that, if you were to string them together, you would almost certainly be the first person to have uttered them in that order. For six months Mal would bark endlessly unintelligible chains of words just to be the first that ever had. Most came from a dictionary, he didn't need to know what they meant.

"Disbelieving diagnosis ferocious atrocious hegemony telephony gripe, never never never, eat fruit until it's ripe."

"Pinecone overthrown on the throne phone home moan drone blown bone time lime zone, oh my haven't you grown."

It pleased her. Mal always gave, but in his own way.

Her devotion was a blanket that smothered but was warm nonetheless. Her life had been sacrificed for the bettering of those around her. In another time, with a candle, a billowing blue dress and a ferocious war fought on a smoky field, she would have been the most popular nurse with every doomed soldier that passed through her charge. But instead she was born to us: her mum, who I could barely remember; Dad; Mal. She'd swung between them on vines, tending them, loving them, leaving with nothing for herself. And now that her mother was dead, and Dad had begun to retreat, to Mal she had devoted herself fully. She knew how to do nothing else.

Five

We were at school when Lou came into our lives.

On those days when it rained for so long that the drains disappeared under puddles, the children were beckoned inside by the teachers. It was with some reluctance that they abandoned the precious fixes that would see them through double maths. But this was the protocol when it was wet: a break time spent watching the louder children carving abuse about the quieter ones in the condensation on the windows.

It was usually about Mal. His refusal to involve himself in the transient social systems of school meant that many a rainy day could be spent watching the words "Mal Ede is a weirdo" run down the glass.

He never even noticed. He didn't care what they thought and they envied that in him. But just as they failed to understand it, Lou understood it completely. I saw it on her face that day, a look like her heart would float upward through her throat, topple from her mouth, clip her front teeth on the way out and drift into the sky. It wasn't love, nor lust, she was too young. But it was something, a seed of a seed that would become something one day.

That day she sat inside the classroom and squeaked her hand across the window to clear a looking glass. The rain drummed down with such ferocity that the droplets smashing into the floor made the tarmac of the playground look like it was boiling. She cupped her hands into the shape of binoculars and pressed them to the pane. Through the dark and wet she saw the shadow of a solitary figure.

Mal. His head tipped back, his mouth wide open and welling up with rainwater that cascaded down the sides of his face, up his nose and filled his eyes. Saturated, his hair made locks of thick dripping slugs, his crisp white school shirt transparent. As Mal regularly refused to reply to his own name when the register was read out, not a single figure of authority had noticed his absence. In fact, the only person in the world thinking about Mal at that one moment in time was Lou.

She watched as the wind propelled the rain against his back. She banged her tiny porcelain hands upon the glass but he couldn't hear her. She rushed back to her chair whenever a teacher or one of those louder boys came by so that Mal would not be noticed by anyone else. And eventually, after more than half an hour, she crept out from the classroom into the hall. Ducking behind a stacked wall of plastic chairs, she meandered through their web of black legs until she reached the far end. There she crouched until the last of the teachers turned quickly into the staff room before tiptoeing quietly across the slippery tiled floors and into the girls' changing rooms. Lou hid behind the door of the lost-property closet until it was safe to emerge, opened the one window that would lead out onto the playground and gently slipped her legs out of it. Unseen she dangled there, half in the rain with her skirt pulled up over her shoulders and her buttocks grazing against the rough edges of the brick wall before struggling free and landing on her bottom in a puddle.

She rubbed her eyes and licked her lips. Tasted like mud.

Picking herself up with a shiver as those first few drops of icy rainwater chased each other down the length of her spine, she walked slowly toward him. She slid her fingers around his and stood there, the two of them side by side, as the beating sheets of rain threatened to dissolve them completely. Mal remained with his face to the sky, clasping her hand in his for fifteen minutes until, as quickly as it had begun, the downpour finished. He released her from his grip and without speaking a word walked quickly back into the building, where he marched straight to the office of the headmaster and demanded to have a lesson on the subject of rain, before passing out on the carpet.

"Excuse me, you're Malcolm Ede's brother?" Lou asked me later that day as I walked home. Her voice and her words hung together in the air like the music of a freshly tickled wind chime.

"Yes, I am," I said. She looked soft.

"My name is Lou," she said.

She touched my arm and she gave me a letter to give to Mal, in a sealed yellow envelope tackily furnished with a single pressing of puckered lips generously coated in thick helpings of bright red lipstick. They were not her lips, for they were not pretty enough, I was almost sure of that. A friend had done it for her. She'd touched my arm.

I pushed the letter into the depths of my tatty hand-me-down schoolbag and ran home at speed; the brief experience of something new, something good, licked lovingly but briefly at my soul.

Six

The pneumonia that resulted cast Mal into the colorful purgatory of the children's ward. Antibiotics and cartoons. The drip feeding him with moisture through the vein that joined the two thin strips of arm on either side of a knobbly elbow saw the disease off soon enough. Pneumonia had torn through him and departed, a viral freight train. Mum was furious.

Visiting hours were 6 to 8 p.m. but on the one occasion I was allowed to come along we arrived half an hour early. I followed Mum and Dad slowly through beige halls with shiny floors. Porters wheeled the oldest people I'd ever seen into elevators on trolleys in much the same manner they loaded silver-boxed meals into massive ovens in the kitchens downstairs.

Soon we came to the wards, doors open. Old men in pajamas, four to a room, too ill for camaraderie, done for. An old lady crying, a massive pot of sweets untouched but for visiting nieces. The smell of clean hands.

I was wondering what wearing an oxygen mask tastes like when I walked straight into the back of Dad's leg, his thigh a cart horse knocking me to the ground. He lifted me by the neck, bitch to a puppy. He had serious eyes and a finger jab because here the building has authority. No speaking, he warns me, no staring, I knew. Like library rules. Like swimming pool rules. I'd never learned to swim.

We found Mal propped up in bed reading a brightly colored

comic and laughing, spliced with a dogged cough. Pleasantries first. How are you today? What did they give you for dinner? Have you made friends with any of the other boys?

"What were you doing out in the rain?" I whispered.

"Seeing how wet I could get," he said.

Mum unloaded a small bag full of toys onto the bedside table and around his feet and we talked about getting well and bravery while he wrestled them free from tight plastic cases. He whined when I touched them. I clung to the arm of a plastic fighting man, just gently between two fingers and a thumb, just to hold it, and he snatched it from me, knocking the table with his elbow and scattering a precarious LEGO wall across the sparkly tiles.

A woman who had shut her own son's hand in the kitchen door that morning and watched as he had two fingers removed that afternoon sucked air through her teeth in disgust. I saw Dad rise, inside and out. He gripped me by the forearm and pulled me toward the door. My jumper stuck to me. My sudden temperature made the wet wool around the neck of it mash the tears colder against my cheeks. Dad slapped the back of my legs and swore and spat,

"Go and wait in the car."

So I did. I was a rolled-up wire ball.

By the time we were on our way home it was too late to make anything to eat. For my birthday meal we had fish and chips in silence.

Lou's love letter, or Malcolm Ede's first-ever piece of fan mail, was pushed into the bottom of the bin when I got in. It was purposely pressed into the rotting meat and bones at the bottom, soaking up the unloved juices of that evening's meal. But not before I pressed it to my own cod-spiced lips just in case.

Seven

With Mal still in the hospital the house stagnated. The colors grew duller, the time would grind, and right from Wednesday onward I dreaded Sunday afternoon. Sundays were merciless. The sofa would hold me down and let the dark get in, and we'd sit in the living room together. On Sundays it felt as though the whole family was breathing in unison, slowly, slower and slower until the evening when we'd fester around the television and fight sleep until it won. The minute I awoke that morning I prayed the day would be over at double speed.

Through the wall was the smell of breakfast and a muffled argument. Mum and Dad, another waste of time. The plaster it passed through shaved the edges off the sounds until they were rendered underwater mumbles. As they raised their voices higher they grew clearer still but I wanted to listen less and less and I tried to stop my brain from translating the sounds as they arrived to me by caking my ears in the soft parcel of my pillow.

"Akeimithoo," said Mum.

"Eedussnikeit," said Dad.

And the day and the context and the worst possible outcome filled my head until it tuned itself in like a radio and I could hear them perfectly.

"Take him with you," says Mum.

"He doesn't like it," says Dad.

Fishing. We were going fishing. I would only hold his hand to cross the road. Mum made me a packed lunch. There were cheese sandwiches and a chocolate bar, a carton of orange juice that needed piercing with a straw and piece of birthday cake, nothing special, just sponge. I ate it in the car on the way and it soaked up the boredom temporarily.

Once we'd arrived, Dad unpacked the trunk in silence while I held the rods. Men who might be friends of his passed and grunted. I worried that I had nothing to talk to him about.

We pitched up on the bank. The thick slops of mud foamed through the gaps in the soles of my Wellington boots. With our lines troubling the flat, brown surface of the canal we picked midges off our lips and flapped them from our eyes. The need for him to speak filled the silence. It made me ache. Litter floated past.

And then he told me a story. It was the most I'd ever heard him say, and it was because Mal wasn't there. It was just me and Dad, and the gap between us where the bridge should be. He didn't know how to build it, but he wanted to try, and the aching stopped for a time. The story was about work. About toil. It had grown inside him so much I was surprised it hadn't torn through his skin and clothes.

Eight

Dad said, "Imagine if you had a photograph of every important thing that has happened in your life. Your first child. Your wedding. A death in the family. Your first job. A car crash. The day you were ill. The night you won a competition. The time you lost a race. Everything.

"Imagine that you carried them in your pocket. Imagine that, depending upon the importance of the event in the picture, the lighter or heavier the photograph became. The heavier the photograph, the bigger the event. Eventually some of the photographs become so light that you don't even realize you never look at them anymore, they just fall out of your pocket and disappear for ever. But one photograph, one of them, will get heavier and heavier, and you'll never lose it, never. One of them you'll always keep, and it will weigh you down until it becomes so heavy that when you think about it, it feels as though your heart is being dragged across the floor. And you'll never be able to pick it up again. This is what happens when you get older. You lose all of your photographs, they become light, they become air, they become indistinguishable from dreams you had and places you imagined. But you can never get rid of the heaviest. My photograph is of TauTona."

The line twitched in the water and Dad didn't notice.

"Before you were born I worked at TauTona. It means 'Great Lion,' they told me. It's a mine in South Africa, just west of Johannesburg. At its deepest it's three and a half kilometers underground. Do you know how deep that is? That's very deep. That's one of the deepest mines in the world. Few people in history have been deeper inside the earth than the men who have been down TauTona. And they go there to collect gold. They dig it out and they bring it back up and it gets sold so that people can wear jewelry and be rich. And it was my job to get them down there safely. It was my job to oversee the building of the cages and lifts that lowered those miners deep down into the earth, deeper than the weight of the world and everything on it.

"It would take one hour to get to where you are going if you were a miner in that lift. That's the descent, and then the long walk to the face of the mine, which, if you're with a good group of miners, gets further every day. Further and deeper and darker, gold doesn't glisten underground.

"That lift drops at sixteen meters a second. A double-decker bus in the blink of an eye. Can you imagine that? That's fast. That's really fast. And I helped to build those lifts. I was there when they were installed. I stayed there for six months. Teaching miners to use them and to maintain them, to make sure nothing went wrong.

"That's what I did, you see. I made lifts. Pulleys and chains and cogs, shafts and drives. The expertise and engineering that goes into the vertical transportation of people. The physics and mathematics of figuring out what force is required to lift what weight what distance. Working within limited space to build a machine that will change lives. That's what I did."

I'd never asked him what he did.

"And it failed one day at TauTona," he said. "One day it all went wrong.

"I'd just finished work. It was my last week in South Africa. I couldn't wait to see your mother, we were very close back then. Before Malcolm. I was maybe half a mile away from the top of the shaft, but I heard it give way. The entire structure we'd created, an immovable force, bent and twisted. Sounded like two trucks meeting head-on, a great metallic roar. A freak occurrence, that's all.

"There were sixteen men in that lift as it plummeted toward the center of the earth. Doctors told me that the force of the fall would have ensured that they were unconscious by the time they hit the bottom. They'd have become five, maybe six times their own body weight. They would never have stood a chance.

"It took ten days to reach them using the parallel emergency shaft we'd built alongside it. Ten days. Of course, we knew they would be dead. When we got there, those sixteen men fitted into an eight-inch gap between the floor of that elevator and the roof. They had been packed into their hard hats. Completely crushed upon landing. There was nothing to rescue, no one to save. We couldn't even bring mementoes for their wives who'd held vigils on the surface since news of the accident first spread. All they really wanted of course was answers, just something, a word or a line for their grief. But I had nothing. See, we didn't know why it had happened. We had no idea why that lift fell with those men inside it, it just did. We blamed ourselves, everyone blamed themselves. But the truth is that I don't know. I don't know if it was my fault. I'll never know.

"See, whichever photograph is the heaviest in the end, that's your legacy. That's what you leave behind. Question is, do you have time to change it? Or do you avoid ever having one at all?"

We caught no fish that day. On the way home we picked Mum up to go to the supermarket, where we bought rich foods to eat to celebrate Mal's return—she loved to feed us—and where Mum would let me think I was in control of the shopping trolley even though I wasn't because she knew it made me happy. She climbed into the car and kissed Dad on the cheek. He kissed her back and smiled. I saw then that we weren't three people who didn't know each other, we just acted like it.

Nine

When Mal returned from the hospital the dynamic shifted to where it had always been, with him as the focal point. His absence had yanked a wheel from the cart and we'd all gotten out to push. With him back, we could all slot neatly into our seats. Things, for a while at least, were normal. Dad was being quiet again.

On the eighth floor of the biggest department store in town we were causing a fuss. Elderly shoppers with a need to concern themselves in matters not of their concern poured scorn from the far end of aisles of soft furnishings. Assistants shuffled shelf stackings and pondered intervening, but none of them ever did. Instead they looked on as Mal and I bounced on brand-new beds still wrapped in plastic sheeting. We'd take turns hiding deep inside piles made of beanbags and cushions, or to toss crisp white sheets across each other's heads, snow in make-believe winter ambushes. This is what Saturday morning always felt like when we were young and together.

Dad would drive us into town nice and early, before the crowds arrived. I knew it was a special occasion, despite its regularity, because Mal would always be dressed when it came time to leave. We'd clamber into the backseat and wave at Mum through the rear window as she stood in the kitchen. She only ever came with us once, and it ended in a row about the color of lino. It didn't really seem worth it after that. Her presence was replaced by the introduction of the shopping list she had written out the night before.

Dad would approach it with military precision to minimize the time spent walking from shop to shop whilst achieving each objective. Once he felt we were suitably trained in this area he'd simply hand the list to Mal, who would take great pride in figuring out what the shortest possible route through town would be, depending upon whether we needed apples, or lightbulbs, or flour, or whatever whim constituted a bargain. On the way home he'd try to figure out the longest route possible too.

This routine allowed us more time for Dad to indulge himself in the only thing he appeared to truly enjoy. Well, there was fishing, but no one enjoyed fishing really.

Ellis's store felt bigger than real life. What it didn't sell, you didn't need. It had men standing at the revolving front doors who were resplendent in red overcoats and black peaked caps. They looked like the soldiers that guard the entrance to a cuckoo clock. Once inside, each of its eight vast floors was a trove of goods lit so brightly that it was impossible to cast a shadow in any direction. Purple velvet ropes trimmed with shiny silver buckles formed cordons around anything that wouldn't survive an errant elbow. I used to think they had been put in place for Mal alone, who often destroyed things of value.

Past the gadgetry and through the food hall we'd march in Dad's tow until we reached our destination, where a rare smile pulled his face taut. Tucked away in the far corner of the store, between the barbecue sets and the heavy-duty garden tools that we pretended were space weapons from the future, were a small set of brass-covered doors so polished and shiny that they caught all who stared into them as a golden sepia photograph. Behind them was one of the oldest lifts in the country.

We'd edge gently inside once it had obeyed our calling, which it always did immediately because, as Dad would suggest, we were the only ones that knew of it. It was always there to greet us on the ground. Inside it was only big enough for two adults, or one adult and two children, a formula that still resulted in Mal or me being tightly packed against Dad's legs. Once the doors had closed behind us the light was that of dawn. It bounced from the reflective silver walls and circled the brass that held the big black buttons in place, playing tricks on your eyes, taking them back in time, making them feel sleepy and warm.

"A feat, boys, of modern engineering," Dad would whisper before lifting one of us from the floor, whoever's turn it happened to be, to the height of the biggest button of all, the one numbered 8. With a clunk and a whir the levers and ropes would gradually fall into place and our ascent would begin. It was fast enough to feel that we were moving but slow enough so as to never know how far we had left to travel. The slightest movement would rock it from side to side and we'd shuffle our weight across it to test the patience of the machine. I worried that those ropes might give way. I imagined the heavy box they carried slipping from their grasp as easily as one might grip a dead pheasant by its foot and tug the cartilage out from the skin that encased its leg. I'd grasp Dad by the knee until the fear passed and he'd place one of his big, rough hands on the back of my head. I'd hear him say "Safest machine in the world, this," though he hadn't even moved his mouth.

At the summit the doors would open slowly and we'd burst from our secret capsule out into the store, greyhounds with a whiff of rabbit, and Dad would tell us off again.

Ten

It was sticky, midsummer, the night before we were due to go on holiday, and we'd both been sent out for the afternoon so that Mum could pack. Not by Mum; she preferred us to stay in. Small flies crawled all over my white T-shirt in one-winged disabled circles and wasps begged at the lip of my drink. We walked for a long time up and down our street, and came to rest on a small wall at the end of it, our energy sapped by the heat. He sat there in the full blast of the sun. I stooped behind him, contorting to fit the shade.

A flash, then gone. Then a face I see, then gone again. I spotted Lou, peering at us, at Mal, from behind the wall of the shop on the corner. Her head bobbed in and out in bursts, followed quickly by that of a friend, and behind that shelter I imagined them giggling.

I pretended not to have noticed for fear that she'd come over to talk to us and Mal wouldn't say anything, instead leaving it to me, and I'd be stuck, I'd have no words, and I'd melt in the heat and she'd be standing hands on hips looking down into the splash of goo where I once was.

Though he wasn't popular amongst the boys, he was amongst the girls, as popular as thirteen-year-olds can be. Where the rest of us were skinny, just ribs draped in wisp, his body was constructed from muscle, every inch of it solid. He carried himself with a poise I'd never manage.

He was good-looking too, unconventionally so, which is the best type of good-looking. Girls liked his chin, and his hair, black and curly, just fell like that. For the same reason, boys hated his chin. And his hair and the way it just fell like that. He was enigmatic. Not to me, to others. He had the right posture, a walk, a way. He just worked. Next to him I looked like I was assembled in the dark from spare parts. Most people knew me as Malcolm Ede's brother. They'd call it, I'd wave and tell them where he was if I knew.

His idiosyncrasies amplified his achievements. When he swam it seemed he swam further than anyone else. An outsider on his own terms, he was free to build his own rules around him, rules no one but him could even hope to understand. Not even me. I was carried in his slipstream, the fluff that blows in through the smallest crack in the doorway if you close it quickly enough.

It felt as though this was his day, and that he didn't want it to end. As if he knew that growing up was dying, not death itself.

Eleven

In the check-in area of Heathrow Airport the airline staff were whispering mangled panicked instructions through dated radios. Which queue? How long? Just calm down, sir, you will make your plane.

Only Dad had flown before, only to unimaginable South Africa and only to return a different man. The routine of air travel, the hurried banality of it, was as alien to us as climbing stairs in preparation for sleep. To Mal, on all fours, the snaking queues were a maze of trees with trunks of legs to traverse. I sat on our suitcase listening to Dad espouse the benefits of a southern Spanish summer. Mum had glazed over, so rapt was she at the idea of stepping from a plane onto foreign soil. In her head it was with dainty ankle, the camera panning up slowly to reveal a wonderful Christian Dior dress in emerald green and half a million pounds' worth of diamonds dripping from a silver chain around an elegant neck, like a starlet to the red carpet of a film premiere. She was so engrossed that she didn't notice the tuts of disapproval being made by the two old ladies behind us in the queue, the whirr of insects in the reeds. Slowly the unrest spread backward down the line until a curt man with damp circles the size of pie tins under his arms approached. He placed a firm hand on Mum's shoulder like one might grip the throttle of a motorbike and registered the unanimous unhappiness of the stony-faced assembly.

"If you cannot control your son," he said, in a way fear dictated he couldn't to a man whose neck was as thick on shoulders quite as wide as Dad's, "then perhaps someone else should." In his hand hung one of Mal's socks.

Our eyes followed the trail of Mal's clothing across the cold marble flooring of the terminal. A sock, trousers that would no doubt soon become mine, two shoes and a T-shirt formed a ragged pathway that led toward the conveyor belt carrying the luggage to the plane. Our eyes reached the thick black flaps of vinyl that formed the doorway just as Mal disappeared through them, flinging his underpants onto the head of the only security guard that had managed to get within ten feet of him with the studied panache of James Bond tossing his bowler hat at the rack in Miss Money-penny's office.

If Mal was to become the first person checked onto a flight as luggage, it wouldn't be today.

We missed our plane. I had been looking forward to seeing how big it was.

Twelve

We screeched into the driveway, where Dad got out of the car and slammed the door loud behind him. This awoke Mal next to me in the back, a wrapped tortilla in a red blanket with badly crocheted pictures of sheep all over it. His clothes nestled in the footwell.

Mum twisted in the passenger seat. It creaked and she blushed. "Malcolm, I think you should go and talk to your father."

Mal slowly climbed out of the car, leaving the blanket on the seat, and walked naked to the front door in full view of the neighbors.

Mum sat quietly for a moment. I watched the reflection of her face in the rearview mirror. The corners of her lips trembled. They made great efforts to leap to the bottom of her chin. Her brow was a concertina, her eyes and nose a-glisten. I laid my fingers on her shoulder gently. Seeing her upset made my lungs shrivel to the size of fists. I took tiny baby breaths so as not to cry. I didn't want to cry in front of her. And when I felt like this I hated Mal. There was such joy in his giving that it was an agony when he took away.

"He's a lot like your father, you know."

She spoke in tones a semi-octave too high. The tears fell from her eyes into the corners of her mouth. Her face wore watery braces. "He can't always get what his imagination wants. That's how life works though. That's how life works."

"Shall I help you tidy up, Mum?" I asked.

If Mal was like dad, I was like her. I was a pleaser. That was where I fitted in.

"Yes," she said, "that would be nice."

Inside the house I took the spray from under the kitchen sink, which was well stocked in neon products with loud names, the forbidden Las Vegas of the cupboards. I removed a yellow duster from the drawer and began to dust the surfaces of the furniture in the living room. Mum's favorite object was a fold-down bureau. It had been made during the war, when all the good material had been saved for use in the war effort, and as such was purely functional. It reminded me of her.

I dusted the skirting boards on my hands and knees, speeding around the floor. I was not doing the job properly but being seen to do the job. At the oven I stirred the mixture and partook of the intense sugary high from licking the bowl clean of the fluffy chocolate mixture. I helped unpack the cases, hung the coats and tidied the shoes. And Mal sat in the bedroom with Dad, their chatter inaudible even to my prying ear at the door, though they were definitely talking because the air had that whistle and fizz of silence with something else in it.

It was my holiday too, ruined. When tiredness took me I seethed and cried, shouted and kicked, and Mum held my head in the warm plate of her lap until I slept. My anger, though, was everything. It made my eyes heat up even when they were closed. It wasn't often that Mum and I were alone. Her gaze felt good. To gaze upon us made her happy, to be our one, our woman. She would have despaired to know how little time was left with things remaining as they were.

Thirteen

That same night was warm and prickly, so Mal and I erected a small green tent in the garden. It was old, Dad had first used it in South Africa, and when you tugged loose the drawstrings of the bag it kicked out a moth-eaten funk that tasted like old dust and made your whole face pucker. The groundsheet had long since rotted to tatters, so we took a gingham picnic blanket from the posh hamper Mum won in a raffle and never used. We flapped it in the air before laying it flat and inviting on the grass.

Like the house the garden was small, and surrounded by other small gardens attached to small houses. We were to whisper because even the slightest rise in the volume would guarantee the complaints of Mrs. Gee.

Mrs. Gee lived in the bungalow next door. If you were to shave it, her head would have been perfectly spherical. With it sat atop her rotund midriff she took on the silhouette of a cartoon snowman. Barely five feet tall, you'd see her in the summer shuffling about the garden, her feet never leaving the floor. The constant *tch tch tch* of her slippers grazing the path served as warning she was coming and meant it was time to dash inside. She wore stretchy dresses that hugged her lumps, the only things that ever held her.

Now in her seventies, she'd lived alone for more than half a century, polishing the taps, feeding the cats. Dad told me she'd been married to a postman on her seventeenth birthday, but that he'd left her that very night when she'd refused to consummate the relationship.

"She'd been returned unopened."

This evening Mal and I hid behind the relative sanctity of the tent's damp canvas wall and spied her shadow in the yard. *Tch tch tch*. She stood motionless, watching the clouds cut across the sky with sourness daubed on her face, sucking on a piss-washed thistle. It seemed she was angry at them for being late, or at the sky for hanging high. Curved bones hunched her shoulders upward to buffer her neck. Her hands were permanently fists. The world was ignoring her until she disappeared. She was one of those people. So we ignored her until she disappeared. *Tch tch tch. Tch tch tch.* Gone.

We clicked our torches on and hung them from the dented metal bar that formed the tent's spine. Neither of us was cold or tired enough to climb inside our sleeping bags, so we lay atop them and the cheap polyester gripped sticky to our skin. We played travel versions of popular games. We didn't have the full versions. We never really traveled.

"Oh." I flinched.

We'd been playing the game for over an hour. I had pins and needles invading my left leg through my big toe and I'd slobbered down my right arm where I'd propped my sleepy head upon it.

"I forgot to tell Mum, at school, they are going to give me trumpet lessons."

"Tell her tomorrow."

"I'll tell her now," I insisted.

I got up slowly and unzipped the tent.

"Play another game of Connect Four," he moaned.

"I won't be long. And I'll get us something to eat, crisps or biscuits or something."

I gently pushed open the back door and made my way through the kitchen, which shone with after-dinner soap suds snail-trekking

Bed 29

their way down clean pots. In the living room the curtains, heavy and old in thick purple felt, were open so as to be able to watch us and the TV-chanted quiz-show mantra. Host says catchphrase, audience replies. Mum and Dad loved but were not united by it, each of them sitting on opposite sides of the room, communicating in random but perfectly understood hand signals.

Turn it up a bit.

Turn it down a bit.

Thingy is on the other side.

What's this?

What was she in?

Is that him from . . . ?

Then they were watching Ray Darling. Newscaster Ray Darling reporting on the issues of the day, his charm tinged with a great unease, his hair a surreal thatch atop the crescent of his powdery face. Dad ticked with frustration as he watched. He had never liked Ray Darling, and by association neither had I. His scripted authority, his wavering interview technique, his flirtation with the poor weather girl. His reek was one of a man petrified of being found out.

Sometimes I suspected Mum and Dad only loved each other during the advert breaks. I waited for one for fifteen minutes. Neither acknowledged me but both knew I was there. Like being on hold.

I returned to the tent. Malcolm was asleep.

Fourteen

"We just have to visit some people, so get up, please."

I was in bed with just a sleepy recollection of Dad bringing us in from the garden. I wasn't sure it still counted as camping.

Visiting people is what Mum called it when she took Mal to see specialists. Behavioral experts they called themselves. We'd get the bus into town, just like on Saturday mornings when the market filled the thin street with the smell of pungent cheeses and men shouting the names and prices of fruit. Bath Sunday nights. Eating fish on a Friday. Bus to town on Saturday morning and home again, carrier bags brimming so heavily with groceries that the handles of them stretched, turned to plastic wires and garroted the palms of children. These were our rituals, the hoops we jumped through.

It was the first day of half-term, and the thought of not returning to school for another week made me feel reborn in an explosion. I slipped both legs from the side of the bed, used my toes to detect whatever I had discarded the night before and climbed quite willingly into yesterday's clothes. Only then did I turn to face Mal.

Sharing a bedroom with him divided me. I'd lie there sometimes, at the end of a happy normal day, and think about how everyone would like to share a room with someone like Mal. Those were the days when I liked him, loved him. Those were most days. Normal days full of nothing unusual. And then sometimes I would loathe it. I'd imagine hitting him as he slept and it would keep me awake, watching him, hearing him, the days when what he did ruined everything. I couldn't wait to be able to escape.

"You have to get up," I said.

He ignored me and turned to face the window. Propped up on one elbow he roughly fluffed his pillow and then pulled it down on top of his head. Any amount of reluctance to do something meant that Mal simply wouldn't get dressed. His nudity, by now, was an embarrassment for everybody but him. What little charm there was in his tendency to disrobe had lain in his choice of occasion but now, now that he was hairy and real, there was no charm at all. If you're naked and an adult, you don't have to leave the house.

I looked at him. His skin glowed a healthy pine. I thought about the time when he was nine and I was seven, and as was the tradition at Christmas up until that point and never again, Mum took us to see a pantomime. Being in the theater felt like being inside a really expensive chocolate box from Belgium, reds and golds and layers of people lining the walls, looking like it could all collapse in one big bite. I'd glanced across Mum's lap at Mal as the lights went down and we were greeted onstage by the forgettable faces of actors too creepy to be dressed as women. I sang and I clapped and I shouted when you were supposed to but in the dark Mal sat silently. No one looked at him but me. I watched him as he slowly moved a hand toward his ankle, hooked a thumb inside his sock and peeled it off with fluid ease. Then the other. As Mum wondered where she'd seen the buxom young woman playing the naive young boy before, Mal balled the socks together. He discreetly dropped them on the floor and let them roll under the seat of the elderly man in front of him. Carefully he wriggled free of his jeans and underpants at the same time, like a butterfly emerging from its yawning cocoon. His best shoes rocked upturned on the floor. Pulling it by the neck, he slid quietly through his cherry-red jumper until, unnoticed, nothing but his lithe torso, bare and unblemished, sat in the chair.

My heart was sagging and scratching the bottom of its case. I was shackled.

Suddenly, the big denouement, where the girl dressed as a boy and the boy dressed as an elf fall in love. The lights came up, the audience was invited to sing. And there is Mal, standing on his chair, naked. He sang.

Mum was stone. I crawled under my seat.

People around us made stunned sounds, a surprise so large it forced noise from within them. *Make it end. Make it end.* The elderly man went to grab Mal's leg, disgusted at his behavior and Mum's inability to do anything about it, but Mal skipped free. And he continued to sing. The big chorus, second verse. He hopped into the aisle and danced along it. All eyes on Malcolm Ede, two shows in the room, one entry price. Women Mum's age jabbed each other in the side and pointed and scorned and tarnished reputations. Men tried to catch him. I cried until we were ejected, Mum scattering "sorry sorry sorry" in our wake.

By the time I'd finished breakfast, toast because there's nothing else in until the weekend, Mum finally had Mal dressed. We walked to the bus stop. We didn't hold hands anymore. I only noticed then.

Fifteen

We waited in the waiting room. When Mum and Mal were called through into the office, I sneaked a glimpse inside it. It was brown and leathery and reminded me of Sherlock Holmes. A miserable-looking spider plant guarded brassy ornaments that hummed with the smell of polish. There were anatomically correct pictures of children on the wall and frosted glass with writing built into the top of the door. It shook as the important-looking man with the moustache slammed it behind him and continued to vibrate like it had eaten Mum and Mal and was chewing them up into a paste, ready to spit them back out at me.

I moved to the corner of the room, where the chairs lining the longest two walls meet in a pile of toys haphazardly plonked there to stave off tantrums. I dug through them briefly, conscious not to show too much enthusiasm for anything I found that was actually meant for really young children, and eventually settled on a yo-yo, only to discover it had no string. And the remote-control car without the remote. And the plastic woman with the snap in her leg that births a shard so sharp you could cut your own throat with it. Broken toys for broken children. I took a magazine that was three years old, torn and faded, and pretended to read it with it right up in front of my face, like the spies in cartoons who have eyeholes through which to study their prey. I peered through the slit by the staple in the centerfold to see what Mal's up against.

There were three other children with three other mums, six sets of eyes wishing they were home. One of them, a young girl with jam smeared into the feathered ends of her hair, rested her head in her mother's bosom and wept the entire time. A boy whose badge said "I AM 8" stared at a yellowing stain on the wall as though he could see the individual atoms swirling through the air the way a bag does in the wind. He was white like milk, topped with bright blond hair and eyes the size of golf balls that a cough could unlodge. His mum ignored him. The third boy was called Ron. As in: "Sit down, Ron!," "Calm down, Ron!," "Be good, Ronald, please be good!" His mother twisted the skin of her own hands as the invisible ants amassed between her fingers. Her shape was rigid, her shoulders great knots and her brain a tug-of-war.

Be Good Ronald was smashing through the pile of toys. He stamped on them, bringing his feet up and marching like a victorious general celebrating the end of a great bloody battle by walking across the broken bones of his enemies. He took the big red fire truck with the little firemen inside long since lost in his chubby little hands, hoisted it above his head and brought it down hard on the floor, where it shattered. His cheeks bunched with delight. His mother mapped her face with her trembling fingers. And then Ronald, naughty little Be Good Ron, took the sharply pointed edge of a small yellow fence that had been attached to an animal-free plastic farmyard and slammed it down into my thigh with astonishing force. It punctured my trousers, lacerated my flesh and drew blood with it as he pulled it back out. I tried not to cry. I held the old magazine up in front of my face just in case, the redundant TV listings hovering inches from my nose. Ronald's mum scooped him from the floor by his arm and struck his behind, leaving a distinct sweaty print on his cheap shiny trousers. He yelled that he did nothing wrong, the little liar, as I carefully slid my hand over the spreading rose-shaped patch on my leg. She dragged him outside, the two of them in tears, and I hoped she'd push him down the stairs.

In the waiting room for children with problems, I was bleeding out of my leg. I was the child, that was the problem.

The big door opened and Mal bounded out, followed by Mum and the doctor, ten pens peeking over the lip of his starched pocket.

When we got home I slung my trousers straight into the washing machine and sat in my underpants on the bed, picking at the nick of skin on my thigh for hours. Then Mal came in to fetch me. I looked down and it had started bleeding again.

"Come in here," he said. "Come and meet my girlfriend."

Sixteen

She was coming through the door and Mum was clapping seal hands, a smile on her face so big her teeth were trying to escape it. Dad, not a man who let his emotions betray him, had risen to his feet in honor of the fact. Mal shut the front door behind them and the grin on his face when he saw Mum's reaction circumnavigated his features. The chemical in my brain that brought jealousy with it had flooded its little storage tank and was flushing around the space between my skeleton and my skin.

"Mum, Dad, this is Lou."

And it was eroding my bones.

In the melee of meet-and-greet, I sat back and watched. It wasn't that she was a girl. It wasn't that she was pretty, which she undoubtedly was. It was that she was with Mal. Not that their relationship was a close personal one, they were teenagers, and that Mal and I shared a bedroom would scupper any plans for pubescent romance before they had even formulated. It was that she was drawn to him the way people were. It was the way he paraded her for Mum's approval, like it was the opening night of his own exhibition. It was the idea of it. I could see what she liked in him. She didn't know what a tyrant he could be. I did, though still what good there was shone through brightest. But I'd never take my clothes off in the supermarket.

I took boundless delight in the awkwardness that ensued.

Mum flapped and squawked, a wild bird trapped in a chimney breast.

"Tea?"

"Comfortable there?"

"Too hot? Too cold then?"

Dad hopped from one foot to the other, peddling small talk. Mum plied Lou with biscuits and questions. I saw Mal's teeth grinding, boats on icebergs, back and forth back and forth.

"So are you at Malcolm's school?"

I loved it when she called him Malcolm. It made his lip curl and his eyes squeeze.

"Yes," said Lou.

"That's nice," said Mum.

Lou absentmindedly brushed the crumbs from the hammock her dress made between her thighs down onto the floor. Realizing her error, she glanced up to see if the crime she'd committed had been witnessed. It hadn't, except by me, but establishing eye contact felt like it would be a pressure I wasn't yet equipped to cope with. Instead I quickly bored my vision into the carpet, lasering an imaginary hole through it.

"Hello," she said to me.

"Hello," I replied, but by the time I'd made the noise it had petered out. It sounded stupid. Worse still, I had nothing to follow it up with. I flirted with the idea of mentioning my impending trumpet lessons but it seemed daft.

I smiled toothlessly until it felt strange for both of us. It went silent for a while and all I could hear was my own breath, so I made an excuse and hid in the toilet until I probably couldn't get away with it anymore. When I got back they were eating bangers and mash on their laps except for Lou, who had the small trestle table, a Jewish prewar one with customarily thick, sturdy legs. She was the guest after all. It's the table Mal normally had.

The quiet, freakish gaps that perforated the occasional sound of the cheap cutlery scraping against our best plates gave me a headache. And then Mal went to the bathroom.

"So are you Malcolm's girlfriend?" wondered Mum aloud.

More quiet. I scrabbled around my head for a conversational tourniquet but there wasn't one. We were bleeding to death. I glanced at Dad, to see his feet disappearing up the ladder and through the ceiling, his dinner just a gravy birthmark on the plate at the foot of his big comfy chair.

"Yes." Lou smiled. Mum didn't stop.

"What is Malcolm like at school?"

It hurt more this time. I longed for the flush of the cistern. The backward click-clack of the lock.

Lou didn't look nervous. She smiled and jiggled a strap of hair from out of her right eye. And when she answered it sounded like lyrics from a pop song learnt from the pages of a teen magazine.

"He's nice," she said. "Better than the other boys."

Mal finally emerged, still buttoning up the fly of his jeans, soon to be my jeans, as he walked into the room. We watched laugh-tracked family comedy together, and Mum offered to make a pot of tea every fifteen minutes until Lou's dad came to pick her up. She offered to make one for him too but he'd left the car running and had to get back for his food. He was having mashed potato with sausages too, he said, and he and Mum cooed over their coinciden-tal dinner plans. Lou did her shoes up and we all grew sad that she was leaving. Especially me, because I knew that now Lou was in our lives, every time I saw her leave from that day on I'd feel the same.

I knew that wouldn't work.

Seventeen

Our school loomed in the background the way a prison presides over its inmates during exercise break. We marched out in a rolling cloud of cold purple knees and icy blue hands tucked into the cheap elastic waistbands of our shiny nylon shorts. The sharp breeze tongued the little scar on my leg to an erect pink mound, my body keeping a record of where I had been and what I had done. That day was sports day, and I had to run but the wind had turned my skin to bone.

My classmates and I craned our necks to the right, surveying the gathered crowd of mums and dads penned in like clucking camera-flashing chickens by reams of multicolored bunting. I couldn't see mine but I knew that they were in there and so I waved anyway, for fear of standing out.

The whiteboard had names upon it listed under different events whose very nature corrupted the definition of sport. Our school year had been split into four segments between which a false rivalry was promoted. I was on the red team. My occasional academic success garnered red points. On red assembly days, it was my teammates who performed in the big old hall. Today I wore a red bib and we huddled together to find out the discipline we'd be competing in. Slowly, amidst the rush and the talk and the togetherness of it, all reluctance to take part began to disappear. This was what all the others must have felt like. I wondered if I could move in wider circles still.

"There you are," said a boy next to me, Ben, fast, sporty and seemingly unaware of intersocial-tier kindness etiquette. He pointed at the whiteboard and I did my best to follow the sniper's sight of his finger but his arm was knocked to and fro by heads bobbing like a crate of apples spilled into the sea. I scanned through Egg and Spoon, Sack Race and Three-Legged Race but couldn't find myself. I wasn't in Long Jump or High Jump. There was no me under Discus or Javelin. I didn't even know our school had javelins.

"There!" yelped Ben again. The crowd had thinned this time and I could look to where he was pointing. There: 4 x 100 Meter Relay. Three names and then mine. The three sportiest boys in the whole school, and then me. Panic racked me, stretched me out as the loudspeaker gargled instructions through the commotion. It was meant to be summer but my breath still condensed against the wind. My legs were speckled purple tinned meats and my stomach nervous bubbles of air in and out and in and out of me. A tapping hand on the summit of my spine sucked me out of a coma.

"Hello," he said.

We'd not spoken before but I knew who he was. Chris. His friends too. They were bigger than me, stronger. When they extended hands I shook them and smiled, and in the back of my head I pretended that they were my bodyguards.

"Can you run fast, Phil?" he said.

My name wasn't Phil, he'd got it wrong, and though it took an ice-cream-scoop-size gulp from my throat I decided in a split second not to correct him. There is no greater test of human character than the riding out of the subsequent seconds after someone gets your name wrong.

"Not really," I replied.

"That's OK. You can go last."

This was good, I thought.

"OK."

"By the time we've all done our legs, we'll have a lead. You just have to run as fast as you can and not lose it."

"OK."

"It will . . . ," he said, as the others turned and walked toward the row of stackable plastic chairs where we were to sit and watch the other events take place, ". . . be fine."

He had a hand on my shoulder; a palpable camaraderie embraced me. It left a brief warmth of friendship in my heart and the prop pride gives wedged tightly underneath my chin. A head rush.

The four of us sat together in a disjointed circle. They joked and I smiled and reciprocated with acute timing. I thought they invited me out with them, maybe on our bikes. In fact I'm sure they did. I felt giddy with the novelty of it all.

"I run like a duck with chewing gum on its feet," I said. They all laughed. They didn't ask me about Mal. I wasn't cold anymore.

Eighteen

"It's going to be fine."

"I don't want to lose it for you."

"You won't."

"I might."

"You won't."

But I might. The trophy, a life where Mal plays a bit part. My life.

I looked to the crowd as I copied the warm-up exercises my new friends were undertaking. I pretended they hurt a little even though they didn't because I didn't really know how to do them properly. What was more important was that, should anyone glance over, I wasn't the only one not standing on one leg, the other tucked into my hand behind my back. We looked like the biggest and clumsiest of the flamingos. I looked like the smallest and clumsiest of the big flamingos. But at least I was a flamingo.

Finally, there was my mum. And dad. He was the only dad there that had brought some binoculars. He felt, I imagined, like an assassin. And Mal lapped at a huge ice cream, the strawberry syrup fringe on it having split into two rival factions. The drip-drip armies raced each other down the brittle cone and through the gaps between his fingers. Mum looked nervous for me. She'd done her hair especially, her makeup too, and she was wearing a billowy summer dress dashed with the colors of burning hot suns. She looked hand-made, a pretty craft-fair doll. I smiled back to reassure her that I was fine, but I was not.

The burst of compressed air sounded as Mr. Thirkell, the wheezing PE teacher, squeezed it through the claxon. He exercised vicariously through us but it didn't show. And that meant it was time to begin. We sauntered toward the starting line. I both wanted and didn't want it.

"Just don't fall over," whispered Chris.

"But if I do, it won't be my fault," I said.

"It won't be anyone else's fault either," he said.

And he grinned. I wanted to ask him if I was still allowed to come on that bike ride should I fall over, or lose the race, or just burst into tears right there.

And as I was thinking, the pistol burst. The four competing colors tore off in pursuit of its echo. A black wave of noise rose from the crowd but in my head it didn't drown out the dull thump thump on grass of their feet, graced with such speed, one I couldn't match with anything but my quickening breath.

Into the second leg. Chris stormed away, catapulted. We had a lead already, the red team were winning, but I grew roots deep into the ground. Perhaps I could just sit it out. He could call me Phil for ever, perhaps I'd get used to it eventually, like the niggling twinge of a cracked rib, perhaps one day it would be there but not there too and that would be absolutely fine.

The third leg. Thud thud thud. My joints seized, a rusted tin man. A scream unheard pumped my lungs to double their size. My ears whistled and the sound of the crowd disappeared. All color leaked from my vision. This wasn't me, I decided. This was some-one else being me. I held out my hand and he was there immedi-ately with a slap that bounced through the air like a gunshot.

And I was running. I was running slowly but I was running as fast as I could. I was running away from Mum and Dad and Mal behind me. I chanced a glimpse over my shoulder and saw blue, green and yellow blocks catching me up with violent pace. I was ahead but less and less so, the timing of my short legs windmilling through the air lapsing in and out of the natural beat my juts of breath made. I was moving. I was going forward. Breaking new ground. I was out on my own. And they were catching me but there wasn't time to overtake me. And they were screaming, and they were screaming because I had won.

Red bibs piled on top of me but my elation lifted their weight and I was dipped in this stream I'd not belonged in and it was carrying me forward. Perhaps I could take this road. Perhaps I was invited. Perhaps this was for me.

Chris cheered and shouted up close to my ear; the flecks of his spittle cooled my heated skin and tickled my neck. I couldn't unclench my hands, they were tight like bunches in girls' hair, and I felt, for a second, like the shaking center of something great. My eyes cried hot tears but before anyone saw I dabbed them into the grass stains on my forearm until my skin was the green of an old bottle.

"Happy?!" asked Chris. It sounded like *Well done*. I nodded. I was happy.

In the crowd I saw Dad, his hand in the air, and Mum, she was clapping to be the last to clap. And Lou, who waved double-handed theatrical air-kissing, the way a famous opera singer would as she disembarked from a plane to greet a legion of adoring fans. But they were aimed at me.

This was life I was feeling. I decided to lie there for a while, enjoying its exciting hand on my back.

nineteen

Day Seven Thousand Four Hundred and Eighty-Three, according to the display on the wall.

It is early morning, a busy one. The medics arrive before breakfast.

There are two ways to get a hundred-stone man out of a house. The way to do it while they're alive is to remove the front of the building. Literally to take it off, all of it, the bricks, the windows, everything. Then you have him bound in hundreds of feet of industrial-strength material, slide specially created inflatable hoists underneath him and gently lift him inch by inch from the bed and out, using a crane adapted for such a thing. Many television companies, private investors and even the occasional celebrity had offered to pay for the procedure in the past. It was, after all, a very expensive exercise. Aside from the building work, you need health-and-safety specialists and medical staff (in case Mal were to have a heart attack, which is highly probable given that he will be moving the furthest he has moved in the last twenty years). You need surveyors and a large police presence to marshal the inevitable throng of spectators. You need to hire portable toilets to cope with demand, extra seats, lighting for when it gets dark and all manner of people and things you wouldn't even begin to contemplate contemplating if you didn't have a man the size of Mal in your house.

We'd been told no long ago. Under no circumstances, no. No,

we would not be lifting Mal out of the house. We wouldn't even be taking the front of the house off. If Mal were to leave this house, it would have to be "the other way." They meant dead when they said that. Not only dead but in little bits in big bags, I guess. Or big bits in bigger bags. The reasons were thus, according to the report that arrived once all of the consultants had been consulted and all of their findings made plain:

> The structure of the house would not withstand the removal of the front outer wall.

This meant that the house would collapse with Mal inside it, the weight of it rolling him outward like an enormous bruised pancake. It made me think about those cartoons where they crush each other with grand pianos and anvils and refrigerators dropped from cliff tops. Except it'd be loads of bricks, and whatever Dad had in the attic. I'd never been in the attic. The second reason was this:

> Physicians found that Malcolm's skin on his back and under-side had grown and developed in such a fashion that it had begun some time ago to incorporate the material of the bedding. The surgery necessary to remove Malcolm from the bed at this stage would almost certainly result in his death from heart failure were it to be performed with him at his current weight.

This was the bit that made me think. Mal hadn't moved for so long that his skin had begun to merge with the linen on the bed. Parts of his back were cloth. All that weight over all those years had welded the two together and made something new. Pressure plus time, just as the earth makes coal.

I watch the expert prepare to slide his hand between Mal and the mattress. His assistants hitch up the overspill of Mal's thick edges, skirting the bed like a vulgar petticoat, and he begins lubricating a latex glove in glossed dollops of greasy clear jelly. He is young and fresh, perhaps mid-twenties, and I smile as I imagine the delight his friends take in recounting the more gruesome details of his perkless occupation whenever their social circle is graced by a stranger. He snaps an elastic band around his wrist to secure the glove in transit and wisely removes his watch, handing it to a pretty young trainee, who smiles because she is thinking the exact same thing as me. He calmly applies his stoic face. Gently he edges in, under heavy, sweeping folds of flab for a short distance until he can go no further. And then I imagine them all as one peeling Mal away from the bed and his skin ripping and stretching like burnt celluloid, an overcooked egg being scraped from the pan. Once the hand has gone as far as it can, and jarred in the flesh bedclothes, the expert beckons his colleague, who drops to her knees and begins sliding a long, thin plastic rod with a cotton-wool tip into the small gap created by the intrepid arm of her cohort. Slowly, slowly, further it goes, swabbing his unbearably pallid skin. Simultaneously they grimace as a long-trapped pocket of air is granted reprieve to greet their nostrils with a sweaty funk. The muscle of it is such that the lady holding the swab rocks backward on her knees with a wince, and the silence is broken by the muffled snap of the plastic tool breaking off somewhere inside him.

The indignity of the whole affair weighs heavy on Mal's eyelids, and he sleeps for the forty minutes it takes for five people in coats to fish out the offending article from where it nestles in a crevasse on my brother's underside. Success is achieved via a crudely twisted coat hanger adorned with bent hair clips belonging to the trainee. She sighs, riffling through a list of other possible vocations in her head.

Twenty

We are used to medics in the house by now. It isn't a big house, ours, a tiny bungalow. But like Mal it had grown.

It had belonged to Mum's mum. Everything retained the essence of her elderly fug, how hands smell of coins long after you've paid.

The room that Mal and I shared had slowly become larger as he did. The kitchen and living room had been knocked through in order to make more space for beds, and Mum and Dad lived in an enormous chrome trailer we'd had shipped over by a woman named Norma Bee in Akron, Ohio. Her husband, Brian, like Mal, had taken over her house, forcing her from it the way all air is expelled from a vacuum-packed bag. When he became too big to be around, she moved into the trailer in the yard and from there she made his meals. Full chickens. Egg whites. Curries, Indian and Thai. Bread, cakes and ice cream in triple portions. From there she fed him. From there she kept him alive. For a time.

A friend she had in Scotland had sent her a small article about Malcolm she'd chanced upon in a newspaper, seeing the similarities between our situation and hers. After Brian's death she donated that trailer to us, a hulking monolith of glistening Americana. Parked out there, a beautiful silver blister on the face of the neighborhood, I used to pretend it was the tour bus of a rock band that were here to perform for me.

When not in there, Dad would usually be found in the attic space of the bungalow. We'd never disturb him, even as children. We'd leave him up there with his paperwork, his books, his maths, his inventions, his tools, his tuts, his sighs and his thoughts. You could hear his anger tremor through the plaster in the walls, the vibrations amplifying it until the house became a giant moan. None of this ever woke Mal.

As Mal had grown he'd attracted ephemera like a rolling ball of dust that bobbles across the floor of a barbershop. Now at the side of his bed there are machines that help him breathe, machines that help him wash, machines that help him eat, machines that help him excrete. Necessary decorations.

And then there are creams and medicines. Lotions to rub on his sores and serums to massage into his skin, all of which Mum did on her own. The latter years of her life were effectively spent basting an enormous turkey in the oven, lifting it, turning it and coating its flesh without the reward of a hearty meal.

She refused to allow others in to assist, and so the list of things on the wall, the list of the chores, the tasks, the things that needed to be done so long as someone's concern was keeping Mal alive, was hers and hers alone to work through.

Feed him.

Wash him.

Change his bag.

Her hands were withered and gnarled, as frail as rice paper but soft and kind and older than she was.

Check his breathing.

Rub his skin.

Change his bag again.

Her hair, once tight and curly, was just wire now, white and unloved. It was the specter of the hair that had been there before.

Shave him.

Kiss him.

Don't cry in front of him.

She was a woman empty, weakened with the weight of a son on her shoulders. Her son Malcolm, the fattest man in the world.

Twenty-One

Mal is still sleeping as the medics run tests. When it seems as though he's stopped, he starts again. The churn of his gut inflates his lungs. Snore growl repeat. Sound as oppression. The army wringing confessions from confused prisoners of war. White noise. I saw it on television once but it had more charm.

Mum is usually in by now, meddling with the curtains so that the sun doesn't lay its rays across Mal's eyes, but not today. I've nothing to do but look at him.

His arms are thicker than my legs. Four times as thick. Five or six, maybe. They look like rolled ham. Mal sheds skin, snakelike, with every move. Each morning he nests upon a fresh coat of it. His fingernails are thick, cracked, yellow and shiny like laminated lumps of cheese. His huge torso is contoured with stretch marks the length and thickness of a cowboy's leather belt. I imagine them tearing.

The folds in his flesh roll over and over like the dunes in a desert. This is my landscape. The nurse who came once to teach us how to use the machinery to dry the sweat from Mal's skin and prevent the irritation that made him feel as though he was being sanded told me a story about a morbidly obese woman from Wales. When she died of a heart attack at seventy-eight stone, forty-five years of age, they found the television remote control lost deep underneath her left breast. I liked the thought of the volume rising and falling as she breathed, of the confusion as the screen went blank whenever she found something funny.

I dread to think what's hidden deep inside Mal's crevices. Small animals pulled into the quicksand of his bulk.

Twenty-Two

Considering that the chance of his getting hit by a bus, falling from a cliff or being randomly attacked on a late-night train is obliterated by his inability to leave the house, there are a surprisingly large number of ways for a hundred-stone man to die. I listen to the medics explain them again.

Obesity such as Mal's—the doctor grimaces—is influenced by genetic, metabolic and environmental factors. Mal is the X on the line graph that charts where the three circumstances must meet for it to happen at an accelerated rate. Morbid obesity involves more than just a lack of willpower or a sedentary lifestyle.

Morbid obesity. Morbid. No other human condition comes prepackaged with an introductory sentiment. This is because, technically at least, obesity is self-imposed. It implies that there is an alternative kind of obesity, a jolly obesity perhaps, or a merry obesity. The kind that middle-aged single people with a good sense of humor have for a brief time before they become so huge and therefore unlovable as to be classified as morbid. Whether Mal is morbid or not was difficult to tell. Selfish obesity would probably have been more suitably coined.

The doctor always comes armed with new-fangled gels, pastes, pills, supplements and creams. He reels off a checklist of invisible murderers.

Coronary heart disease

Hypertension

Type II diabetes mellitus

Hyperlipidemia

Degenerative joint disease

Obstructive sleep apnea . . .

Check check check check check check.

Today's special from the menu was gastroesophageal reflux disease. Heartburn in most, in Mal it had become an excruciating, angry, fire-breathing dragon. Manifested, it felt as though his heart was having great plumes of black oil smoke blown straight through it, ending only in the temporary reprieve of a hot, grotesque burp.

When he wriggles, his bellies ripple like imaginary stones have been skimmed across them. Past him I see the glass stained in crow. I see its carcass smothered across the patio. I see a cat plucking at its entrails with the rabid fluster of a banjo player.

Past that I see the chrome trailer bouncing light back across Mal's naked girth.

And then, past that, I can see Lou.

Lou.

She's back.

I blink four or five long, squeezed blinks. I turn my head from side to side. And when I come back to where I'd seen her, she is gone. It is a phantom and a memory and a cruel trick of my mind on my eyes. The picture of me and her is the one I carry, the one that weighs me down. I've loved her for such a very long time.

Twenty-Three

All I knew about Mum and Dad before they had children I knew from the stories Mum would tell Mal in bed when we too were young. Sharing a bedroom, we'd listen to her until one or both of us slept. It was soothing. She was womb. They were just snippets of stories but they could be pieced together easily to form some semblance of a history.

Mum met Dad just after he'd finished school. Mum hadn't been to school for years. Her mother had been ill and her father had fled long before. Mum cared for her mother on a full-time basis, nurse, maid and daughter. Dad was popular. He was good-looking and muscular. Mum had no friends. She'd needed Dad, and he was there at the right time, but he'd come to need her equally. Dad had proposed to Mum just before he left to go and work in South Africa.

"He missed me terribly whilst he was there, and I likewise. He used to like being at home with me. I used to cook huge meals and we'd sit down together and eat them. I used to care for him. Mother him. When he was away I barely knew what to do with myself. All I had was my mother but she was too ill by this time. Could barely recognize me, poor woman. And it was me that had bathed her since I was small. I would just sit with her in the house, poor woman, and bake and clean and care for her like I always had since for ever. And wait for him to come home. I just wanted to look after him. I'd been caring for my mother for so long, it was all I knew how to do."

We always stayed still when she spoke.

"When he came home, he was never really the same again. Poor man."

Mum would sit with Mal on her knee, a ventriloquist in silhouette. She would reward him for sitting and listening with sweets. He wouldn't fidget. I'd rattle the bored jittery beat of a letterbox but Mal would be calmed, a hen underneath a dark cloth.

When Dad arrived home, we'd eat until our sides ached and slumber drugged us. Mum would care for us all, and we left behind those times when the length of a day was an indefinable prospect.

In the months after my sporting triumph I'd grown in confidence, testing the warmth of teenage spirit. When Lou and Mal left the house I'd ask her if I could go with them. She always said yes, and I knew from that she liked my company as much as I craved hers. I couldn't think of others'. Hers was everything, everything but mine.

Mal's reluctance to have me follow them around subsided quickly upon her insistence. As the two of them walked hand in hand, like fifteen-year-olds do, I would trot along behind them like a stray cartoon dog with the scent of sausages, but I'd try to stay closest to Lou, where I felt most welcome. Mal mewed his annoyance. He wasn't embarrassed to have me with him. What other people thought wasn't his concern, and he didn't have any friends he felt any immediate desire to impress. It was more that when I was there, Lou was divided. He didn't consider me the threat I wished I were, he just didn't seem to realize how much she loved him already. I did. It felt how it did to be bereaved. To talk to her would alleviate it, so I did as much as possible.

We went to the fair. It was an early autumn evening, and as we walked through the quiet streets the tiny embers of incinerated newspapers brushed our faces and hair. Everything felt quiet and still but the air was brooding, like there was a fight in it somewhere that you could smell on the wind. I walked four paces behind Mal and Lou, just far enough away to still hear the snippets of conversation that were not meant for me.

The fair was erected twice a year in the grounds of the town's leisure center. It was a shambles of broken bulbs misspelling the signs on the rides and within minutes the lush green grass turned to a sodden mush chicken-pocked with footprints. Girls with their hair scraped back so violently it threatened to rip their forehead from their face. Boys with industrial amounts of product lashing their hair short and neat and only ever forward. Walking amongst them, dressed in whatever ragtag ensemble he'd dug from the cupboard—sports socks in school shoes, airtight jeans, Dad's white shirt far too big and a leather jacket that a trendy new sleuth might wear—with the hair and the walk and the girlfriend, Mal looked every bit as ridiculous but at least he hadn't tried.

"What are you fucking looking at?" came a voice.

It was fake anger, you could tell. A bet possibly, or a challenge. But it was being directed at me. It brought that feeling, the rush of feeling you're in danger, real, physical danger. I sped up to catch Mal but he had stopped and I dared not look behind me. Everything quickened. Mal didn't speak, he just stood there, looking back over my head. Slowly inflating his chest, proud and peacock. He looked huge, fierce. I peered up at his face but he didn't acknowledge me, he just stared and stared and stared. I'd done five blinks and looked back down but in that time he'd done none. And the voice behind me was having the gall drained from it.

"What?!" it shouted, the same as before but with the power taken out.

Mal's hand held Lou's hand and her other hand suddenly held mine. It felt like six years were whipped from the calendar of my age. I turned around slowly.

The voice was that of a boy, maybe my age. He did the beckon of fighting, both hands cupped with come-here fingers. But he looked scared now, and the gaggle of idiots he'd attempted to impress looked toothless and lame. Mal stared. Slowly they dispersed into the lights and the signs and the chances to win things. The flurry of panic slowly subsided, segued into admiration. I looked up at Mal. He didn't say anything.

"Are you OK?" asked Lou.

"Yes." I nodded, trembling.

"Come on," she said. "Let's go and get something to eat, that will make you feel better."

The two of them held hands as we sat down at a small table, subconsciously dictating the seating plan. My breath was still hurried. I tried to relax as I looked at the menu through a biting stink of fried onions. The fat, smoking man scraping charred bits of meat around the dirty black hot plate with a gardening tool made life itself seem unappetizing. We ordered three hot dogs with the ten pounds that Mum had forced into Mal's hand. Each of us took it in turns to approach the van and slather the cheap meat in almost translucent, possibly toxic tomato ketchup. The bread felt damp and remembered your fingerprints.

"I don't know why people bother," said Mal.

A warmed knob of butter slipped from his bun and landed with a plop on his knee. He then scooped it up on an expertly hooked finger and dropped it back onto his sausage.

"Why people bother what?" said Lou.

"With the plan."

"What plan?"

"Well . . ." He considered the question, took another bite and swallowed it down with a deep breath. "These people, they're our age, yet they're just biding their time until they think it's acceptable to commence a plan they've got figured out for the rest of their lives. They get older and start drinking. They meet someone and get pregnant. They work and work and work. Buy a house and sit in it in silence listening to the baby cry. Have another one to keep it company. Waking up early, going to work, packing a lunch, coming home, watching the television, paying the bills, thinking they're happy, having another baby just in case. No thanks. And they're all in such a rush to do it. I mean, look at them."

I followed the invisible death ray from Mal's pointed finger-tip as he pontificated, then he dropped his hand to Lou's thigh, where it was before. He gripped it tightly like he always did. He was always holding her in one way or another. Lou looked at Mal and shook her head.

"That's called growing up," she said.

"That's the prize for growing up?" he said.

"It's not a prize, because it's not a competition. It's just what people do, Mal."

"Yeah, well, there are no winners. Sounds like bullshit to me," he said. "Why would so many people stick to a plan that hardly ever even seems to work? If all adults were walking around with-out so much as a worry, or a personal tragedy, or even a shit day in the office, then I might get it. But they're not. Why would you chase something that turns out to be so fucking awful so much of the time? Looks like a let-down to me."

After we'd all discarded half a hot dog each, I followed Mal and Lou around the grounds of the fair. I won a cuddly toy I was much too old for by fishing plastic ducks out of a children's pond. I remembered just how impatient fishing made me, how impatient I could get. I gave the toy to Lou and she said that I was sweet, then kissed me on the cheek, just a little peck, which I got a bit embar-rassed about. Next, Mal drew quite a crowd, hitting a large foam pad with an over-sized wooden mallet to ring a bell. The rising strip of lightbulbs declared him Superman and a small, tinny alarm sounded. People all around us clapped and cheered and whistled, and Mal stepped down from the plinth looking happy again. He won an enormous toy, much bigger than mine, which he gave to Lou and I watched from the corner of my eye as she gave him a kiss to say thank you. I'd have hated to be caught.

As we left, having only been there for half an hour, we walked past the same group we'd encountered as we arrived. They said nothing. The once-brave young soul who'd goaded me shuffled his feet in the mud and looked at the sky. His friends all began to laugh when he accidentally stepped in dog shit.

For the first time I thought I saw Mal, older, something manifesting itself. And for the first time I saw why Lou loved him so much, my eyes opened to it.

Twenty-Four

Dad would be out working more often than not. He would travel the country, visiting elevators, mostly enormous ones meant for no people or lots of people at the same time. Some nights he would be in strange hotels, somewhere else but with the same curtains, the same manufactured darkness in the mornings. He would call and talk to Mum on the phone. She always worried whenever he was away, happier when we were all around her. She would say "I hope he's not sad," and to think of him sad made me sad. He looked big and old, like an elephant on the plain, its mate taken for her tusks.

On Mum and Dad's twenty-fifth wedding anniversary, Dad was in. He came in from the bedroom. He was wearing a suit, light gray with a sheen through it, and a metallic-colored stripey tie. His shirt was buttoned right up to the collar so that the girth of his neck filled it and spilled over. The tips of his fingers were reddened where he'd been flustering over the cufflinks before asking Mum to deal with them for him. His trousers were too tight and his hair was combed back with water so that when it dried it naturally bounced into a wiry quiff, offset on either side by the first footprints of male-pattern baldness. He looked smart; I'd never seen him in a suit before.

"Tell your mother I've gone to start the car," he said.

Mum was wearing makeup, purposeful and neat. Her cheeks, decked in blusher, were the kind of rose-pink you see on birthday cards that pensioners send to you. She wore lipstick and it felt like it was the first time I'd ever seen her with lips. The heels and shoulder pads were thick and generous sandwich slices, salad spilling from the sides. Her skirt and jacket were the same gray as Dad's suit. Together they were a dull postcard from a county bored and staid. She rooted through her handbag, checked her purse and checked again.

"Where are you going, Mum?" asked Mal.

"Out for a meal," she said. "I told your brother to tell you."

She hadn't told me, though, because she'd been too busy thinking about everyone else.

"I've done you dinners, just warm them up, and there are cream slices in the fridge for afters, but we won't be late anyway. Please try not to make a mess, and try not to break anything either. I've tidied up today." She tidied up every day.

The beep beep beep of the car on the drive, the chug of its engine and the dizzy petrol smell of it starting up meant she had to go. She stooped to kiss us both on the cheek. I rose to it, a strained neck like a chick getting fed muddy wriggling worms, still warm, from the beak of the huntress mother. Mal slunk lower still into the chair and wallowed in thick silence. When she could bend no more she planted a kiss on the top of his head, right in the center of his shiny, black, angry mop of hair. All of the commotion and the noise followed Mum out of the house, and as the door closed we were suddenly shut off. Mal didn't say a word.

"What shall we do?" I asked Mal. I waved my hand in front of his face as though I were testing someone's claim to being hypnotized.

Mal stood. He walked to the bottom of Dad's ladder and, putting one foot before the other, began to shimmy up it. We'd get in trouble for this. I followed him. He placed the flats of his palms against the underside of the hatch and eased it open slowly, pushing it upward until it fell upright against something else and stayed there. The hole in the ceiling, like a lone telescope on a hill, begged us to look through it. So we did. I followed Mal up, my eye at the level of his tattered socks as we ascended, not knowing what we'd find. And then, as quickly as I'd started to follow him, I stopped. This was all that was forbidden. I couldn't anger Dad.

"Come on," he said. "Come on. Let's go up there."

I shook my head and jumped down the few steps I'd taken to the floor.

"Just come on," he said.

"No, Mal. Let's sit down," I countered, turning back toward the living room only to be stopped by him grabbing my arm, his fingers rigid and with the strength of a man determined to burst a basketball using only his hands. He launched me onto the floor with a stern push, about-turned and marched out of the room.

I wanted him turned to powder. I grabbed my bike and pushed it through the front door onto the path outside without a thought for putting my shoes on and rode into the street.

It was three hours and ten minutes later when Dad's car trundled around the corner of our road. I'd been patrolling it, rolling slowly up and down its length, the way every house looked the same, watching the birds swoop down toward the big glass doors at the front of ours and pull suddenly into last-minute climbs.

In the dark of the night the light from the headlights formed a veil around me that lurched a hard right into the driveway. The clicking of the seat belts preceded the clunking of locks and the perchunk of the doors opening.

"Where is Mal?" asked Mum. Dad rolled his eyes. Not "Where are your shoes?" or "What are you doing out here?"

"Dunno," I said.

With a twist on her dainty heel, she gathered pace toward the house. I went to follow her but Dad stopped me at the door with one hand rested on my chest. His suit felt nice as it brushed the skin of my arm. I'd never known him to feel nice before; his clothes were normally heavy with a rough musk.

"Don't go in there," he said.

"OK," I said.

We went to the car and climbed inside. It still smelled sweet, like perfume and wine, as though the car was holding these scents in its lungs for as long as it could manage, worried it might never get to inhale them again. Through the glass doors I could see the shape of Mal under his quilt, his naked leg poking out from the side and the rise fall rise fall of his breathing underneath it.

"You know I love you, don't you?" Dad said. And I said yes, I knew. "And Mal too," he said. And I said yes, I knew. "And your mum, I love your mum," he said.

I sat and listened as he spoke. He spoke so rarely that, even if it was for a short time it was how treasure hunters must have felt when their gadgetry beeped and their hearts leapt like salmon through their insides.

Twenty-Five

Dad said, "When I met your mother, I loved her immediately. I needed her. Do you understand? There was nothing else."

I felt a bit embarrassed, like I was watching them kiss.

"Out at TauTona, she was all I thought about. I wanted to be back. It was hot there, arid. You would wake up in your hammock in the morning and it would be so saturated with sweat that you could wring it out like a towel you'd just dried yourself on after a shower. And it would stink. Of heat. Hot smells. Of men in the morning, the large tents we set up fumigated by cigarette breath. I just wanted to get back to your mother.

"When the accident happened, when I found out, all the while we were trying to save those men, I realized that it wasn't for me. Life, I mean. Depression, I guess that's what they'd call it these days, something bloody stupid like that. Bet they'd ram you full of sugar pills, send you on your way. Well, I don't know about that. I felt like I wanted to be a child again, when everything is painless and easy and done for you. I wanted it all taken away. The badness, I wanted it stopped. I remember wondering why anyone would want the responsibility of other people's lives on their conscience. Do you see? You will learn this. And Mal. My parents taught me that when I grew up, the world would be my oyster. I wouldn't tell the same lie to you. TauTona taught me that.

"Everything you imagine about the future when you're young makes everything that happens afterward a cruel disappointment.

I watched those women crying on the surface. I watched their colleagues crying underground. I watched hopelessly as our futile attempt to reach those men got nowhere at all for hours on end, and we knew they were dead. No one signed up for that."

From the car I looked out through the big glass doors and I watched Mum, perched on the end of Mal's bed, rubbing his feet. She smiled at him. Her tears ran strings through her makeup. Dad sighed. It meant "Look at her." So we both sat there and did. It seemed inappropriate that the lamppost outside our house had a broken bulb and that she wasn't bathed in light, like you'd see in oil paintings of angels. She cared for him and in return he was all hers. She saved him from an outside world he wasn't ready for.

Twenty-Six

Day Seven Thousand Four Hundred and Eighty-Three, according to the display on the wall. I rarely look at it anymore.

Mum arrives with breakfast once the medics have shipped out. My legs are still rigid and painful from my time asleep.

Food is Mal's clock. Mum is in and out of the kitchen. The turning on of taps, the scratching at of pans with scouring pads, the metronomic clicking of the ignition on the hob teasing the storm-blue gas into a happy marriage of heat and light. All these sounds had a Pavlovian chime.

Mal burned such little energy that his sleeping patterns were in disarray. He drifted off, illuminated in the glow from the television, which would blast out old movies until four or five in the morning.

He'd wake again at about eight to be met with a huge cooked breakfast, all the colors of an artist's palette as he sits at an easel to paint autumn.

A brief doze afterward meant he'd rise again for lunch, often finishing mine. This would set him up nicely for a steady flow of chocolate snacks, ice cream and cakes. It was less a third course, more of an obstacle course.

At dinnertime came the truly gargantuan portions that would serve to impress even the most experienced historian of royal medieval banquets. Any lingering tastes were soon destroyed by perhaps another full tub of ice cream. This was known as pudding in the evening, unlike when he'd quickly consume the very same of a morning. Then it was simply ice cream.

Further snacking ensued, crisps, a pork pie or two, yet more chocolate, until suppertime, when typically Mal would revisit the leftovers of his dinner. Before retiring herself, Mum would litter his bedside table with enough food to carry him through the night.

A visiting doctor told me once that Mal's horizontality meant he wasn't only prone to growing outward faster than was normal but also that he was becoming taller as a result. We all grow at night, by fractions of fractions of millimeters but come the morning, when we finally stand, the growth is compacted again by our own weight. That, he said, is why astronauts often return to earth from space half an inch or so taller than they were when they left, which must be odd, he joked, when they come to kissing their wives hello.

I watch Mal inhale his breakfast. He follows this by quickly wading into the enormous chocolate cake Mum has made, scooping it with clawed hand and shoveling the crumbling thick brown sponge mixture into his mouth with the jerky precision of an industrial digger. His mouth opens so wide that I can see the point where his tongue emerges from his lining. He's just a couple of degrees away from owning a flip-top head. That he doesn't must be attributed to evolutionary oversight. The survival of the least fit. The caramel adhesive that holds the cake together drips from his fingers, dangles in strings from his lips and clogs the wiry clumps of hair on his chin, but undeterred he spoons in more and more, even before he has finished with the previous mouthful. His arm repeats that same motion with clockwork regularity.

I am taken aback as I am every morning by the deterioration in the health of Mal's skin. Where once was florid boyishness is now a ruddy, mean-spirited mess. The lack of fresh air has turned his face into a miserly wallet for dirt and sweat and grease. The resultant clusters of immature acne glisten at the sides of his nose, growing like a coral reef across his chin and down his neck, blinking in the sunlight as they slowly marinate in their own juices. Acne at forty-five makes me feel better about living with my parents, living at home with my brother, at forty-three. Marginally. My broken legs ache but also mend.

It was her love that was killing him. Mum.

Twenty-Seven

The visual stimulus of watching Mal be bathed wrenches my stomach up into my esophagus. He looks like an enormous sea monster caught and displayed in a Victorian museum of the grotesque.

Mum pushes the bedroom door open with her foot, carefully carrying a bowl of warm soapy water that splish-sploshes about in it from side to side, occasionally making brave leaps in huge teardrops of freedom. It is spiked with a special antiseptic lotion and smells of clean. She sets it down and begins work methodically. I look on from the armchair in the corner of the room.

She starts with his face, stroking the wet flannel across his brow and down his cheeks. He wheezes like dust-caked bellows, in and out, in and out, all of his effort consumed. She slides a hand under his left breast that hangs flaglike and slowly lifts it as though it is a rock in the garden and spiders might dash out. It wouldn't surprise me if they did. Underneath that fold the skin is as white as an institution, racked with scabs and scratches, deprived of all sunlight and free of all life. Tenderly Mum dabs the area with a soaked sponge. Her eyes are cold and spent.

The other colossal breast. Done. Armpits. Done.

Next the folds in his arm, which she sweeps for gathered fluff and finds enough to make a scarf for a doll. She puts down her tools and forces an arm underneath the fleshy ring of fat that divides the four different segments of his belly before dousing the newly exposed flaps in more warm lather. And then down further still.

Mal closes his eyes. Mum approaches his gusset. She pushes her open hand into the massive mottled midsection, kneading it into position as it closes around her wrist like the soft gummy jaws of a manatee, and takes a towel to Mal's privates, the infected blisters he's never actually seen.

Then, as best she can, his back and underside, the chafed bottom of his legs, the edges of his buttocks that jut out like blocks of porky shelving and leave the sheets sodden with the sweat of a great weight not allowing the heat inside him to escape. As she moves a wet wipe once more around his chins in preparation for his shave, it expels a bubble of trapped air with a shrill whooping sound. It is a noise that never loses its novelty. Smothering the lower half of his face in thick slabs of foam, she carefully runs a razor around his outline. His skin has stretched and is thin and feeble, so he cuts easily. Occasionally I'd see the blade jar, a deep red trickle of blood blending with the foam like a death in the snow.

I refuse to watch as she trims his toenails. Likewise as she empties his bag.

Twenty-Eight

Tick tock tick tock.

Mum finishes cleaning Mal just as the psychiatrists arrive. I let them in. She tells them they have until the TV crew get here. There are two of them, a man and a woman, and they both accept a slice of cake out of politeness. Rather than look like she isn't eating it, the woman wraps it in a piece of tissue she finds in her handbag and pretends to save it for later, sliding it into the pocket of her jacket. Mum, out of equally painful politeness, pretends not to have noticed and then absentmindedly offers her another portion.

I hear Dad move across the floor of the attic that moans and groans when he doesn't sit still. He hasn't been down all day. I wonder what he's building. I go to sit with Mal and watch a worm of saliva maze its way out of his stretched, wet lips. It makes me retch dry nothings up my throat.

The door opens and the psychiatrists enter. I love this part, the look on their face when they first see him. Mal is naked. They see his feet first, disappearing under the hanging sleeve of the fat on his legs the way a snake eats a sheep whole. The growths and deformities caused by poor circulation chart a route up him to his knees, huge, flattened spheres of flab the size of satellite dishes, the bony caps long since buried.

The woman raises her hand to her face, aghast. The smell hits her. Not uncleanliness, not godliness either. An impassable waft, sweat and odor, a clotted, hideous force. She might faint, she might not.

Up past his thighs is where he really begins to spread but they're covered by the changing blubber of his many bellies. The occasional purple vein careering through them near the surface is worked to bursting point. The stretch marks, the thickness of tires, worn like sashes around his huge, flappy tits. The crumbs in his chest hair, his eyelids half-cocked.

Bed and depression are inexorably linked, the experts are explaining as they sit in the two plastic chairs Mum has placed at Mal's side. His head rocks over to look at them as though it's toppled under the weight, and I think about how weird it is that his features have not grown in keeping with the expanding face they sit on. It is, she says, "A vicious circle, really. Staying in bed, the constant malaise of it, the deregulation of the body clock, the lack of movement, it makes you depressed, an imbalance of hormones." She tries to look Mal in the eyes, and in the eyes only, but she fails and pans down and up him. Her voice is sweet. She could be describing the feathers on baby ducks, rather than the fragile mental state of a man who hasn't gotten out of bed in twenty years.

"And then, when you're depressed . . . ," she continues, speaking in unison with the metronomic nod of her colleague, who can barely bring himself to look up, ". . . the natural instinct is to hide away, to find solace in lonely comfort. To go to bed. It's a vicious circle. But you already knew all this."

She goes to hand Mal a leaflet but her dainty wrist accidentally brushes the saddlebag of fat that hangs precariously on the side of the bed as she leans in and she drops it. It lands in the center of Mal's chest and lies there, open on a picture of an obese man. It's like that feeling of being flanked by mirrors on either side, so that you can see yourself duplicated into infinity. Mal brings up his arms to reach it but he can't with either, and he's powerless. It occurs to me then that he can't even clasp his hands together in prayer, should he want to. Eventually I stand up, even though it hurts my legs to do it, and remove the leaflet myself.

"Sorry," says our guest.

"That's OK," says Mal. His breath is a heavy wheeze. I fold the leaflet into the back pocket of my jeans.

"So we'd like to ask you some questions," the man says. He has a clipboard perched on his lap. Attached to it are questions written by someone else. The man might as well be a computer. Or a pen. "They'll help us to understand where you are at mentally."

I look into Mal's eyes every day. There is nothing wrong with him. He isn't mad. He wasn't mad when he was a child, he isn't mad now as a great big deflated hot-air balloon of skin. This isn't what we need to discover. You can't get the right answers unless you ask the right questions. And there is one. Why?

I stand up slowly, the pins in my legs grating, and edge past Mal's disgusting feet. I step over cables and trolleys, creams and serums, and open the door.

"Will you ask Mum to come in?" says Mal in a breathy whisper of exhaust fumes. He likes an audience. He always liked an audience.

"OK," I say.

Mum is in the trailer, where she always is, facing the wall above the oven like she always does. It is always hot in here, the glass in the pictures she's hung to make it slightly less plain permanently steamed. A picture of Mal clings to the wafer-thin wall above the fridge. In it he is five and naked. Dancing at a birthday party, knees bent, elbows out. Adults form a circle around him and clap as he performs.

"Mal wants you to go into the bedroom," I say.

I massage my forehead with my fingers roughly.

"Did they finish their cake?" she asks.

"Who?"

"What do you mean who? The doctors."

"They're not really doctors, Mum."

"Of course they are."

She has both her hands on her hips, the way you imagine the housekeeper always does in Tom and Jerry cartoons but you only ever see her ankles.

"They're not, Mum," I assure her. "They're just reading out questions from a piece of paper. They can't help."

"Don't be so bloody silly. Should I take them some more cake?" she says. She has already prepared a trayful. She arranges it in a semicircle around a freshly brewed pot of tea. It looks beautiful. It could be an advert for tea and cake.

"Yes. Yes. If you like," I say.

She gathers up some napkins. She's always on crumb duty. God, she looks old.

"Mum," I say.

"Yes?"

"I need to talk to you."

"Yes," she says. "Let me take this tray through. You know what he's like if I'm not there. How are your legs today?"

"Fine, I suppose."

"You'll be right as rain in no time, love. You'll be skipping. And they'll give you some work at the shop again, part-time maybe, I bet."

She edges out of the trailer, pushing the door open gently with her back. As soon as she's gone, it snaps back into place. I can't remember a time I was in here alone. The thick wooden furniture makes me think of America. Everything seems more substantial in America, their furniture objects of sturdiness, reliability, things your leaning can depend upon. It makes me think of Norma Bee, whose trailer it once was.

I look out of the window onto the lawn for a new angle on where I thought I'd seen Lou. She isn't there.

Closing the curtain, I scan around inside. None of Dad's stuff appears to be here. The bed looks slept in by one. It isn't a place graced by the heavy hand, clumsy foot and poorly folded clothing of man. It feels sterile and weak, trodden down and used. Dad has been spending more and more time in the attic. I decide to pay him a visit and make my way, slowly, back into the house.

From the bottom of the ladder I can hear Dad behind the hatch. The calming tap tap tap of a hammer at a quarter of a swing, or the end of a chisel. Tinkles of bolts and screws.

I bend my painful left knee and lift my foot up onto the first flat rung of the metal ladder. It feels flimsy and dentable, like a tin man, and that it might rip from the ceiling and come crashing to the ground. My dad would open the hatch to find me lying twelve feet below him, a pile of metal and cut bleeding body parts, a mangled robot crash. But it doesn't fall, it stays rigid. He steps over my head, unawares. The wood sucks in and out. Sawdust raindrops land in my hair and filter through it to rest on my ticklish scalp.

With both palms rested flat against the undersurface of the hatch, I wait for my time. And I wait and I wait, until I hear Dad has sat down in his squeaky old chair up there that I imagine to be coated in tattered leather but I cannot be sure. Then, with all reserves of my energy and calm, I push upward from the elbows and the power in my legs against the battered metal ladder. But nothing moves. A heavy weight rests on the hatch, an immovable one, and I am denied.

Catching my breath, I stay up on that ladder for a few minutes, unsure of what to do or where to go, feeling like a child again, remembering that I am a man. Eventually I hear the bedroom door open, the test over, and I slowly bend my sore knees down the steps. Nothing seems wrong when the two psychiatrists pop their heads around the edge of the living-room door to say good-bye to me. The man has a thin streak of chocolate above his lips, just underneath his nose. Both Mum and his colleague have been too polite to tell him.

When they've gone, I peer back up at the hatch in the ceiling.

Twenty-nine

Being a teenager was boring more often than not. Sitting in silence I'd listen to the mechanics of my own body. I liked the fizzing of my stomach acids forcing tiny little growls through my throat. I enjoyed the dull wet slop it made when I allowed my mouth to fill with saliva and then swallowed it all in one exaggerated motion, like a chick necking a beetle, unhindered by peristalsis. Occasionally I could hear my own heart beat with a strength that would move my body involuntarily, thud thud. If I thought too hard about it I'd notice a faint clicking in my head, the ticking over of my brain. I liked, for a time, to be alone.

Mal had reached a plateau, a compromise with life. He began spending more and more time at Lou's house. Her dad even let them share a bed. He was perhaps too apathetic to object, or just not in control. They could never have done the same at our house unless they wanted to share the room with me.

I wouldn't have minded.

His prolonged absences left Mum bereft. She took a job cleaning in the evenings at the office of the local mayor. She'd discard the empty brandy bottles hidden in the toilet cistern and pretend, as he leered drunkenly over her petite frame, not to have noticed his disgusting purple nose, which wriggled with broken veins.

Even Dad wasn't around as much as he had been. He had recently felt able to return to the deep shaft mines of South Africa, though this time far from Johannesburg. He had been employed as a consultant on the sinking of a new lift shaft two miles into the center of the earth. Things seemed to be working. There was convention. There was rest. Nothing unexpected. It was as though the house was waiting for an almighty cloud to fall across it. One that never arrived.

And so I spent a lot of time on my own. I'd think of all the things I wanted, trapped inside my fertile teenage mind.

I'd sit and wish that I was Mal, his hands clumsily wrapped tight around Lou's wrists. Using his nose, no . . . my nose, to brush aside her hair and gain access to her earlobes. Slipping a finger, and then two, and then a readily cupped hand, beneath the underwire of her bra. Roughly tugging at it in the hope it might unclasp and excitedly peppering her breast with openmouthed kisses. Tentatively sliding an open palm past the elastic of her soft knickers. Taking what I found fully in my hand and gently searching it, hoping secretly for a guide, a sign, a map of exactly what to do next. Then finally finding out on my own when what's in there accepts me, draws me in.

And then alone again, on my sofa, hoping for nothing but Lou's dad's sudden change of personality, or sudden development of any at all. Him barging that bedroom door down as fearsome as a rhinoceros, grabbing Mal, not me, by the neck and holding him high against the wall. I mouthed the words he'd say: "You ever touch my fucking daughter again!" I'd picture Mal crumble as Lou realized the error of her ways. She'd dash quickly from her house to mine, to find me alone, asleep in an armchair, and take me in her embrace.

I woke to find Mum was home from work early. It was Shrove Tuesday but she'd forgotten to buy eggs. We had an apologetic-looking plate of chips and beans while she told me what the mayor's breath smelled like. The orange sunrise of slime had dried and cracked and stained our plates and was long since cold by the time Mal walked in through the door and she stood to make him some dinner. It was almost midnight and she'd waited. She offered, he smiled and was fed, so she was happy.

When he'd finished eating, Mal placed his plate on the floor at his feet. The thick juices on it slid back and forth. Without asking, Mum, who'd been watching from the doorway of the kitchen, brought him two thick slices of soft white bread, light and fluffy, cloud-tasting, to mop up the remnants of his meal. He did, letting the softened, torn slice slip down into his stomach, where it ballooned as would a sponge to his wetted inner workings.

More bread was broken, offered and declined. Mal rubbed his stomach, tracing the lines of its distention with his forefingers. Ice cream was proffered as an option. He accepted and Mum, smiling, swung toward the kitchen.

"You're getting fat," I teased but it was barbed with malice and he knew it, he could feel its claws on its way across it, playful and nasty, catlike toward his ears. "Now you've left school, if you just sit there all day, you're just going to get fatter and fatter."

He moved to respond but Mum got there first.

"There is no rush, Malcolm, you know that." She nodded toward him.

"I know," he said.

"And stop winding him up, he's done nothing to you," she said, aimed my way.

Mal went to bed before me, as did Mum, and I sat up late, the flicker of the television strobing my face in the dark. When I eventually retired I found that Mal had emptied my pillow of feathers. Too tired to argue, I sank to my knees and slowly picked them up, one by one, stuffing them back into their case until I had at least a chicken's worth, which I slept on, restlessly, for what felt like seconds.

Thirty

A ferocious banging at the front door jerked me from a dream instantly forgotten. A feather was congealed to my dry, sleepy lip and it removed a layer of skin when I pulled it off to speak.

"Mal. Mal."

"What?"

"The door," I said.

I could tell that he wasn't awake, nor asleep either. He was a gargling confusion.

"What?"

"The door," I said again.

Then there was more banging, a bunched fist hammering against the wood, making the metal of the letterbox swing noisily.

"The door, Mal!" I shouted through clenched teeth, aware that whoever was on the other side of it wouldn't be looking for me.

He threw a leg from the bed, then another, and with a yawn took his quilt under both arms like a huge padded shawl and, still naked but for that, walked out of the room to the front door.

I heard Lou's voice and rummaged in the darkness for a pair of trousers. The legs were turned inward and knotted, and I rushed to force my feet through them, blood through arteries clogged with cheesy dollops of fat. Their steps approached. I buttoned the trousers at my waist with farcically good timing as the pair of them emerged through the door. Mal had his arm around her shoulders, like he was holding her together, and she was crying. His arm was big and strong and her slender neck rested against it. It looked like he was leading her, dazzled, from the wreck of a car crash. Except that he was naked and dragging the bedclothes with his right foot across the carpet. She didn't seem to notice, her hands were closed around her face like a book. I bent my stomach and arched my back. I made myself small. I did my utmost to become assimilated into the shadows formed in the corner of the room by the splicing of the moonlight through the window by the curtains.

"Sit down," he said. Lou perched on the bed. He enveloped her in his might. "Tell me what's wrong."

She stammered, her voice mired in the back of her throat. Slowly she cleared it, got stronger and began to speak of what it was that brought her here in the middle of the night.

"Mum has gone and left him," she said.

Mal had told me once about Lou's mum. He'd called her selfish and arrogant and bullish, and it was obvious from the times when her dad would come to pick her up from our house that it was him Lou would turn to rather than her. Now it seemed it was Mal rather than either of them. Mal rubbed her shoulder. It fitted perfectly inside his palm. And after some deep breaths she spoke again, and I realized I was hearing only the end of a long-standing inevitability.

"After you left tonight she told him. Just like that. She walked into the living room, and she told him. She said she was going. Leaving him, she said. That she'd been with someone else, for years. That man, the real estate man. The estate agent, the one with his face on the signs. Him. And that's why she was never there. And that's why she didn't love him anymore, because he just sat there in that chair watching television. She said she couldn't remember the last time they even spoke. And then she went. She left."

Lou's shoulders shuddered like her spine was the pump-action arm of a shotgun. I shrank smaller and smaller in my bed and listened.

"What did he do?" asked Mal.

"Nothing. He did nothing. He didn't flinch. He didn't move or raise his voice. He didn't even speak. He just sat there like an empty shell. Like a ghost."

Her lips flickered as she inhaled a sob and a silence where a wail was expected.

"But it's not his fault. She did that to him. She broke him. He would just sit there all day because he didn't know what else to do."

He massaged the thin muscle of her upper arm in his hand, up down up down as though he were raising a flag, and she leaned into it like a cat, back flexed, to a fond leg. She cried more and the words sounded watery.

"He loved her. It's like she's killed him and left him alive at the same time. She was never there. She was always out. Always with him. And Dad knew, all this time he knew."

There was quiet for a while but for the gentle, tired whimpers she made.

"The woman he's devoted his life to, and he never gave up because he believed that he loved her. Total devotion, and slowly it broke him. Can you imagine that?"

Mal told me once she looked like her dad. Never her mum.

"I tried to hold him but he didn't move. He was never really there. Now he never really will be."

She nestled her head in Mal's neck and he embraced her. It was as if he had grown around her, like ivy, like exactly what was needed at exactly the right time.

I pulled my own quilt up over my head and thought until I could hear the two of them sleeping. That poor man.

In the morning neither of them had moved.

Thirty-One

Though I was never destined for the summits of academia, the older I got the more I enjoyed school. I sought and needed it. But it was not what I learned that I'd remember, it was the proximity of that lesson to the first time I felt a girl's lips placed upon mine.

Sally Bay, Sal, was in my class. She wore makeup, the pinks and blues of a parakeet, which bestowed upon her an allure the other girls hadn't yet figured out. Boys liked Sal so much that a playful punch from her was consigned an altogether different meaning. Even if it hurt, it was a pleasure. It was attention. It was everything that I'd wanted but had lost now that Mal's was being so frequently shared, and that because of him Lou would never give me.

It was a warm spring day, the air swirling with pollen and floating seedlings. We were sitting in the park, me, Sal, Sporty Chris, others, pulling those thick yellow strips of straw from the ground with sharp tugs, the way one might pluck the coarse hair from a pig's back. People were disappearing, home for tea, for television, other callings, until there were just the two of us left. No boys to say funny things before I'd thought of them. No braggarts, no liars, no better faster stronger runners, jumpers or thinkers, just me and her.

We were spread out on the grass, unnaturally, pricklingly close. So close I could hear the short bursts of her quick, crisp breath, and it was exciting.

"Have you ever kissed someone?" she said.

"Ha!" I snorted. "Yes," I lied.

The anticipation suddenly sawed into my skull a headache, a mouth full of frozen ice cream.

"Want to kiss me?" she asked.

I turned to face her, our noses almost Eskimo lips brushing. Her eyes were closed, a thick pastel blue. Her face was warmed by the sun and tiny flies buzzed whirlwinds at her ear. You, I thought, you, are the most normal person I know. And I liked it.

I licked my lips, not too wet, and then padded them together just how girls did to remove the grease of a purple cherry lipstick like the one she was wearing that made her lips look both alive and like plastic. And then I pursed them, like in magazines, and drove them forward slowly, like in soap operas, until the faintest of contact was made.

"Wait!" she said, and she pulled the coat she'd been using as a pillow up over our heads, as if to prevent the sun from playing witness to our illicit little tryst. As an added bonus, in the unthinkable event that either of us would open our eyes midway through the act—or, God forbid, both do so at the same time—the terrible embarrassment would be muffled by the dark.

And then she drove forward herself, her hand tentatively resting on my belly so as not to embrace it but to be there, scared and rigid. I repeated the act, mirroring her movement but taking the utmost of care not to accidentally brush her breast. Instead, and much to my instant regret, my hand came to rest on her bony rib cage with the static positioning a sprinter might adopt at the starting blocks. She smelled like teenage woman, sticky in the back of my throat. Her lips, as they came to mine, were slightly open, warm and syrupy. Mine, no saliva, were dried instantly so that we scratched and jarred together until I too was coated in a layer of her balm. And soon we were slipping off each other, our bodies wrought iron but our mouths two eels. Our jaws two engines, pumping away, sliding in and out of each other's hopeless youthful timing.

I opened my eyes as the cymbals clashed inside my head. This felt wonderful. I looked at her, and though I couldn't see I forgot very briefly everything else that had ever mattered and enjoyed the moment so completely that tears pretended they might form in the corners of my eyes. It lasted mere seconds.

She pulled away and giggled. I smiled back. And then a blankness caked me. I knew nothing to say. There were no correct noises, nor incorrect ones, to be made. Just the rustle of the long grass and the last dregs of pleasure. But I had to speak, to rescue us both. And so I panicked. I imagined Mal speaking to Lou.

"Do you want to come to my house?" I said. But I wasn't him and she wasn't her. And I was fifteen. And this was ridiculous.

"Erm . . . no," she said. She was blushing. "I can't. I've got to go home."

She climbed to her feet, said good-bye and waded through the long grass circle our supine bodies had carved on the ground. Home. But it had been instinct, nothing more. Drummed into me over all these years, an unease with the real world that only then could I start to abandon. Home had always been safe. Home had always been easy. But I didn't want easy anymore. I wanted to lie in fields, kissing girls.

I watched her leave. I imagined Lou's back.

Thirty-Two

An hour after my first kiss, the residue of euphoria still remained, the way it does when you're lucky to still be alive. I walked slowly home as the sun set and the sky dozed a melancholic purple. I was blessed with a new confidence. I imagined myself in an old film, doffing my cap to ladies and jumping into the air to bring both heels together with a charming clickety click. I pictured myself swinging effortlessly around lampposts for the full three hundred and sixty degrees. Maybe twice. I was grace and cool. Something about the evening had aroused in me an untested superpower. I felt the faintest tingle of it across my forehead and down each arm.

I turned into my street in time for the sunshine to outline the chimney stacks. Dad was sitting in his car, the door open, his legs swung to the side the way you'd lower yourself into a well. He was smoking a cigarette, the ghost of which made fragile designs. I hadn't even known he smoked. He did that Dad nod, a neatly compacted "Hello, how are you?" that signaled some level of familiarity. He looked heavily weathered, a stranger almost.

"You're just in time for dinner," he said, then bounced the butt of his cigarette against the drain.

Dinner was an unloved oven-ready pizza. Pineapple chunks flanked slithers of sore-looking meat, glazed in a shiny coat of grease and sitting on an old, chipped plate Dad won in a raffle. The television was switched off and we were perched on each side of a haggard, square, self-assembly trestle table we never normally used. It didn't bode well. Happy families eat off of laps. I took extra time to chew through the lightly browned cheese and thick crumbling crust in the hope that it would render me exempt from any duty to break the silence. Dad examined the serrated edge of his knife before buttering another piece of bread.

"So," he said to me. "Today? Good?"

"I saw the careers adviser," I said.

I'd decided that now was not the time to mention that, after lying in a field with a girl and almost feeling the outline of her tender young breast, I'd been forced to stop off on the way home and look into the mirrored window of a hairdresser's to be sure that my bottom lip wasn't smeared in makeup. It was. With his eyes he goaded me, implored me to recount my day at school. And so, for him, I did.

"So what is it that you would like to do?" she'd asked me.

My school careers adviser, a woman named Ms. Kay, who, when asked the same question hadn't responded "Be a careers adviser," seemed surprised that I didn't have a ready answer.

She was dressed like an art deco supervillain, powerful clashes of blacks and whites topped neatly with a slick, angular bob that danced against the side of her head as she strode purposely about the corridors. She had pretended not to notice the gross caricature of her that someone penciled on the wall next to the door of the staff room. There were few in existence who wanted to be elsewhere for so much of every working day as Ms. Kay. Adult life for her had been a huge disappointment. It had failed to keep a single one of the promises it had made to her and liked to rub it in by forcing her to spend most of her waking hours with those of an age that facilitated the enjoyment of being alive.

In the sterile environs of her office she'd spread pamphlets on the table, detailing all manner of career paths I'd never entertained. She was busy talking me through them, making no pretense at having any passion for her vocation whatsoever. Not that it mattered to me, I'd stopped listening some time ago.

"Are you even listening?" she asked.

"Yes," I said.

I was actually thinking about Lou. That beauty, the poise of whose cheekbones alone (they formed the perfect gradient, pulling tight the skin around her cherubic chin) made dizzying bursts of adrenaline burn through my heart.

"What do you feel that you are good at?"

Pretending to listen.

"I'm not sure," I said.

Ms. Kay cleared the pictures of plumbers, electricians and builders from the table, slotting them back into the corresponding files on the bookshelf. It was a process she'd be performing in reverse just five minutes later. She walked to the window, removed a smear from the glass with the cuff of her jacket and turned to me.

"Do you know . . . ?" She paused. She sounded like she had too many teeth in her mouth. "Do you know what your brother Malcolm said two years ago when I asked him what he'd like to do?"

I'd no idea.

"Malcolm is unemployed," I said.

"'I'd like to change the world,'" she said. "And do you know what I told him?"

"No," I said.

"'Don't be ridiculous.'"

She thrust a leaflet into my hand as I walked through the door. On the front was a photograph of a man carrying a box, looking bored. I could only presume that the box contained his will to live. He looked a little like Ms. Kay.

My family, at the dinner table that was so small our knees knocked and locked together, received only an edited version of this story. I left the part about Mal out of it but I thought it to myself and I watched his face as he was reminded of it, his eyes dropping to the piece of cheap cubed pork that lay alone on his plate.

Thirty-Three

Without the qualifications or inclination to go on to further education, after leaving school I grasped firmly to the floating detritus in the undercurrent of dead-end jobs. I resigned myself to two years of soul-destroying tedium before I left home. Everyone else seemed to be doing the same thing. This is what people did, some of them forever.

I found a job in a butcher's shop where the floor was a sticky bleach smell but never clean. The walls smelled of that waxy meat odor. So did the radio and so did the mugs from which you drank piping hot tea. To the touch, everything felt clammy, like holding a wet, raw kidney. By the time I arrived home from a day's work the skin on my hands was a torrid blue from digging through freezer cabinets and covered in cuts and slices from the sharp, spiteful edges of frozen livers. My apron would be swiped with blood from helping a colleague, Ted, for whom conversation was limited to sports statistics and different cuts of meat, carry on our shoulders whole sides of beef between the delivery truck and the walk-in fridge. We looked like pallbearers on a farm, I joked, which he didn't get.

I liked Ted. Ted listened while most were simply waiting for their turn to talk. If he didn't know about something, he didn't feel the need to misfire conjecture into the discussion. He was honest. He had a big honest face and a big honest chest atop legs as sturdy and true as tree trunks. He reminded me of a faithful St. Bernard digging through Alpine snow to find his buried master. It was on the first day that I met Ted, covered in blood after shifting the hollowed carcasses of lambs all morning and with his outstretched hand dripping, that I decided to make him my best friend. Always covered in blood. I called him Red Ted.

Red Ted didn't care who Mal was. He didn't ask at any point. Even years and years later, after Day One, and even much later still, after I'd been to America and returned, broken, Red Ted would drive me to my hospital appointments in a car that was too small for him, dropping me by the door. He never asked about Malcolm Ede, even though everyone knew about Malcolm Ede by this point. That's why I liked Red Ted. That, and his name.

Red Ted was twenty-two. He too had fallen into butchery upon leaving school, employed by the man who owns the shop to lug the bins full of bone across the yard without slipping over on errantly discarded gristle and breaking his gargantuan back. Soon after he'd joined, the owner had developed chronic arthritis in his fingers through years of exposure to cold, cuts and the infections the two bring when married together as they were here. Faced with a choice between closing the shop and giving it over to Ted, he chose the latter, mindful of the fact that few people were more trustworthy. There were also few who were more adept at carving meat. Red Ted, with a small curve-ended filleting knife clasped between his thumb and forefinger, could remove all of the bones from a chicken, neatly and wasting none of the tender meat, in under a minute. I remember wondering, all of those years later as I watched Mal expand, how much choice meat Red Ted might be able to remove from him, and how long it would take him to do so.

"Not that long," he replied matter-of-factly when I asked him once, as though it were as normal an act as rolling a loin of pork, or preparing some thinly sliced lamb cutlets. He could do a cow in just under an hour.

"There is someone here to see you . . . ," Red Ted announced one day, in his customary baritone. When he shouted, it was the pull-string horn of a speeding train.

"Who is it?" I asked.

I was brushing the cold, slimy, golden jelly from a roll of freshly cooked turkey with the back of my hand. To stop, clean up and reapply my hairnet only to find it was Chris, or Sally Bay, or any of the others who'd pop by unannounced in the hope of scoring a free sausage roll, would have been pointless.

"It's Lou."

I straightened my apron, dosed my hands with bright blue sanitizing powder that burped chemical bubbles on contact with the hot water on my skin and threw my hairnet aside. A look in the mirror. A rub of the hands. One more straightening of the apron and a deep, deep breath. It felt like I hadn't seen her properly for a while, since Mal had all but taken up residence at her dad's house.

"Hello," I said quietly, emerging to her surprise from the doorway underneath the futuristic neon blast of the fly-murdering machine. It buzzed like its victims. She turned.

"Hello. How are you . . . ? I like your apron."

I laughed. "Thanks. I'm good. You?"

"Good."

"I take it you've not come for some sirloin."

"No."

"We do excellent chops."

Adult conversation. With Lou. Funny. Clever. Light, not too serious. For the first time. She smiled. My mind lit up and in my ears came the organ music they play at American baseball games when a home run gets hit but my face stayed collected. I wondered why you never feel like you're maturing, you just wake up one day and you've matured. Well, almost.

"Have you heard from Mal?" she said.

"No," I said. "Not since yesterday. He ate all my biscuits."

She laughed again. I get cartoon pound-signs rolling around my eyes, my mouth a frothing fountain of animated golden coins.

"Oh. Well, we've found a place to live."

"Right."

"We were wondering. Wondering if you could do us a favor?"

"Sure. OK. What is it?"

My heart began to hurt. I almost turned around to check that Ted had not jammed his cleaver through it. I could see this coming. I was at least three seconds ahead of the world.

"We were wondering if you'd tell your mum the news?"

Thirty-Four

My walk home from the butcher's that night was prolonged by the lazy warmth of an orange dusk. It was stretched beyond recognition, like the walk behind a family hearse.

By the time I was home I was a wreck. I forgot to take my overalls off. A dirty apron. A splattered white coat. Boots dashed with the ghostly spots of the bleach Red Ted would use to clean the floor. A white netted hat with animal blood coagulating on its rim. I looked like a mental umpire.

I took off my stinking boots outside and placed them neatly side by side at the step leading in. With surgical care I slid my key into the slot and turned it. Inside I found Mal, surprised to see me, loading a cardboard box with an assortment of uncoordinated clothes.

"If you're here . . . ," I said, "why do I have to tell her?"

No room for hellos. No time for how-are-yous.

"Because she's not here," he said. "She's at the mayor's office, working, and I won't be here when she gets back."

"But you can be."

"But I won't."

He scooped entire bundles of his own things from the wardrobe with both arms, as though shifting boulders with a growing urgency, and with no regard for the sharp creases and folds Mum had loved into them dropped them into the boxes arranged on the floor until they spilled out over the sides. I flung my bloody hat onto the bed but it rolled onto the carpet. I sat down where it landed and watched him as he packed.

"OK. I'm going. Tell her I'll be back tomorrow to get more stuff." He waddled through the door, a box under his arm, Lou waiting in a car parked in the street. "And tell her it's fine. It's normal, that's all. People leave home all the time."

He shut the door behind him with his hooked left foot. He'd gone to enter a world he never before wanted to be a part of. He'd started his run-up with a plan to make a dent in a surface he'd once told me wouldn't bend.

The house felt dormant. I could hear the dull mechanics of the clock on the wall. I could hear the bubbles pop pop pop in the can of cola Mal had left on his bedside table, and I silenced it by drinking it down in one go.

Thirty-Five

Mum came home late. Her key rattled loudly in the door, her bag swung on the peg meant but never used for hats. In one practiced move she scraped her flat shoes from her heels with the other foot until they plopped to the floor below her and chased them with her big toe to their hiding place like they were mice. Before they'd touched down her feet were already in new slippers. She shuffled into the kitchen. In the flicker of illumination she filled the kettle with water and switched it on, the opening bar to a piece she knew well played out again then by the kitchen orchestra she conducted. Clicks and whistles and beeps. The thump of tins in bins and the clack clack of a chopping board fighting a knife.

I sat quietly in the living room.

An omelette for two, mushrooms, lightly salted. I'd meant to bring meat for her.

"He's gone," I said.

"I know," she said.

That night in bed I heard her cry as she folded her clothes with meticulous care and put them to sleep in a deep wooden drawer. I heard it close. I fell asleep.

Around three hours later there was weight on my bed, a hand on my shoulder, a kind whisper of, "It's just me, don't worry." A shadow part caught by the light through the window made the half of Mum's face it hit moon-colored. Nighttime chameleon.

"What's wrong?" I said. Sleep talk, slow and tired and confused.

"Nothing," she whispered. But there was worry in her voice for a bird flown. If I'd been Mal, she'd have sat there all night. I fell asleep again and she left.

Thirty-Six

Day Seven Thousand Four Hundred and Eighty-Three.

I stumble about the house in a melancholic stupor that stops me from feeling the breeze of daily commotion as it passes. Mum runs between the trailer and the bedroom, trays of food wobbling like the jowls of a huge, slobbery bloodhound. I stand still at the foot of Dad's ladder, still unconquered. I was silly to even attempt to scale it, I think, my legs as they are.

She doesn't notice me scrabbling through the airing cupboard, where I discover my trophy from sports day all those years before. It wears a cape of cobwebs and nestles in the damp bedding of old blankets and children's toys. I am, for ten quiet minutes, an archaeologist of my own childhood. I brush clean the dinosaur bones of the times it wasn't like this. I piece together the broken pottery of the long days our family would spend together and wonder just how it had been smashed into so many tiny fragments as to have become unrecognizable. This was, perhaps, a job for a better archaeologist than me.

I hear Dad clambering about the attic still, the tools in his work belt angrily striking at his hips clank clank. And as I lift my crisp white butcher's overall from the radiator and violate it with cruel, urgent creases, I walk to the window.

Lou. I'd not imagined it.

Lou. Right now.

Lou. On the lawn.

Day Seven Thousand Four Hundred and Eighty-Three, according to the display on the wall. I see Lou.

Thirty-Seven

She stands there in the sunshine, looking much the same. Still that pinprick of light in her eye, her thin porcelain neck a matte white, rolling into sharp collarbones in an angle-free descent like the ornate, curved legs of a Victorian coffee table. Lou was beautiful. Some people are so attractive that looking at them makes you feel as though your own skin doesn't fit properly, and Lou is like that. She has blond, tumbling hair that wisps and frays as though she's washed it in the sea each morning, combed it through with the finest shells and rinsed away the foam in a freshly formed rock pool. She looks like a mermaid. Her eyes are mint green, her nose straight and strong. Back then, before she left, I would look at her every day and still find new secrets, new details in the shapes she made.

I wave, clumsy and graceless, unsure. She waves back a smooth, elegant half-moon. I can see her at twelve again.

I look at my watch to record the time. All around me is noise, this endless cycle of ordinary repetitive action by which our extraordinary lives have become defined. But no one seems to have noticed her out there, certainly not Mal, whose snore has refired once more.

Mal. I dreamt sometimes of standing on him, my feet disappearing up to ankle height in his flab, schloop schloop schloop as I stepped, like in quicksand. Losing my boots in his belly, wading through his fatty quagmire, being pulled deeper and deeper into his gut until I was, at waist height, halfway inside him, clinging to

Lou by the wrist and trying to pull her out. But she's disappearing, and I pull and pull and sweat and struggle but it's hopeless, and soon she is gone, eaten up by his skin, lost in the marsh of his great stagnant body. And by then it's too late for me too, and I follow her down inside him never to be seen again.

She is still there and waving back. This sight, it lifts and swings me through extremes of hot and cold. I know then I still love her. I know then this is coming to an end.

She is wearing sunglasses, big ones that panda-circle her eyes. She gestures, a flattened hand turned on its side, chop-chop-chop. To meet her at the butcher's shop. And a time. Eleven o'clock tonight. After the interview is finished, of course. And then she turns and walks, stepping over the guy ropes of the tent on the lawn. Soon she has disappeared, my phantom limb lopped off.

"Where are you going? You can't go anywhere. What about the interview?" Mal says as I struggle to bend down over my stiffened legs in their surgical scaffolding and put on my shoes in the bedroom. His voice, powerless, wafts through the tires of flab that hoopla his neck.

"Out," I say.

"You never go out," he says.

"You can talk."

We both laugh. But I'm not going anywhere just yet. I wouldn't miss this, the interview, the big reveal, for the world.

Mum is on her hands and knees by the side of the bed, unraveling wires and tubes dreadlocked together from the back of Mal's machines. They bleep a perpetual chorus. They remind me of the doctors who have now all been and gone. Now on to the serious business.

The stretched patches of hair on Mal's enormous chest are turning silver. Clinging in amongst them are the charred crumbs of well-cooked sausage and the crumbly sponge morsels of last night's cake. Red Ted would need to dig for a long long time to find Mal's bones. Burst a spade with a sharp downward jab through that dirty, thin top layer of skin. Force the shovel with his foot through the sinew and the meat. Lift, drop and dig, spooning out the maggoty-white tubes of fat. And dig and dig and dig until he hears the chink of his blade upon the skeleton, the treasure, all that was there in the beginning. A journey to the center of the earth.

"Where?" he says.

"Where what?"

I know how he hates it when I understand what he means but implore him for a clearer definition anyway, hates the effort, hates the energy he must summon to expand his diaphragm, lift his rib cage and make words.

"Where are you going?"

To see Lou, I think.

"Out. After your interview, I'm going out," I say.

He curls up the chubby elbow of his nose and purses his lips. His shiny, sweaty forehead ruffles in frustration.

"With your legs?" he says.

"Yes, with my legs. I can't go out without them."

I look round at the walls and the floor and think about how long I've been here. I look at the display on the wall, the bright green liquid crystal shining down, illuminating Mal's cavernous navel (by now stretched to the proportions of a medium-sized oven dish). I look at the huge, tattered pile of news cuttings forming a paper staircase up the wall. I look at my tiny bed wedged into the far corner. I hear Dad through the ceiling, hammering, clink clink, dragging a weighty new contraption across the floor he drilled holes in. The dusty leaves of wallpaper dying and dropping off, the autumn of the decoration. The sacks and sacks of mail from all over the world. The adult nappies. The dirty, dirty plates.

I pull on my other shoe, neatly weaving the laces like spaghetti through the holes in the leather. But I am early, very early. So I sit back on my bed and I watch Mum help Mal suck dry spoonful after spoonful. A glinting chain of saliva sends a tractor beam between his gums and the silver. His swallow expels a bass heavy grunt, like an elderly cow hitting the floor, in anticipation of rain one last time.

Thirty-Eight

Houses have, in the memories of the bricks, an ability to return to normal. To withstand death and loss. To return to a shape like a spring or a sponge. An innate power to survive even the greatest erosion. That's what our house had, and when Mal, its beating heart and vibrant mind, had departed, it didn't keel over and die as it would have seemed fit to. Instead it regenerated, the way the human body can its liver.

Mal visited, as he promised, which would always cast the spell of a toothy grin across Mum's face. They would sit and talk for hours, her checking he was OK, him keeping her updated on developments.

"I've got a job in an office," he said. "It's boring but I just keep my head down and promotions happen pretty fast."

A smart haircut had crept up behind him and fixed itself to his head. On a few occasions I'd pass him on my way to work, me on my bike, him in Lou's car. A tie wound round his bulging neck, the top button forcing his Adam's apple further up his throat like a corset might a plump bosom.

He looked like a black-and-white edition of Mal, an official version. Government sanctioned. One hundred per cent approved. On the ladder. Moving up. Ticking the boxes. Nine to five. Friday lunchtime drinking. Pay slip, mathematics. Bills first, play later. Die now, pay later. Coming home, feeling tired, plan the dinner for next week, go to bed. Wait for the weekend, DIY superstore, clean the house, dread the feeling, Monday morning alarm clock blaring. Big shop, big shop. Try to save up if you can. Summer holiday or broken boiler.

But Lou. He had Lou. Slowly she began to visit again, with Mal, each occasion doing a little more to melt the frost that had collected on the moment. Mum did her best to pretend that it had never been a problem, that she'd always been perfectly happy for Mal to leave. She wandered through her days, seemingly untouched by the news, untroubled by whatever went on around her. Serving up huge, elaborate dinners for me and Dad, happy to see us eat them but all of the time becoming more and more insular as the world she'd created slowly left her behind.

Dad, quieter and quieter still, would spend longer and longer periods away from home working. On his return he'd be up in his attic, building and making but quiet all the same.

The glue where Mal had been had dried and flaked, disintegrated.

It felt as though I was the only one participating in family life. Still living in the house, fearful to leave Mum on her own, I began to build myself my own little part of adulthood. The more Sal Bay came to stay, which she never did for the night but rather when Mum was out working late, the less I'd imagine that she was Lou as we lay together on the bed. No longer awkwardly but lovingly, tenderly. Normally.

In return for helping him continue to build the business on behalf of our arthritic boss, Red Ted gave me the absolute minimum amount of grief and let me work whatever hours I felt suited me. Occasionally, say after a hard day's pulling the muscles from the legs of turkeys, talons still attached, in preparation for the Christmas rush, we'd head into town and get drunk together. Sometimes Mal would come along too. Life trundled along with a steady momentum. And though I thought about Lou, I was happy. Just as I knew in my heart and my bones and the fibers of my being as a child when Mal was about to turn an ordinary day into an extraordinary one, I knew it would happen again. And it would shake this steady ship, this steady boring ship, until we all fell off it. This sailor's life was not the life for us. I wasn't sure if I cared whether I'd drown. Maybe I already was. Just bobbing, waiting for the lifeboats to be deployed by whatever Mal did next. I knew that if this was how I felt conformity's dull itch, in Mal it was an agony he couldn't let persist. We were just waiting for the need to scratch it to become too big to take.

I was happy to wait, in the meat and the boredom and the wanting Lou. The heaviest photograph had not yet been taken.

Thirty-nine

One day I was tapping my fingers on the radiator like a tin-ribbed xylophone. Its cold metal vibrated, left hanging robotic melodies in the air. Mum was cleaning, rarely rising from the mists of sprayed polish and only to wonder aloud about the whereabouts of Dad, who had gone merely to Ellis's store and should have been home by now with more dusters. The one in her hand splayed wet and limp and matted with swaths of black muck and hair. She barely applied pressure to it, just swept it back and forth along the mantelpiece.

I watched the particles of spray that kicked up into the air have tiny dogfights so intently that when the phone rang it was a fire-cracker. I answered it.

"Get your shoes on," said Mal. "We're going on holiday."

Then he hung up and all I could hear was the telephonic purr of a conversation ended, and all I could feel was a rush.

Lou's old blue car sidled up to the curb, contoured with great silver scratches that ran in zigzags as though they'd been put there by the thin-tipped sword of a flamboyant matador. Mal was in the passenger seat, his tidy hair now a mess, bearing his teeth like an excited chimpanzee. He was wearing Lou's coat, a grand purple piece of cloth with three chunks of golden button at the top. I wished I could hide notes in her pockets. I climbed into the back-seat, stuffing my bag into the well by my feet. Lou grinned and kissed me on the cheek. Her hand rested on Mal's thigh and when he spoke she squeezed it.

"Where are we going?" I asked.

"To the sea," he said.

The old car hacked, reluctantly pulling into the road with a spectral smoke path behind it. We drove past Dad at the end of the road. We pressed the horn and waved. I banged on the windows until the glass shook and the rubber around it loosened. But he didn't notice. His chin almost touching the steering wheel. His thoughts not of the road.

"Go on then," I said to Mal as we gathered speed. "What's going on?"

I could feel all the bumps and jolts of the drive compounded in my buttocks, the springs stacked loose in the seat jabbing pins into the meat of my calf.

"I've sat in an office answering a telephone all week. A twat selling shit he knows nothing about to idiots who have no idea. Lou's been counting other people's money behind the counter in a bank and you've no doubt been fingering your way through the insides of a cow." Lou grinned. "I'm not going to spend the two days off I have a week looking forward to the five that follow, am I? So I thought we'd just get out of it for a while. Be somewhere new. See what we can find. See what there is to discover," Mal said.

"Get drunk on the beach?" Lou said.

"Yes. For a start."

Through the windscreen the sun cooked the soft hairs on our arms. She kept her hand tight on his thigh. He stroked the back of her neck. Even on the motorway and during the high-speed entrances and exits, the noise and the zipping-by.

When we arrived we parked by the ramp that the lifeboats use to enter the water. A large man and his friend were trying to sell cheap watches from the boot of their car, saw us get out and called Lou over. She went, not through intrigue but through politeness, and surveyed the range of junk he had displayed on a small rug. There were dank silvers and golds, like a collection of foils, worthless and gaudy. I followed her; a sensitive barometer for the out-of-place urged me to.

"Any one you like, love?" he said. His head was misshapen by bulging veins. All about him but his thin pink lips seemed brutish.

"No, thank you," Lou said.

He held her arm just above her wrist. I was rooted.

"Come on," he said. "I'll give you girlfriend prices."

His friend behind mooched. He laughed on cue but didn't realize it, and behind his eyes he was replete. My fingers fidgeted in my hands. I looked to Mal but he'd gone to find a machine to buy a parking ticket from. I looked to Lou and he was still holding her arm. Not how Mal held it. She was brittle with fright, like he might snap her, and her eyes widened to invite me in but I was powerless and it was all so fast.

"No. Thank you," she said.

She pulled her arm toward herself and stared. And he did the same but so much more powerfully. Because he thought he was a man, and because he thought that those not in his image were not. I was not in his image. I would never be in his image. My anger clogged my throat.

"Come on," he said.

His face was up next to hers, his head square, blocky, twice the size of Lou's. I saw his breath hitting her skin, refracting the day's heat. I saw the missiles of spittle launched from his mouth, landing on her eyelids clenched shut, tight like bulldog clips.

"At least give me a smile, beautiful."

I burned a fury at seeing her wronged. A fog had befallen me and it was thick. I heard his friend laugh again.

"Or a kiss."

He closed his eyes too, and pursed his lips, and I wound up a coil of all the force I could muster, clasped my fingers together and pulled back my arm, ready to unload it.

Then Mal, Lou's purple coat hung like a cape from his neck,

his hair a blackened unruly weave, his shoes odd, stepped out smoothly from the afternoon as though he'd been there all along, part of the car or just of the day. He lifted one leg behind him until he was shaped like a bow, leaned in and kissed this thug full on the mouth in a short, quick burst. And he was the man, he with the least concern for any notion of how he as a man should behave. Before either of them, their heads like knuckles, could do anything about it Mal grabbed the lip of the rug from the boot of the car and pulled it sharply. A hundred poorly made watches crashed onto the cement and shattered in cheap shards.

Mal took Lou and we all ran together toward the beach. They gave chase but we lost them in their confusion. When we were far enough away, we stopped to quickly pull our shoes off and then carried on running, this time even faster, until they were gone. In safe distance, laughter having outfought the fear, Mal dropped the bag he'd been carrying on his shoulder and we sat to catch our breath, amazed and in love.

Forty

By the sea the breeze was a racket. It was already edging toward the remnants of the afternoon, and so the beach, or what little there was of it, was clearing of people. Those who remained watched as Mal made a great show of creating a sandy mosaic from the towels he'd brought with him. Me and Lou sat on the floor and laughed some more and were warmed by burying our feet.

We drank the wine Mal had hidden in the boot of the car as a surprise and rested until all of the sky was the color and texture of clouds with nothing to break them into small floating pieces.

"Do you like this?" asked Mal.

Lou's head was on his belly.

"What?" I said.

"This, what we're doing now. This middle part."

"Of course I like it . . . But the middle part of what?"

"Of life," he said. "This is the bit after the time you can't do anything for yourself and before the time you have to do anything for others."

He stroked Lou's head. She closed her eyes like she'd heard this before, or as though she was remembering an argument, words exchanged.

"I love this bit," he said.

"What makes you think you have to change?" Lou said.

"But you're expected to," he replied, "and you will have to. Maybe one day you realize that everything you thought was coming to you, everything you'd been promised, just isn't going to happen. And maybe when you realize that, maybe settling down is just what happens. Maybe that's when you admit defeat. When you become a horrible, lecherous prick selling cheap jewelry out of your car in a car park. That's when you know that it's time to put your hands in the air. Give up. Move on. Life is over and it's someone else's turn."

She was warm in his voice and his touch and the way he thought.

"Right . . . I'm drinking sand here." Mal stood up and the final drips from his upturned glass parachuted to the floor. "I'm going to get more wine. And chocolate. Guard the towels."

"What kind of people would steal towels?" shouted Lou, her voice snapping at his heels as he jogged down the beach.

"Wet people," came the response after we could no longer make him out in the dark of the evening. And then there was silence for a second.

"Lou," I whispered. "I've never been to the beach before."

She sat up straight and incredulous.

"Never?!"

"Never. I nearly did once but Mal was naughty and we had to come home."

She laughed. "Do you think he's OK?" she asked.

I stalled. "He'll be fine. He's only gone to get some more wine."

"No," she said. "Generally, do you think he's OK?"

"Of course. Why wouldn't he be?"

"He's restless."

"He's always restless."

"But in work, and at home. I don't think he's happy."

"Don't worry," I said. "Mal was always this way."

I imagined her head on my stomach, me underneath her with my arms crossed behind my neck and the sky above us blackening until we fell asleep right there on the sand. And us going home together when we awoke. There was more quiet, and I watched on her face the inner whirrings of her decision-making process, whether or not she should tell me whatever it is that's opening and closing the gates of her thought. And then she opened her mouth to speak. I imagined a ping, the cartoon lightbulb of a new idea.

"Last night," she said, a beat and then another, "I told him," and another and another, "that I wanted to have a baby."

I became massively aware of my own body weight, sinking.

"Oh," I said.

"He was just quiet. He didn't really respond. He took all of his clothes off and he climbed into bed. I just presumed this was what would happen, that we would have a baby eventually. That's just what you do, isn't it? And when he woke up this morning he was different. Like when we were younger. He just insisted we do this. He didn't even mention what I'd said last night. It was like he'd just reverted."

The sea hissed. Foam fizzed on the beach.

"Has he spoken to you about it?"

"No." I shook my head. "He never really speaks to me."

I gently lifted my feet so that the sand fell through the gaps between my toes in ticklish waterfalls. Lou quaffed the remainder of the plastic tumbler full of wine she had in her little hand.

Forty-One

When Mal arrived back with a plastic bag clanking with colored glass tucked under his arm, I did my best to act like all me and Lou had spoken about was the lapping of the waves of the sea I'd never been in. The darkness landed like a pillow on our faces, and though we'd known it was coming we were surprised just how quickly it arrived.

"You were gone for a while," Lou said.

"I stopped off at the car," Mal said.

We sat and we drank, the conversation flitting happily through topics, a giddy moth between lamps. There was smiling and laughing until it came to three in the morning, when still it was not cold. The wind too was calm. We began to wane as sleep started to take us, and with a towel over her face to protect her eyes from the emulsion of the moonlight, Lou fell to slumber on the sand.

"That's it then," Mal said. I sensed he'd continue, I sensed he had something to say and that he would as soon as he had poured the last droplets of wine from the bottle into his cup. For the first time today he was not smiling. "Back to work."

"It's not all that bad," I said.

"But it's not all that good either, is it?" he said. "It's not the stuff you read about in children's books. You're not the astronaut or the explorer. All this . . . bills, kids, marriage. It's not good enough. What will there be to remember of a mediocre existence?"

I didn't know I'd fallen asleep until the sun rose and poked its hot fingers through my eyelids, massaging my eyeballs until I was awake. Lou and Mal both sat there, stretching, emerging. Her hair was thick with sand. And still there was no one around. It was early. We filled our bags with towels and bottles and walked slowly, quietly, back to the car. I imagined we were returning to a military homecoming on a big ship in the sea. A million cheering people were lining the walls of the docks with flags and banners and kisses when we moored. I was still in this daydream as I climbed into the car and barely noticed the small crane that had been deployed to retrieve the watch thug's vehicle, which rested in the shallow water at the bottom of the lifeboat ramp, all the ticking in the back of it having ceased.

Forty-Two

For all the powers of recall our house had, Mal and Lou's had none. When they left it, it was as though they were never there, the walls having never heard them speak, earless. This was the blight of the young modern couple. The table everyone else had. The chairs that came with it. Stock glossy pictures on the wall of couples they don't know in places they've never been. Starter furniture.

We sat at the starter table drinking cheap wine from starter glasses. Lou was out, at a training course to assist her in working as part of a team in the bank. I'd not invited Sal to Mal's house. I'd see her later. She'd begun to talk about us getting our own place together. It was an impossibility, unless it could be paid for in minced beef. Besides, the desire was not there, the flame low. I'd toyed with the right way to let her down a final time. Perhaps that night.

Despite the weight gain in his gut, Mal looked gaunt. His cheeks sunk into dark hammocks across his bones so that if it rained you'd be able to lie him down and pool water in them. Around him were piles of ironing. The fridge was all magnets and bills. A voting card hung among them for a date that had been and gone. The floor was strewn with fast-food cartons and shoes. It was Friday night, Mal's twenty-fifth birthday. After work he'd untucked a creased, dirty shirt from his trousers and partially loosened the horrid checked tie around his neck.

The calendar that hung from the shabby notice board in the

kitchen featured twelve cute kittens. One played with a ball of wool. One peeked from above the rim of a wicker basket. One fell asleep next to a puppy. Each month was marked by Lou's careful hand, an elaborate matrix of ticks and crosses.

"Are you trying for a baby, Mal?" I said, drawing him out.

"We won't call it 'Baby Mal' if it's a girl."

He seemed dour. We started to walk home, my home, to his birthday party, where Mum had spent the day blowing up balloons with all of the gust in her lungs and Dad had been dozing gently in his chair to the hiss and crackle of an old record player he'd found and repaired. One compilation of the Glenn Miller Band's greatest hits played quietly, over and over again, on repeat.

"What's wrong?" I asked.

The night was cold, and though it was only just dark the walls and the fence posts shone with an early frost. My warm breath spelled out my words in frozen mist.

"Did Dad ever tell you his story?" he asked.

"What?"

"About TauTona. About the mine and the accident."

I'd had no idea that Mal knew it too. We'd never discussed it, which seemed odd, but then we'd never discussed Dad either. He was discussion-proof.

"Yeah," I said. I faked manliness, not knowing why.

"About the photographs. About the things you leave behind."

"Yeah."

"Well . . ."

He stopped. We stood there, both hands in pockets, holding identical poses. I didn't feel the cold anymore, just the needle-jab ache of the icy breeze in my ears.

"What if you knew, now, that you wouldn't leave anything behind. That you couldn't leave anything behind. That no one will remember you, and no one will have anything to remember you by. That you are, in fact, just someone who was there, and that's it."

"You're being stupid," I said. "What does that mean?"

He didn't look up. Neither of us did. We stared at our feet by the yellow beat of a vandalized streetlight. A deep breath. Not a sigh but almost.

"I kinda think . . . ," he said, and it was paced, more considered this time. "What is the point?"

I was frozen. My tongue too stiff to make the vibrations and shapes that form the sounds I needed to say *Please, Malcolm, shut up*. The water streaming from our eyes in the wind was only just too heated by our skin to turn to ice on our faces. And so I raised my fingers, two of them, gun-shaped, to his lips to stop him from saying any more. We walked home under the umbrella of his arm around my shoulder, and it felt bigger than it ever had.

Later, we were sitting on our front doorstep. His twenty-fifth birthday party. Mum was ferrying great silver trays of snack foods above our heads, perched on the bent tips of her long frail fingers like I'd seen the waiters do in posh hotels on television. Dad was sifting through a stack of vinyl he'd picked up in a secondhand shop, hoping that the people dancing in the living room don't stop all at once. Red Ted, Sal, Chris, Mal's boring work friends, the guys that Dad goes fishing with, weaving arms and kicking legs. Strangers talking the international language of drunk. But none more drunk than me or Mal.

"Do you not see?"

Mal's breath was hot and cloudy in my ear, a great boozy fog. My eyes fogged and then cleared, rolling around my head, awry projections.

"Do you not see?"

"No, I can't see."

"Well, I can," he said. "And that's the point. If you can't do what you're meant to, why do anything at all?"

He was inches from my ear, shouting into my skull. It rested and wobbled on my knee. Mrs. Gee, next door, was banging a "keep it down" rhythm through the thin plaster. No one could hear it. That her old bones could muster the strength to thump the wall was commendable. She would have been better off not doing it in time to the music. Mal was pointing but I couldn't focus, my eyes had abandoned their posts. I'd a limp cigarette in my mouth but was lighting my chin. He was still talking, I was sure, but it was just noise and I tried to concentrate until slowly it sharpened and shifted and began to make sense. I didn't even smoke.

"NMMMMMMMmmmmmmmnddddddd sswwwwoooork in . . ."

"What?"

Where had the cigarette gone?

"What?"

"Have you been listening?"

"Yes."

And I wished I could understand.

"I work in a chair. I fight on a computer game. When I vote, it changes nothing. What I earn can't buy anything. Maybe my purpose is to give purpose to others."

It kind of always had been, I thought, but I couldn't verbalize the notion.

"What?"

I fell back until my dizzy head rested in a pile of strangers' shiny work shoes.

Moved around. Glass of water. Sally kissing me on the forehead. Fleeting glimpses of landmarks I only half recognized on the long road back to sobriety.

It was later. The house was empty. The music was gone. I was on the settee and it hugged me, still dressed, unsure whether the phone had just started ringing or whether it had been ringing for hours. I picked it up.

"Hello."

My hand was numb from where I'd slept on it, drool had trickled around the ball of my thumb like an ornate Indian decoration.

"Hello . . . Malcolm? Malcolm?"

Lou, her voice was a bullet with an urgency I wished was for me.

"No. It's me. Lou? Mal is in bed. I think he's in bed. What time is it?"

"Can you fetch him for me, please?"

"He's in bed. It's his birthday," I said.

The semiclarity of sudden drunken awakenings.

"I know. Can you get him for me? I need to talk to him. It's urgent!"

New sincerity that was there before I heard now for the first time but I was drunk and none of it mattered.

"OK."

Standing slowly I gripped my belt and turned it around my waist ninety degrees, a heavy sundial, until my jeans no longer twisted the skin on my legs. I heard Dad snoring softly in the attic, tools in hand. With a gentle push I opened the door to our room to find Mal asleep on the bed, naked, the crisp linen sheets draped over him. He seemed heroic, albeit briefly. In the armchair next to the bed was Mum, her hand resting on his, her head tossed backward in slumber, the conversation they had left to drift there in the chilled night air.

The sight spun, twirled and threw me drunkenly. I landed face-down on my own bed and fell asleep instantly, oblivious to my clothes, the open windows, the voice repeating the words "Hello? Hello? Hello?" through the telephone receiver propped on the arm of the settee, but not to the knowledge that things were about to change.

I dreamt about Lou again.

Forty-Three

By late morning Mum had already woken Mal but he hadn't yet emerged for breakfast. She reasoned that he must have a hangover, unlike me who, though twenty-three, was still bathing in the wondrous period of grace life gives you where the morning after the night before is little different from the morning after the night before that. But I'd seen hangovers on Red Ted. That slow agony. Those tired weary bones, frayed tempers, black hounds. I sympathized. Which is why I didn't protest when Mum, as Lou called again that morning, explained that Mal was asleep and curtly took the phone off the hook. Still inebriated as I was, I thought nothing of it at all.

We waited until early afternoon. Mal's present, wrapped resplendently in crisp gold paper and shiny red ribbon the width of a horse's mane, lay idle in the middle of the living room floor. I could barely resist the urge to unwrap it myself as the sun ricocheted off it but I managed to leave it be. And then Mal's gift, and the fact it was wrapped, became a smaller issue altogether.

"He said he's not getting up," Dad said.

"Until when?" I said.

"Never."

"Never?"

"Never."

"Never?"

Mum took our words with her as she walked to Mal's room,

where she remained for more than twenty minutes until, at Dad's behest, I eventually followed her in. I carried Mal's present under my arm but my mind was no longer on whatever sat inside it. She kneeled at the side of the bed, cupping his hands in hers like she had been the night before, when I found them. Malcolm stared up at me. He was naked still, the quilt kicked off and twisted like a white doughy plait at his feet. It was as if he had suddenly jettisoned all things with the swift wrench of a lever.

"Get up," I said. "You have to get up."

"Why?" he asked, reserved, calm. Infuriating.

"Lou's back today."

"There is nothing," Mal said, "that I can do about that now."

Forty-Four

Day Four.

Mal never asked for anything, confident as he was that it would just come. Instead he lay quietly, watching television, waiting for something and nothing.

In the kitchen the night before, Mum and Dad had had the biggest argument I'd ever overheard. Dad, his loft, his work, his fishing. Mum, the cleaning, the cooking and Mal. All history born of conflict.

"Stop cooking for him, waiting hand and foot on him, and he'll have to get out of bed. Don't you see?" Dad had said. Not for a second did he consider that this might actually happen.

"He can't starve," Mum said, her voice shaped powerfully.

"He won't starve!"

"He's my son and I'll look after him if he needs looking after."

"You're a fucking martyr, you are!"

"Go up in your loft. Don't you worry about anyone else."

The next morning I asked Mal to stop. To get out of bed and carry on. I reminded him about his flat. About his job. About Lou. I begged him. But it had begun. It had most definitely begun. I just hoped that his interest would wither and die like a seed planted in alien terrain.

"Get up."

"No."

Goaded, I grabbed him by the ankle and in one almighty pull

heaved his muscular naked frame from the bed and onto the floor at my feet. My hands open, I slapped and scratched at his face, head and neck as he wound fetal around my legs. I jabbed at his chest with my heels, pinching his stubborn flesh between my shoes and the floor. Exasperated, I slapped at the red handprints around his ribs, at the cut above his eye. In that instant I felt like beating him to half his size. I pounded harder and harder into his chest, thud thud thud, then dropped to my knees, vacant and breathless.

Dad rushed in and all but tore the door from its hinges. He put both of his enormous hands upon my shoulders and lifted me out of Mal's reach. Mal clambered slowly back into bed and pulled the quilt up over his cut, swollen face.

Pushing me into the kitchen, Dad ran my bruised fingers underneath the cold tap. He didn't need to speak.

Hours passed before I poked my head tentatively around the bedroom door.

"Hello," he said, something of a surprise, the will of a brother to forgive another.

The flesh that framed the socket of his right eye had swollen and blackened, his naked chest was pocked with deep red grazes and tiny star-shaped formations where dried blood had collected after I'd cut into him with the heel of my shoe. He seemed completely nonplussed by the fight or by the arguments but what frustrated me most was that he'd ignored all attempts at communication from Lou. She had called at the door upwards of three times a day so far, alerting us each time with that same rat-a-tat-tat. Dad would always be in his attic, which would clang with dropped tools, the mesmeric rolling sound of loose screws spiraling about the frail wooden floorboards.

Mum would be similarly noisy in the kitchen, smashing pots and pans together, blaming them for a burnt cake or oversalted bread sauce. I imagined that when she wasn't there they all sprung to life, their handles and joins forming smooth-edged eyes, noses and mouths like in a Disney film. I imagined they all congregated around the wise old talking oven and moaned about how hard they were worked.

It would instead be left to me to answer the door to Lou. I didn't mind. She'd cry, I'd hold her. She'd ask to see Mal. I'd inform her that he didn't want any guests and apologize and apologize again. Mum would lock the bedroom door with the small bolt she'd asked Dad to affix. I'd get the words *Let's run away together* stuck in the tastebuds on the back of my tongue.

One week in, he'd still not changed his mind.

We were playing chess. Mal lay nude under a white cotton sheet, draped over him so neatly that from a distance he looked like a fallen pillar crumbling in an ancient lost amphitheater. I'd pulled a chair to his bed and turned it around so that my legs straddled the back of it. Mal's failure to appreciate the rules of a game established for many hundreds of years meant that the levels of concentration required when playing chess against him were of lunar-module-landing intensity.

"Your move," said Mal.

"OK," I said, glancing down at the board and then back up at him. I posed no threat whatsoever.

"And if she comes, I can't see her."

"Are you going to tell me what you are doing?" I asked.

He didn't answer.

Lou arrived again eventually. Her eyes were tropical spiders, red rings with feint black legs.

"Why?" she asked.

I said I didn't know.

"I love him," she said, and then she wept.

Every last ounce of what was inside of me squeezed up inside a tight rubber ball and bounced around my body.

I watched Lou leave, back to her father. So did Mum, through a slit in the curtains.

Forty-Five

Within a year our lives had changed immeasurably. In this short time Mal had become our sun, our lives in his orbit. The rings we were forced to travel around him were getting smaller and smaller, pulled in more and more tightly.

It was early evening and I was trying to watch television, scuppered by the clacking of scissors from the bedroom. Mum was cutting Mal's hair. He'd expressed no desire for any particular style, or even to have it cut at all, so Mum stuck with the textured, messy short look that was customary and achieved mostly by accident. I got up to ask them to be a little quieter. As I walked through the door, from the corner of my eye I saw her dig a smaller pair of scissors from her bag and start on his toenails. His toes, pendulous troll dollops.

"For Christ's sake, Mum, do you have to do that now?" I said.

"If you don't like it, go elsewhere," she said.

Elsewhere. This was my bedroom too. I didn't need to say it. Mal stifled a giggle. I playfully slapped the remote control against his knee and hoped it hurt him.

By then I noticed his nudity only intermittently. He was always naked, and he was always there, but even Dad seemed comfortable with it, in a way. Those pale gangly legs dangling from the sides of the mattress had become as much a part of the bedroom as the wallpaper. I understood how the children of nudist parents you'd see on daytime talk shows would appear almost to be feigning their embarrassment. It was just a body, sticks of meat.

There was a knock at the door in a rhythm we didn't recognize. Each of us froze, gawping at one another as though someone amongst us might be psychically linked to whoever was visiting. No one said a word.

Another knock. I switched the television off and stepped over Mum as she knelt at Mal's feet. Mal didn't flinch one iota. I peered out from behind the curtains in the hall.

Another knock, needlessly harder and more urgent this time, so I swung the door open to catch them unawares and took some delight in that first embarrassed grunt that emerged as the stranger at the door slammed his knuckles into nothingness. His movement carried him forward, the feeling you get when you step onto a broken escalator your legs expect to propel you. The visitor's hand ceased just inches from my face. Normal door-answering etiquette had been temporarily reversed. It was now him that needed to say something before this entire situation began to acquire even a jot of normality.

"Hello," said the man.

He was flanked by a much smaller man with a boom microphone on a pole and a much larger man with a camera on his left shoulder, the muscles in which were visibly bigger than those in his right shoulder.

"Are you Malcolm Ede?" he continued.

I recognized him from the local news on television. His name was Ray Darling. His hair was combed into a side-parting straightened with mathematical precision but it was obvious that he wasn't wearing a toupee. Mal owed me five pounds.

"No, I'm not."

"So you must be Malcolm Ede's brother?" he said.

It was the first time I was ever asked that question in that way.

"Yes. Yes, I am."

He raised an eyebrow to a right angle, offering it to me. Now we're friends.

"We hear that Malcolm is involved in some kind of protest?"
he said.

Protest. I'd not thought of it as that. Sometimes around Malcolm I could barely think at all.

"No."

"Can we come in?"

(He starts off kindly.)

"No."

"Are your parents here?"

"No."

"Your mother is."

(He changes direction.)

"How do you know?"

"What is it then?"

"What?"

(He confuses you.)

"We hear that your brother is refusing to get out of bed."

"I don't know."

"What is he doing?"

(A hard question, followed by a harder one . . .)

"Please."

"And more importantly, why is he doing it?"

(. . . there it is.)

"I don't know, now please . . ."

"People are talking . . ."

(Just like on the television.)

I slammed the door hard. Through its bulk I heard Ray Darling force his mute colleagues to agree that this house, our house,
was a house full of "fucking weirdos." The very same Ray Darling
who looks like he is wearing a wig even though he's not.

Forty-Six

On the news the next evening there was a war. There was a politician's deadly sex game. There was a strike at the fire station. There were some football fans feeling aggrieved because a team from their local area had been beaten by a team from a different area. There was a woman who was famous but nobody knew why. There were predictions about humidity, a brief problem with the sound and a deaf man doing sign language in a shirt that fitted too tightly.

And then there was a piece at the end.

"Malcolm Ede . . ." said Ray Darling.

"That is definitely a wig," said Mal.

It wasn't. I had seen it up close. He owed me five pounds. Ray Darling's face shone like a great pumpkin lantern.

". . . hasn't got out of bed for a whole year, according to local sources. As yet no one in the Ede household has been able to comment on what his motives are. He is not believed to be ill."

They showed footage taken from over the garden fence, of Mum trimming Mal's toenails the night before. She stopped eating the meal on her lap. The blood drained from her every inch. Disbelief dripped from our three mouths, agog.

"Jesus fucking Christ . . ." came the call from the attic. "Did you just see that?"

The entire house seemed to buzz, as though the light of the sun was focused upon a pin-size spot of it. Dad even descended, albeit temporarily. He looked at Mal, turned to me and said simply, "Who?"

It wasn't Lou, I told him. We hadn't heard from her for months. I'd tried to visit her at her house. Her dad had told me she'd gone away but I could still smell her perfume in the entrance to her home, even above the scent of his cigars.

"Mrs. Gee," croaked Mum, her knife and fork still equidistant between plate and mouth. "Mrs. Gee."

Mrs. Gee knew our business. Mrs. Gee loved to talk. I imagined her watching the news, thinking *If only I was Ray Darling's age,* her hips creaking like a trapdoor.

Forty-Seven

Day Seven Thousand Four Hundred and Eighty-Three, according to the display on the wall.

I sit in the corner, still toying with my shoes, not thinking about the pain or the metal in my legs but thinking of going to meet Lou. For weeks Mal's interview had been all that had occupied the muddled space in my thoughts but now she pulled my eyes elsewhere.

There had been three thousand or more media requests before. Every day they would clog the answering machine, hair in a drain. Over the years they had become more frequent, swelling in direct proportion to Mal's epidermis. Television companies from across Europe and America would lavish us with praise and gifts to try to secure exclusive rights to his story. The wolf-eyed representatives of tabloid newspapers would arrive with suitcases full of money in return for Mal's words but Dad would turn them down with the shake of a finger and a closing of the trailer door. In response they would scattergun that cash, buying rumors and lazy old lies from those who professed to know us. On a regular basis, the day after their rejection would come front-page splashes of salacious old nonsense, all of it a variation on something printed in the same newspaper a few weeks before.

Someone once told us that when a story about Mal was splurged across the front of a magazine it sold a third more copies. I obviously had nothing at all in common with the vast majority of the general public. Second cousins we'd never met would appear on daytime chat shows or trashy magazines, talking of how Mal would seem whenever they came to visit. Liars. Weeks later they would be spotted parking a brand-new car in the center of town, their infant children in dirty shirts, sucking on hyperactive fluorescent lollipops.

Still, in the house we felt safe. Closed off.

Not today though, Day Seven Thousand Four Hundred and Eighty-Three, according to the display on the wall. Today was special, because Mal had agreed after all these years to allow a news crew into the house.

Mum pulls the fresh sheets of the bed up over Mal's body, stopping short of the final tug above the face that denotes a passing. The medics are gone, the psychiatrists too. The room is tidy, the bed made. Mum is in her best dress (a pink number she's had for more than fifteen years, with padding in the shoulders and over-size pretend flowers soiling the front) and Mal is tingling with the prickly heat of nerves. I look out of the window and see how unsuitably calm the weather is. The sun is shining outside. It doesn't feel like the day of a grand denouement. Those days are windswept and plagued by rain. This isn't the weather for something incredible.

After an hour of waiting, there is an unfamiliar knock on the door. I get up to answer it. I slowly pull the handle back to be met with the older, ever-more-orange face of Ray Darling. He looks like he's been painted with the sealant used to protect wooden fence posts from the elements. With him are a cameraman and a sound technician, the same two from all those years before. He waltzes straight past me toward Mum, who stands at the end of the hall outside the bedroom that grows inside the house like a baby in the womb. He clasps her small, blue-veined hands in his monstrously hairy fingers and kisses her on the cheek. The sound of his lips meeting her face feels like a chop to my windpipe. A large blue badge on the lapel of his blazer catches on Mum's cheap embroidery and brings them together with a not-unfunny awkwardness. His badge says "Ray Darling!" It has an exclamation mark on it.

"Please, go through," she says, gesturing toward the door after unattaching herself with a blush. So begins an event.

As Ray Darling and his team set up the equipment around Mal, making the bedroom into a black operating theater, they make pleasantries. Mum makes tea and Mal makes no effort whatsoever. Edged out of the room, I take the keys to the trailer from Mum's handbag and slip quietly through the front door, where the atmosphere is high. People have been gathering for hours but not one of them notices me emerge.

There are maybe a hundred people standing and waiting. Today could be the day they'd find out if they were right or wrong. When the bookies who have revelled in Mal's cause célèbre will make or lose their money. When a hero's status is confirmed or when a disappointment is unleashed that will rival ten thousand badly planned New Year's Eve parties.

I walk the short distance up the shaky metal steps into the trailer and close the door, locking it behind me. From out of the crowd, suddenly I am totally alone.

I switch on the television. Ray Darling's fluorescent face flickers and then shines.

Forty-Eight

Fulsome beads of sweat map Mal's emotionless face. On television he looks even bigger. His arms appear as bags of salt swollen to splitting. The physical stress of the occasion makes it too much for him even to hold his mouth closed. The lighting makes the insides of his cheeks glisten as the spit runs down them. His eyes are dust bowls, sunk back into his face like the ugliest of dogs. Inside and outside the trailer is a silence and only the whir of the camera zooming in on Mal's flabby face, played through speakers an industrious neighbor had hung from his window, mean anyone is sure that their ears are working. And then Ray Darling speaks. His voice sounds thicker and more rounded than it does in person. That's what television does.

"Hello, ladies and gentlemen," he says, and for the first time I am part of the world looking in, rapt.

"I'm Ray Darling, and soon I'm going to be talking live, exclusively, to Malcolm Ede. Since his decision not to get out of bed on his twenty-fifth birthday over twenty years ago, Malcolm has grown to weigh more than a hundred stone. He has captured the imagination of all who hear his story. But the question is why? Why did this normal . . ."

Hardly.

". . . twenty-five-year-old take a decision to end what normal life he had? Why is Malcolm Ede in bed? Join me after this short break to find out, for the first time."

An ice cream dessert.

Microwave meals.

Do-it-yourself mini sandwich snacks with processed cheeses for lazy parents to slot into the lunchboxes of children with limited palates.

All advertisements for food. Clever.

"Welcome back. You join me in Malcolm Ede's bedroom. Hello, Malcolm."

Mal blinks slothfully. He swallows and it lasts a lifetime. His appearance is greeted by enormous cheers outside that tremor through the glass and into the microphone dangling above him to be blasted through the speakers and back out with a bass tone into the crowd from which they came. He doesn't answer. I grip my own hand, pinch the fingertips, look around the trailer for something to clench and find an apple. I break its skin.

"How are you today?"

No answer. Ray Darling's lips slowly nosedive down his chin.

"OK . . . well, the question everyone is asking is, of course, why?"

Mal's mute face fills every screen.

"Malcolm?"

Ray Darling's badge tilts at an angle so that you can't read it without turning your head ninety degrees to the left.

"Malcolm? Why did you decide not to get out of bed?"

Mal breathes out slowly, like a blimp deflating with a pinprick.

"Are you going to speak to me, Malcolm?" says Ray.

This really hurts. And then suddenly relief, a great wash of relief.

"Mr. Darling," says Mal.

A studied pause, nice.

"Please, call me Ray . . ."

A smile, some vindication.

"Mr. Darling," says Mal.

It's so beautiful, my head aches.

"Yes?"

"May I ask you a question?"

"Of course, Malcolm. Of course."

This feels like the center of the world, the start, the pop before the biggest bang.

A pause. A beat.

"Are you wearing a wig?"

Forty-nine

The laughter outside is uproarious. It reverberates around the silver skin of Norma Bee's trailer, making the china plates vibrate on the plastic kitchen surfaces like chattering winter teeth. With the corners of my sleeves I dab away the tears of laughter that outline the shape of my nose and I think about how much Norma would have loved what Mal just did to Ray Darling on live television.

The excitement is such that not a solitary figure in the crowd gathered outside the front of the house notices me slip surreptitiously from the door of the trailer and into the bustling marketplace of commotion they've created. I lock the door behind me and stand there, surveying the moment. Then I feel a huge friendly hand on my shoulder. I turn to see a man whose face I recognize. He has been here before. A few times I'd woken to his face pressed against the window. Looking at Mal's stomach. Looking at the pins that pierce my legs. His fingernails are yellow and cracked and home to small semicircles of dirt and mud from the grass. His hair is long, matted mazes, confused and tangled and greasy. His skin is a sun-wrinkled suitcase leather. He looks and smells and moves like the outdoors. Even his breath smells like outside, like air and peat and grime that wriggles with life inside it.

"Hey, man," he says.

"Hello," I say.

"You're Malcolm's brother, right?"

"Yes."

He smiles a green-toothed grin.

"Wow. Did you see the interview?"

"Yes."

He looks at my legs.

And then he asks me a question. A flurry of hits, a combination of blows.

"Why did you come back from America just to live in that room with him?"

Slowly heated needles pushed quickly through my heart. Every bad memory I've ever forgotten jammed onto a hook and dragged backward through my brain.

"That's not why I came back. Look," I say, polite but pretend, a robot butler. "I'd love to stop and talk with you but I have to go inside now."

"No problem, man." He grins a toothless, graveyard smile.

With my eyes to the floor I trot through the crowd, mapping the pathway until I am at the front door, which I shut behind me, hoping that the amount of people outside will have diminished by the time I have to go and meet Lou later tonight. I think that I am back in the bubble, and I think that the peace is inside it but I am wrong. Raised voices crackle through the plaster in the walls and skim off the glass in the windows. Volumes of mighty anger, panic and fretting. I slowly, with the tip of my longest finger and the sense of a bigger dread, push open the small wooden door between me and the racket.

Ray Darling is clinging to Mal's left elephant ankle with both hands, his fingertips leaving deep indentations in the chunky flesh sheath of it. His cameraman and soundman pull with all their strength at his belt, trying to drag him away, but his wrath is too great and suspended between them and Mal it's as though he grips for dear life to an immovable lamppost in a hurricane. His face is burgundy, his eyes bloodshot, and he shouts jets of vengeance. They are so loud that they lapse in and out of sense.

"How fucking dare you! How dare you!" he screams, tearing the sheet on Mal's body to the floor. Despite the best efforts of his two larger sidekicks, Ray Darling is slowly clawing his way up Mal's wobbling, quivering frame. "Make a fucking monkey out of me!" he roars, his hands dug deep into Mal's belly as though he were digging his way through a pile of warm clay. "Bastard! Bastard! You great, fat, horrible bastard!"

I see Mal break sweat, unable to move, the vast hundred-stone umbrella of fat that covers him pinning him to the bed. I picture Ray straddling Mal, leaning down and biting off his stubby nose. I imagine him splashed with Mal's blood, it dripping in thick red jewels from his mouth as Mal, underneath him, suffers a massive heart attack that judders through him, flushing out the remains of life.

Mum is wailing. She has accidentally hooked her foot through the dense nest of wires between Mal's machinery and the television equipment that has been set up for the broadcast. I watch as her feet become mummified with cable and in a great flurry she is brought crashing to the floor, grabbing and tearing down the curtains leading to the front lawn, where by now a small throng of spectators remain, drawn back by the din.

They peer in through the glass. Mum wrapped in curtains and brightly colored wire. Mal, enormous, naked, terrified. Ray Darling, clinging to the heavy flaps under Mal's armpits, spewing vicious obscenities at my brother, his tormentor. Two fully grown men unable to stop him. Me and Dad, bemused, only now springing into action.

Dad jostles for position with the soundman in order to get at the legs of Ray Darling. I wrap both my arms around his neck as though I were squeezing him python-like to his death. The four of us holding him and still he scraps. Then there is a tearing sound as Dad attempts to haul him away from Mal by the back pockets of his trousers, ripping them off to reveal a skinny, hairy pair of legs and a discolored off-white pair of underpants, which finally saps the fight from Ray Darling and presents me with an opportunity to settle this once and for all.

Dad lets two policemen in to find Ray Darling, exhausted and in his dirtiest underwear, lying spread-eagle atop the naked blob of a hundred-stone man as I pull the toupee from his nasty orange head.

As Ray is arrested, Mum puts the curtains back up. Mal's laughter sends currents bubbling through his soft juicy pulp.

Fifty

One year in, a circling of the sun, Mal was twenty-six. I watched him digging through a birthday toffee pie and ice cream. His head seemed to hang too loosely on his neck. It was eight in the morning. Mum brought in a great silver sack full of presents that left cheap silver glitter twinkling on the bed, all dry and dusty, the way you'd imagine the surface of the planet Mercury. There were chocolates and socks and things women buy men without interests. And there was a long, rectangular package, about the size of a case you'd keep a snooker cue in. I perched on the edge of my bed, my legs thrown over it, feet hovering just above the floor as though a dummy across the lap of a ventriloquist. And I watched. That he could bear to open a present so slowly and carefully carved little nicks in my impatience. Eventually, having opened one end of the gift, he slid it out of its Christmassy holding like he was removing a thigh-length leather boot from his leg.

"It's a clock," said Mum, her hands excitedly clasped at her chin, overjoyed to have us all here.

Even Dad was present, unable to work temporarily after twisting his ankle falling down from his ceiling hatch. He sat in the corner, his head rested on a flat palm and bent elbow, in wonder at how grossly happy she seemed. At how gripped by cheer she had been for a whole year.

"A what?" asked Mal.

"A clock. We had it made for you. A friend of your dad's, from

South Africa, this is what he does now. He makes clocks. But not ordinary clocks. Special clocks. Like the ones that do the count-downs, the big ones, on New Year's Eve, just before the fireworks go off . . . Doesn't he, love?"

Love. When she called Dad "love," I knew fondness. Few things so endearing grew more so the sparser and more meaning-less they became.

"He does, yes," replied Dad, still unmoved in his chair, never a word wasted.

The flecks of glitter chased each other around in the shafts of sunlight piercing the window.

Mal turned the cumbersome black box over and around, inves-tigating and probing it for a switch or a button, whichever gave it life, as Mum hurriedly unwound its cable and slotted the plug into the wall. With a click the two of them were suddenly illuminated in a comic-book green that bounded off every wall. By the time it reached Dad, gently swaying in the rocking chair by the television, it was a dull pea color, highlighting his wrinkled brow and making him look the wicked pantomime witch.

YEARS MONTHS DAYS HOURS MINUTES SECONDS

Tick tock tick tock, Mal's life in liquid crystal. Mum lifted the small black plastic flap on the back and poked a finger around the tiny buttons buried there until there was a beep a whirr and a click.

ONE ZERO ZERO ZERO ZERO ZERO

She twirled the smooth plastic dial.

ZERO ZERO 365 ZERO ZERO ZERO

Day Three Hundred and Sixty-Five, according to the display on the wall.

Dad stood, smiled and left the room. I followed him. It struck me then, for the first time as I shadow his movement left leg right leg, that I was bigger than him. That I probably had been for some time. And that it seemed he was withering away, a stop-motion image of a flower turning from yellow to gray and into powder as the wind sucked it up into the air. I wanted to wrap my arms around his neck, push my heart into the back of his chest and share with him my life force. I wanted to lift him atop my shoulders, right there in the living room, revive him, give him back what he lost. What all sons secretly wanted to do to their fathers, to make him the champion. But he looked beaten, by time, by events. By whatever he lost one day and never got back. I followed him into the kitchen, where he rested a rough, haggard hand on the metal skin of the kettle to check its temperature and flicked the switch regardless.

"Are you OK?" I asked.

"Yes. Yes," he said.

I wanted to tell him that I wished we talked more but had he been to ask me "What about?" then maybe I wouldn't have known. Every day I left him there when I went out in my apron to work, and every day he was there when I returned. What wage I earned would be spent hastily, out with Red Ted, who would drive us to satellite towns, and we'd go to bars and clubs where the music was too loud, communicating with imperceptible gestures. It was cheap at home, I'd reasoned with myself. I'd no responsibilities, no matter how much I might have wanted them. There was the difference between me and Mal. And, I wanted Lou. Everything I did was designed to help me forget the fact as cheaply and as quickly as possible.

"The clock," Dad whispered. "Your mum says she thinks it will make him realize how stupid this is. That it will make him get up. If you ask me, I think she might have set him a challenge."

A shrill yelp screeched out from Mum's throat, raking the lining from the inside of her lungs. Dad, pouring from the kettle, scalded his hand on the spout.

"What's wrong?" he shouted, louder than I'd heard him since the day he tanned my hide at the hospital, and we ran through the living room to the bedroom, where, standing at the window, palms fastened to her cheeks, is Mum.

The shock of what she'd seen had apparently tapped her for blood at the ankle, her face a mint white. Mal, naked, had the bedsheet pulled up and over his face. His fingers gripped it at the top for fear that someone might whip it away, a magician at a dinner table, leaving naked Mal, the plates and cups rocking gently but still on show.

Dad and me walked to the window and pulled the curtain further aside. Out there on the grass, our grass, was a tent, pitched and lived-in.

"What on earth is that?" Dad asked.

"A tent," I said.

"A tent, yes. But what is it?"

"It's a portable piece of camping apparatus used for shelter." Malcolm laughed.

"I know it's a tent. Of course it's a bloody tent," Dad said. He was pointing at it through the window as though I wouldn't have noticed the landscape that had been mine for so long suddenly had a new addition. "What is it doing there?"

"I dunno," I said.

Mum sat back on Mal's bed. It was though she'd drawn the curtains to find a full chorus line of can-can girls pumping pom-poms. She was ashen.

The tent was small and white, looking from a distance little more than a fly-wing-thin sheet tossed over a couple of twigs. To try to sleep in there in the heat of the midday summer sun would have been hellish. But then, for one reason or another, camping had never seemed to me like a good way to have fun. As the clouds moved across the sky, this tent, barely twenty feet away from where we were standing, was illuminated. And in it, when I stared hard enough, I could see the silhouette of a solitary figure, an outline I would recognize by clearest day or darkest night. But I didn't even need to say it.

"It's Lou," muttered Mal from underneath his cover. "That's Lou's tent. I recognize it. That's Lou, I guess, inside it."

Mum rocked back on the base of her spine. Dad brought his hand to his mouth. I saw he was surprised but more than that, mischievous perhaps, enjoying the presentation of a hurdle, anything to softly prod the cradle.

And I felt elation. Sweet, powerful elation. Elation just to see her again.

Mum rose fast and drew the curtains back across the glass, leaving the room lit only by the bitter green glow of Mal's twenty-sixth birthday present. We stood there, in a row, basking in the ambient light, the fact that it was Day Three Hundred and Sixty-Five, according to the display on the wall written large across us all.

Fifty-One

"You're not going out there," ordered Mum.

I was scrabbling through the pile to find my shoes as Mum, in pointless protestation, pulled the bolt across the front door.

"What are you doing that for?" I said, annoyed.

"Because you're not going out there," she said.

Her teeth gnashed. I couldn't figure out whether she was angry or afraid. Regardless, my decision was made.

"I'm going to talk to Lou!" I shouted to Mal in the bedroom but more for Mum's benefit. He didn't answer.

"Well, I'm going to call the police," she snapped. "It's trespassing, technically. It doesn't matter who she is. That's our front garden. She has no right just to turn up and pitch a tent there without our express permission. She has no right at all."

As she talked I listened less and less, until eventually she became background noise. I could see her pursed lips forming little shapes. I could see her slender eyebrows snaking. I could see the wild gesticulation of her hands cutting the air in an angry dance. But it meant nothing to me.

"Mum," I said, "do whatever you like, if you think it will make life easier." I felt big, readied. A man. "But I'm going out there to speak to Lou. Let me find out what she wants."

Mum's head bowed until her chin rested against the sharp bony plate of her chest and her force field, which until now I'd not been able to detect, slowly disappeared. Steadily, and without meeting my eye, Mum shuffled into the living room. Dad waited there with a hot cup of tea in his hand for her, his timing impeccable. Mal still hadn't said a word. As I pulled on a thin summer jacket to combat the brisk morning chill, I peeked through the gap above the hinges of the bedroom door. The sheet was still above his head and only his swollen traffic-light-green feet were on show, poking out from the edge of the bed like the upturned heads of two rakes in the grass. Begging to be stepped on.

Removing the latch from the door a nervous sickness growled in my stomach, so I waited and swallowed and waited again until it eased to a gentle purr. And then, slowly opening it, I trod out into the cool baby steps of the day. Only when I heard the hairy crunch of the bristled doormat underneath my feet did I look down to find that I was accidentally wearing odd shoes. I was thinking about Mal as I crossed the small stretch of grass to the tent, where I heard her humming, a siren singing me to shipwreck.

Standing outside, I cleared my throat. It sounded horrible. Apprehension wriggled and popped in my legs.

"Hello?" she said.

"Hello," I replied.

My fingers fidgeted at my sides, jerking the way a quick-draw cowboy's would at his holster when there are fractions of seconds before he or his foe fire the first and fatal shot at high noon. The zip began to unfasten from the inside. I watched it crawl down the tent, and then there she was, sitting in the porch of it.

"Hello." She smiled. "It's good to see you." She remained amazing. "You're probably wondering what I'm doing here."

My voice box filled with thick impossible foam, and so I just nodded like the stupid greedy dogs that waited for Red Ted to sling malformed sausages from the doorway of the butchery.

"Perhaps," she said, moving aside, "you had better come in."

I dropped to all fours.

The tent was little bigger than a coffin and had that stifling smell of hot vinyl. In the pockets of the lining were a few supplies. Food, flasks, water bottles. A mirror. Clean underwear. Magazines. A picture of her dad that had fallen from her purse. He looked sad and thin. A pillow. A sleeping bag. Wet wipes and cosmetics she didn't really need. I sat facing her as she tied her hair back, quickly and professionally so that not a single strand of it still hung down over her face when she'd finished. I'd rehearsed this and rehearsed it again but only ever in my head. Now I'd arrived at the show, in costume, only to find I'd had my lines cut without my prior knowledge.

"How's Mal?"

"Fine," I lied.

Truth is, I didn't really know.

"Do you think I can see him?"

"I don't know. I don't think so. I mean, well . . . It's not just you, Lou. He's not had any visitors. None at all."

"I see," she sighed.

"So," I wondered, "where have you been? What have you been doing?"

"I moved back in with my dad."

"How is he?"

"He just sits there and thinks about Mum. Like he's waiting for her to come through the door, and if she did he'd just stand up and put the kettle on like nothing had happened. I think he thinks bad things like that don't happen to people his age. He's wrong. It can happen anytime, I suppose."

I wanted to tell her she was doing the same.

"I guess that's love for you," she said.

I wanted to tell her that it wasn't but what did I know.

"I've tried to forget him." I could see it in the contours of her frown. In the pressure in the S-bend of her tongue, coiled up like a viper in her mouth. "This isn't what was supposed to happen."

"You won't be able to forget here. Camped out on our garden," I said.

The cogs and pulleys and chains of my body geared up to perform the simple pattern of movements required for me to land a caring, conciliatory hand on her knee but the engine didn't fire and I remained rigid in my place. She stayed quiet. Sat there, rocking her heels to and fro, clacking them together like Dorothy from *The Wizard of Oz*, which I'd seen on television once. A childhood trait of hers kicking through into womanhood.

"What are you doing here?" I said. "I mean, the tent and all. We were all a bit surprised."

"I know, I'm sorry. What did your mum think?"

"She was going to call the police."

"Will she?"

"I doubt it."

"Do you think I can speak to her? I'd like to."

"I've no idea," I said, unable to find inside me the correct way of saying no. It was not in me to explain just how things had changed, just how normal Mal being in bed had already become. "So, why?" I asked again.

"Why am I here?"

"Yes."

"I still love him, I always will. And so a little piece of me will always be here. This tent will be here to remind him, for as long as it needs to be."

I pushed my two upper front teeth downward into my smooth bottom lip. Then came the beep beep and third impatient beep of a car on the road outside. I poked my head out and saw Red Ted, ghouls of smoke pumping from his exhaust pipe. He was chomping contentedly on a snack-size pork pie with the circular jaw motion of a giddy camel and listening to some meaningless foreign sporting encounter on the radio.

"I have to go to work," I said.

Lou didn't say good-bye. Instead she laid her hands out on the floor in front of her, rocked her weight onto her arms, lifted her bottom into the air and leaned forward to kiss me on the cheek. It remained there, that feeling, long after the contact was broken. I copied her grin, magnified it and sent it back in her direction. Then I backed slowly out of the tent so as not to knock it to the ground in my clumsy odd shoes and zipped it up behind me with the caring hand of a newly qualified surgeon. If I could have told her that I loved her, perhaps that would have lasted a lifetime too. The trouble was that there wasn't room in her for any more. Mal's love had taken it all, and now it was squatting inside.

I climbed into the car and dropped my head to Red Ted. He didn't mention the fact that I had just emerged from a tent on my own front lawn, that my shoes were two completely different colors or that a beautiful lipstick butterfly has landed on the side of my face. It stayed there all day, basking in the sunlight that fell into the shop.

Fifty-Two

The tent stayed. I thought of Lou every time I left the house. But I didn't leave. There was nothing and nowhere to go to as grand as what I had imagined. My friends from school had mortgages and children. Maybe Ms. Kay had been a shepherd, her advice a path to fuller pastures, advice they'd taken while I hadn't. I knew regret a little but something magnetic had moored me, its anchor in my thinking. I had friends, though. At least I wasn't Mal.

Mal's body had begun to morph. I noticed how the fat had started to gather first around his hips, swallowing up the lines where the tops of his legs bookended the trunk of his stomach and would have plunged into the trousers he never wore. Soon I could trace with my eyes where Mal's body had become misshapen, the workings of his metabolism shot through with sloth.

I would see passersby point and nod in the direction of the house as they strolled past, pointing at the tent, glaring from the pavement through the window to where Mal lay. Mum would be tending him like an emperor penguin plodding through the snow, careful not to let any camouflaged predators pounce upon its egg.

Day Nine Hundred and Fourteen, according to the display on the wall. People in the town knew Malcolm Ede by name and name alone. He'd become gossip, a myth, an eccentric or a crank. Some who discovered I was his brother would come by the butcher's shop to ask about him.

"A fiver's worth of braising steak. Are you Malcolm Ede's brother?"

Yes. But you knew that already.

"A chicken. A big one. For roasting. For Sunday. So how is Malcolm these days, anyway?"

"Fine, just fine, I've customers to serve."

"A pound of Malc . . . minced beef, please."

As it grew more and more frequent, Red Ted agreed to man the front of the shop while I remained out back, preparing meat, cleaning up and placing orders for stock. I'd listen through the wall to the people asking about someone they didn't know who isn't actually doing anything. This was what fame was.

"Are you Malcolm Ede's brother?"

"No. My name is Ted. I have no brothers."

"Are you sure?"

"Yes."

"Who is Malcolm Ede's brother then?"

"Who is Malcolm Ede?"

"You know who Malcolm Ede is."

"No."

"Yes, you do."

"No, I don't."

"You do. The guy that's stopped getting out of bed for no reason. His girlfriend has a tent on his lawn."

"Could be anyone."

"Not really . . . He's been in bed for ages and his girlfriend has a tent on the lawn."

"Yeah, precisely."

"So you're definitely not his brother?"

"I don't have any brothers."

"Oh."

"Here you go, eight pork-and-leek sausages, a pound of lamb

mince and a pound of stewing steak. I've got no idea what you're talking about. I don't know anyone called Martin."

"Malcolm."

"No, my name is Ted."

I loved Red Ted.

And Mal grew bigger and wider and rounder and heavier. Like a colony of ants, we worked and lived and fed around him, pretending that everything was normal, which in the strangest of ways it was.

Fifty-Three

In Dad's car it smelled of tobacco and pungent breath mints designed to disguise the smell of tobacco. I liked neither but the two combined were an olfactory delight. They brought to mind times I wasn't even born to enjoy. The smell of Dad's youth decades ago, before the firstborn. The seats were brown and the air was still. The ashtray's stinking guts spilled out their sterile gray carpeting all over the floor.

"Come fishing. It's been a long, long time since you came fishing," he'd said.

I'd resolved to bring him further into my life, and for me to worm further into his. Fishing was the price I'd pay. I had stalled long enough, pretending on previous occasions that I was going to see Sally, whom I'd not seen for almost a year. I'd stay at Red Ted's house.

Soon my wealth of excuses was diminished by my rising guilt and I found it in me to feign interest in the fishing rod Dad had apparently designed and built in the attic. It was, he said, his own combination of pulleys and cogs and wheels. It meant that he could lift bigger, heavier fish from the water with far less effort than was normally required, and lift them safely and quickly to the bank without any fear of their falling free. It was a feat, I was sure, though I'd secretly always wanted those fish to escape. I'd look into their horrible beady death eyes. I saw how they hated the air.

We were sat on the bank, the two of us, listening to the plink-plink of the line tickling the surface of the water. And there was a peace. The rare kind of peace Dad spoke in.

"I went back there, you know," he said.

"Where?" I asked, his interjection into the nothingness having taken me aback.

And he began. And I listened. It seemed that even the fish slowed as they swam past.

"TauTona. South Africa. To the mine. I went back there three years ago, just before Malcolm got into bed. I didn't tell anyone. I lied. I said I was going up north to help build a new lift, do you remember? But I didn't. I went back to TauTona. I went back to where the accident happened. I had to go.

"It was the same heat, kneading your skin. The heat there, it grinds you down and makes you slow and weary. And it was the same dust in the back of your throat. It was that same feeling that was there when I left, of something that had happened that would never be forgotten, of something that we'd always carry. That weight, as heavy as the day that the chains snapped. As heavy as the day it happened."

I wondered if Mal would ever hear this. I wondered if he went to bed so that he'd never have to go fishing again.

"Do you know, they never took anything out of the ground there? It was just too deep. Too dangerous. The sixteen men that died in that lift, they are still there now, impacted three and a half kilometers inside the earth. We could reach them but we could never take them home. And I went down again. I stood on the platform of the lift in the emergency shaft that I made, and I went down again. So deep that nothing can live there. Not insects. Not light. Just memories. So deep that there was nothing but the twisted metal and the stale smell and the dust and the dark and the pain in my heart. I went to see if I could take those men from the earth, if I could finally bring them home and lay them to rest. If I could give those women with their candles and their headscarves something real to grieve. But I couldn't. Nothing could. All was gone.

"That night there was a remembrance service. I was invited. In a small gray church by a river. A corrugated tin roof and a cross made from cheap wood with chipped paint. And I went. I wore a suit with a yellow flower, just like they do to remember in Russia. I'd always liked that. Not black. Yellow.

"And at the front, on the first two rows, were the sixteen widows of TauTona. Sixteen still-shattered faces. And I thought to myself, you know, I can't be like them. I can't carry this picture around inside my head for ever. This grief. I thought, one day, and I don't know when or what, but I'll have to do something, something great, something new and wonderful, if I'm to leave TauTona behind. If I don't, there'll always be seventeen men there underground."

We drove home together, the silence restored, and shared a grilled fish, with cake for dessert. Afterward Dad climbed up into his attic to make some adjustments to his rod from the equations he'd formulated while testing it out that afternoon.

Fifty-Four

On Day One Thousand Four Hundred and Sixty-Five, according to the display on the wall, Mal received his first proper piece of fan mail. Mum picked it up from the doormat, scowled and carried the envelope into the bedroom, where I was donning my work overalls and Mal was hastily devouring a second bowl of custard, the remnants of it collecting in arcs at the sides of his mouth and leaving him with a golden smile.

The letter rested on top of a cushion, the way you'd think the Queen received her mail. Short of a silver letter-opener with which to carve a neat incision, he licked the crumbs from the knife he'd used to butter his precustard round of thick white toast and slotted it inside the envelope. With a quick jerk of his thickening wrist he stabbed it open, murdering it so that its papery innards plopped out onto his chest. Mum offered to read it to him, as though he couldn't himself. He agreed, which pained me a little.

"'Dear Malcolm Ede,'" she began. "'I just wanted to write to you to let you know that I heard what you are doing and I think it is wonderful. I'd love it if we could become pen friends, and if I could keep you company while you do what you are doing. Lots of love, Amy Lam.'"

"But you're not doing anything," I said, adjusting my apron to straighten the twist in the strap that runs behind my neck and holds my shoulders.

Mal shrugged.

"That's OK," he said.

I felt my lips clamp. I was well practiced in dealing with Mal's idiocy but not the greater idiocy of anyone inclined to try to be his friend.

"I'm going to work," I said.

Red Ted left the shop early to go to the tattoo parlor. He said he'd always wanted a tattoo and had been held back because he couldn't settle on a design. In the end he'd opted to keep it simple and was, he told me, going to have his name written across his back.

"I suppose that could look quite good," I said. "It's a cool name, Red Ted."

"No," he said, "just Ted. You are the only person who calls me Red Ted."

Alone and slow on customers, I thought about the fan mail, about Amy Lam. Mysteriously buoyed, I picked up the phone and dialed Lou. It seemed like legitimate news, something to say, which I'd vitally lacked. A man answered.

"Hello?" he said.

"Hello," I said. "Is Lou there, please?"

"No."

"OK. Can I leave a message?"

"Yes."

His answers crashed in before my questions had finished, forcing them off the road. He was old, his voice raspy, definitely a dad and not a boyfriend. He was forgiven. I couldn't bring myself to say my name because I would only suffix it with "Malcolm's brother," and so I said, "Tell her Malcolm has fan mail."

"OK," said her dad, ringing off.

When I arrived home that evening the sky was pink and the smell in the air that distant bonfire stink of danger. Mal was watching two-part detective dramas and Mum sat at the ornate rolltop desk Dad had been bequeathed by his own father, a black fountain pen in her hand. Her fingers were colored white by the scars left by the burns from the cooker and the iron. She was writing a reply to Amy Lam, happiness on her face, a reason in her evening.

I removed my shoes and blood-dampened clothes by the front door and jumped when someone knocked on it. I opened it to find Lou. Her smile was huge, impossible and lovely. We sat in her tent with a torch and played cards and I told her about the fan letter that arrived. She laughed along with me at it and I masked my delight at what I considered a breakthrough.

Fifty-Five

Lou flopped a waxy two of hearts onto the floor. It directed the light from her lamp against her chin like a buttercup. She lay on her front, hitched up on her elbows. I loved her shoulders and her cleavage, the dive of her bones. I loved the ski-jump plunge of her back, from her neck to her buttocks. I loved the three moles, a constellation on her cheek.

"Can I ask you a question?" Lou asked.

"Of course," I said.

Something about Mal, I presumed.

"Why do you stay?"

I crinkled my nose and licked the glossy insides of my teeth. Mal had asked me this once, and I'd stumbled as the answer evaded me.

"Is it because you're in love with Lou?" he'd said. I'd nodded and my heart had cracked.

He'd closed his eyes.

"You could leave," she said.

"I know I could. Anytime." We both sat there, trapped in the time and the conversation. Together. "So could you."

"I have."

"Not really."

The dinking of a fly trapped between the outer layers of the tent.

"We both could," I said. "Something big needs to come along to knock us out of orbit."

"Like an asteroid?" she said.

I heard that same sadness in her as was in me. It seeped and was on both our skins. The will to escape without the power to enact it.

"Yeah." I smiled. "Like an asteroid."

We'd both basked in the warmth when Mal turned it on us. But she was blocked, unable to see around Mal's expanding waistline to what lurked in his shadow. Me. It was time, I thought, to show her that I could give her that same warmth too.

"Lou," I said but unaware I was to speak she spoke too.

"I guess I'm more like my dad than I knew," she said.

Fear let itself into me, and the confidence that came so briefly expired, died and rotted. Like her dad, she'd never given her love to anybody else and now she didn't know how to. That is what joined us inexorably. Neither had I.

"I love him," she said.

To love someone is to watch them die.

So we floated in stasis together, for days and weeks and months and years. Lou chained to Mal, widening like the flourish of bubbles on a wet bar of soap. Me to Lou, the metal of the chains thick and heavy. And we waited for Mal to take the lock in his hands, spin back the steel cover on the hole and produce the key. If he would unlock it, I could have taken her away. An arm underneath the crooks of her knees, the other a scaffold for her shoulders and back, and I could carry her. Without the shadow falling on my face, she'd see the love in me. She'd grip my hair in her fingers and know this time was wasted. But he didn't. The asteroid would come from elsewhere. From America. And the time it would take to get here would mean the crack in my heart grew bigger still.

Fifty-Six

After that first letter arrived, like a finger widening the hole where a tooth was knocked out, more and more dropped through the door and onto the mat. It slowly became an occurrence of such regularity that it was added to the list of chores Mum was to complete upon rising.

Get dressed.

Make Mal's breakfast.

Collect the post.

We were having calls from the post office, questioning the influx, as if to check we were suitably deserving. Letters came from as far away as Australia. I saw postmarks of all colors and patterns. The rainbow squiggles of Japan. The red-yellow sunburst of Alaska. The criss-cross mint-cool blue-green thatch of Peru. The world dropping through our front door in tiny jigsaw pieces. Dad would save the stamps. Nameless heads of state. Placeless landmarks. Inventors, engineers and thinkers whose existence was not even in our time.

Some days I arrived home from work to find the corner of a room brimming with bulbous black bin bags, rustling and shifting. They bulged like the humongous eyes of giant flies. They spilled and rolled and moved. Their outline, like Mal's, was becoming a lumpy unnatural changeling. Sometimes I would find these big black sacks in the garden, breathing in the heat of summer, or caked in thin white frost come wintertime like a Scandinavian licorice.

Mal didn't read the letters. His fingers had grown too fat and stiff to hold something with the fragility of paper. He'd once worn a silver ring on his right forefinger but it had long since been swallowed up, his skin and flesh having grown over it, incorporating it into his all-consuming mass. He was part jewelry. I looked at his chin. It blended almost seamlessly into his shoulder blades, and I imagined his body consuming itself, the edges smoothing out. There was no outward evidence that he even had bones in there anymore. If he were to live forever, perhaps he'd eventually become one huge, amorphous pink blob. A globe without oceans. I imagined that belly of his wriggling and moving until it spilled open to a yawning chasm webbed with bloody strings, like a toothless old man, his gummy grin full of toffee. I imagined it spilling a sea of pearly white eggs across the bedspread, full of larvae that became insects that became clones of me, Mum, Dad and Lou.

My mind was wandering in this way when I heard, above Mal's foul and coarse snore, Dad shouting from the attic.

"What on earth!"

I opened my eyes and listened to the tinny clank of him trundling down his ladder into the kitchen, where, since I'd been secretly awake, Mum had been putting the finishing touches to a cake festooned with rich cherries. Breakfast.

"Yorrnomgooindulikeiss."

Dad's voice, muffled and squeezed through the insulation of the walls. Eventually I understood: "You're not going to like this." I pulled on Mal's old jeans, my wardrobe long since bolstered by his renouncement of clothing, and walked slowly to the window. I glanced to check he hadn't stirred.

I was the fearful shake of red hands awaiting a caning at the thought that Lou may be gone. I took the cord of the curtains and opened them steadily, as though I were master of the red crushed-velvet drapes, twenty feet tall, of a stage in a town where the theater was the oldest building. As though my drawstring were a thick golden plaited rope I needed both hands and all my might to unfurl from its great wound wheel in the ceiling. As though whatever lay outside for me was the opening night of a show and me and Mal the audience brimming with anticipation hot and sickly like an illness.

Behind the glass, behind Lou's tent on the grass was another. Big this time, in the professional camping shades of blue and gray, its ropes taut and poised on the ground like the legs of a praying mantis, its silver pegs sharp and shiny like claws. A green-toothed man sat outside it with his girlfriend. They were cooking sausages on a small gas stove, the blue flames fingering the bottom of a rusty pan.

I nudged Mal's chubby knee with an outstretched toe that peeked from the hole in a sock he used to own.

"What?" he muttered, an angry shaven bear.

"Look," I said, and gestured with the same toe like it was a stiffened finger. He followed the line of its nail to the view.

The way settlements become hamlets become villages become towns. Landing at the biggest river. Staying where there is action and food and reason. Mal. Dust and rocks and comets caught in the path of a comet hurtling nowhere.

"And what do you think about that?" I asked.

The light from the window hit his face in golden rafters and made his pupils expand and retract in perfect circles.

"It's nothing to do with me," he said.

"It's everything to do with you, Mal. That's why they're here. Because of you."

"And they can leave if they want to."

He turned, his white naked back, blotched with ink-drop red

blurs and the blackened heads of deep buried filth, facing the window.

"So can you," he said.

By the time I arrived home from work, dried crusty lamb's blood worn like a shawl around my shoulders, the second tent was gone, their fun had. And with the trap being open would come the opportunity to limp away.

Fifty-Seven

Day Three Thousand One Hundred and Eighty-Five, according to the display on the wall, started as I was accustomed to. Mal, bigger even than yesterday. Food. Work. Red Ted. Talking continuously about those two beacons of masculinity, football and meat. I never thought I'd be a butcher at thirty-one but I was good, really good. I thought about getting my own shop one day. I battled the inertia that prevented me and didn't win. Then home.

Red Ted pulled neatly alongside the pavement outside our house. Lou's tent was illuminated by the security light Dad has installed on the roof. I eased myself out of his shattered old car and walked down the path toward it.

When I get there I see spread all around it the tatty remains of shiny black plastic and envelopes torn hastily in two, the way presents are supposed to be opened—with the excited talons of a child. Inside were four more sacks, their contents all over the floor of the tent like a soft paper mattress. And amongst it sat Lou on a throne of neat handwriting and goodwill.

"What's going on?" I said, though my face asked it first. "What are you doing here?"

"Hello!" She beamed. I'd meant to say hello. I'd not seen her this happy in just over three thousand one hundred and eighty-five days. She looked great when she was happy. "Guess what."

"What?"

"Your mum came into the bank today."

"She doesn't even bank there," I said.

"I know."

"What did she want? Please say it's not a loan. If she wants a loan, she can have one of mine. I have lots."

"Two things. She said now that so many letters keep on arriving, well, there's no point in fighting it anymore." I waited for her to say she'd been inside to see Mal but she didn't and I was relieved. "She wanted to know if I wanted to help."

"Why today? She's never wanted help before," I said, sitting just inside the front of the tent, crossing my legs as though I were a child being read to in a classroom and leaning into a plumped bag of post.

"I guess it's all getting too big."

"Mal?"

"Everything. She said there just isn't the room or the time anymore. So I'm going to help her answer some of these letters."

"You're mental," I said.

I felt like she'd escaped a riptide only to be torn away in the grip of a fierce undercurrent.

"Why?" she said.

"Are you serious?" I squirmed, anxious not to sound too negative.

"Yes, of course. Why wouldn't I be?"

Defensive. Uncomfortable.

"No," I stammered and bit my lip and opinion. "No reason at all. I think it's good. Great, I think it's great."

For one of Santa's elves. I thought of the relationship between fat men and large quantities of mail and wondered what made it so.

"Yes," she said, the purity of her unabashed joy massaging my sore, brittle cynicism.

"Yes, it is," I said.

Then she rallied.

"And she wanted me to come and talk to you."

I felt like I'd been powered down.

She shuffled through a neat pile of paper on her lap in search of something and I drummed tense little fingers softly against my thigh, wallowing in my helplessness. I drew neat little triangles around my kneecap with my thumb. Then Lou discovered whatever it was she'd been searching for.

"Look," she said, thrusting another torn-up envelope into my hand with a letter hanging out of it.

The bright red-and-blue postmark was American, the neatly stamped words AIR MAIL telling me it was better traveled than I was.

"What is it?"

"It's from a lady in Ohio. She read about Malcolm in a newspaper. How weird is that?"

I nodded and agreed but Dad's stamp collection was led by an army of Lincolns. It was stewarded by a whole troop of Edisons and flanked on either side by Washington after Washington after Washington. His stamp collection was a parade of founding fathers. Mal received letters from America all the time.

"Just read it," she said, and so I did.

Day Three Thousand One Hundred and Eighty-Five, according to the display on the wall, I read only my second of Mal's fan letters. Unless you counted the one Lou had passed to me at school when she was twelve, which these days I didn't.

Dear Mr. and Mrs. Ede,

Unlike the others it wasn't addressed to Mal, a unique approach to fan mail. Boded well.

My name is Norma Bee, and yours is a situation to which I can wholeheartedly relate. I live in a trailer in my own yard in Ohio, America, because my husband grew too big. I mean very, very big. My husband grew to 1,288 pounds. People who'd not seen him in years stood no chance at all of recognizing what he had become.

I screwed up my face into a puckered sour ball.

"It's amazing, isn't it?" said Lou.

"It's horrible," I replied but I couldn't take my eyes off Norma Bee's frank, captivating scrawl. "Has Mum seen this?"

"No."

I read on.

This may sound strange to you. This may sound odd or perverse or even upsetting. Or, as I dearly hope, this may make some kind of sense. Regardless, I'll continue. Just six weeks ago I entered my husband's bedroom with a stack of blueberry pancakes, smothered in thick maple syrup and sugar, to find that he was dead. He had suffered an aneurysm and hadn't even finished his breakfast of bacon, eggs and waffles. He could eat twelve eggs in a sitting. Our house is small, and as my husband grew large and needed more and more space, it no longer became possible for me to live there comfortably with him. And so I began entering competitions to win myself a trailer. I would enter all kinds of competitions. I'd enter cake-baking competitions, raffles and mostly painting competitions (I love to paint and my husband used to be my favorite subject—I've painted him over thirty times). Seven years ago, with a painting of my beloved Brian, I finally won one. It is a glorious Airstream trailer with a marvelous kitchen inside it and it's where I have lived ever since, using it to make the meals for my husband in the house and to sleep whenever I got the opportunity. But now, of course, I have no need for it. Since my husband died, I like to sleep in his old bed. He was in that room for twenty years, and that is the closest I can get to him. It's with this in mind that, having read about

*you both and your son Malcolm in the newspaper, that I thought
of you. I'd love to offer you my little trailer. I'd love to have it
shipped over to you, so that, if you need it, it can continue having the purpose for you that it once had for me.*
My contact details are on the back of this letter.
God bless you,
Norma Bee, Akron, Ohio, USA

I used my fingers as pincers to scour the envelope and pull out
whatever it was I could feel still left inside of it. Two Polaroids
fell out into my lap. They were memories of an enormous Mr.
Bee. Rolls upon rolls of mottled black skin. His face segueing into
hanging fat breasts and a monolithic tummy comprising separate
slabs of hulking meat. On his face was a smile and in his hands
two cream cakes, white and fluffy, as though he'd reached into the
heavens for a scooping of cloud. And then there was another photograph, quartered and folded. Lou took it and opened it slowly,
smoothing out its petals until she could lay it flat in front of me, a
photo of an exquisite oil painting of a silver trailer nesting in bright
green grass to the backing of a wide blue American sky.

"Why not?" asked Lou. "Wouldn't be the first strange thing
on your lawn."

Fifty-Eight

Mal was surprisingly awake on the day that the builders came to demolish the wall that separated our bedroom from Mum and Dad's. He lay there and watched with the sheets lapping at his body like a great lumbering walrus emerging from the ocean. The dust in the plaster woken by sledgehammer upon brickwork made him sneeze so hard that the sheet fell to the floor and the builder pretended (badly) that he hadn't noticed.

Mum wasn't convinced when Lou gave her Norma Bee's letter, vehemently refusing to have anything to do with Norma Bee's very queer little life. She did not see her own reflection in the mirror of it. Besides, it distracted her from the job at hand, Mal. Dad, meanwhile, embraced it as his own special project. He had friends in shipping, having himself sent huge metal structures all over the world, and enlisted them to help him bring Norma Bee's gift to us.

Dad paid Red Ted to drive with him to the coast, where our great metallic pod was arriving on a huge blue liner. By the time Dad and Ted arrived home, a crane was on hand to lift the trailer into position, for which Dad was in its cabin with the driver, entranced by the systems of levers and combinations of pulleys and wheels. A crowd gathered. I watched with Lou as the trailer swung through the air like a glamorous silver wrecking ball, catching the sun as it slowly spun and turned, bouncing its harsh light into the eyes of everyone who had come to watch. Slower and slower still it was lowered toward the floor. A team of men in fluorescent jackets stood on the ground to guide it carefully into place. A camera crew gathered behind a cordon of plastic yellow crime-scene tape and they filmed the entire thing.

Finally, when it was all over and the crowd began to disperse, I found Dad, his hands on his hips, surveying the land like a conquering emperor a new domain. In his eyes was a mad inventor glint.

"Did you see that?" he asked, hopping from one foot to the other like a sand lizard. "That was amazing. Did you see the crane? How it lifted the whole weight of this caravan like that? It wasn't even a big crane! See, you can't do that with lifts because they're stationary, but for a crane to be able to pick up and move something like that, with just ropes and wheels . . . Essentially, of course, that's all it is. Well, for a crane to be able to do that, and do it that easily, it's a fe—"

"Feat of modern engineering," I said, faking a yawn that he didn't notice to amuse Lou if not myself.

"Yes, exactly that, a feat of modern engineering. How I would love to make something like that. Amazing. Could you imagine?"

"No, Dad," I said, secretly glad to be warmed by the reigniting of his imagination. Far too long had passed since his body registered such a feverish chemical rush. I could almost see him glow. I could sense the beginning of the fading of TauTona on his face.

"Seriously," he said, because he didn't know that I'm taking him seriously and I didn't show it. "It's all about weight and space but . . ."

He walked away, still talking, his words a slow jet behind him.

Later that night, as Mum and Dad got ready to sleep in the trailer for the first time, me and Mal watched their silhouettes shuffle around inside of it like in a Victorian children's puppet show.

Fifty-nine

I'd been home from work for ten minutes when the doorbell rang. Lou stood there in a floor-length overcoat, collar up around her face, eyes perched on it, round and pointed at the ends, a cat's mouth. The heat from inside the house climbed out over her.

"She's dead," she said.

"What?"

Images of all the women I'd known flickered through my mind. Of Sal, whom I'd not seen or thought about in so long. Of Mum. Of Mrs. Gee, who probably was. That was it, small roll call.

"My mother is dead. She died last night."

She was still smiling, though I couldn't see her mouth. My stomach rolled.

"Oh." I offered a hand, automatically, conciliatory. She took it in hers, folded it around mine like an oyster. "I'm sorry," I said.

"Don't be."

"How did you find out?" I wondered.

She still held my hand and ran the ball of her tiny thumb across the scarred, cold brim of my butchered knuckles.

"I went to visit my father this morning," she said and dropped her head for the first time at his mention. "First time since I moved into my new place. I couldn't open the door for the pile of post behind it. The carpet was covered in packets of food and rubbish, bottles and ash. It stank. And he was in the corner, in the same chair in the same clothes. I knew she'd died. I knew it. But you know what? I'm happy she's dead. Now she's gone, he's cut loose."

"How?" I said, as though I only ever knew one word.

"Cancer." And I could see it in the back of Lou's gladdened, pretty eyes.

A bobble became a bump became a lump became an aggressive tumor in her hot breast. It had eaten through her with its mighty jaws in no time at all until her skin remained just hangers for her bones and all the fight left inside her was with her own regrets. A karmic tumor. It unfurled in my imagination like a flag to some memorial. On her deathbed she had asked to see her daughter but the message of her illness arrived too late, unable to make its way through the chicanery of the relationships she had busted to reach Lou in time for her to make it to the hospice. Not that she'd have gone. Just as Lou's mum hadn't been there when Lou most needed her, Lou was absent when her face was all that her mother needed to see.

I could picture it. In those last moments she had worn the over-bearing guilt of abdicating her maternal responsibility around her neck, an anchor that weighed her to the bottom of an ocean of dark thoughts. And I could see that this made Lou pleased. I could see it in her as she smiled at me and let go of my hand.

"I can't end up like my dad," she said. "I can't let Mal take me with him. Perhaps it's time for me to leave."

Then I realized she had let go of my hand, that mine was still cuffed to Mal and hers moved freely away. My cellmate's pardon granted, I slunk into the darkness of the corner as the bars slammed behind her. I wanted to run out behind her, roll like a commando through the gap in the door. But I was weary. It was there, as always in my head, the invisible barrier between the opportunity and the grab I wanted to make for it. Tired.

Mal had been in bed for ten years. I climbed in beside him.

Sixty

It had been a year since the death, the carcass mulch. The tent remained idle, a collapsed lung on the yellowed grass. When the low breeze blew southwesterly, sweeping the walls at the side of our bungalow, the tent would breathe. Over Mal I watched it as the display on the wall went click.

Lou would call to see me at the butcher's. She still asked after Mal but less and less so. "He's OK," I'd say, hollowed by the effort. She told me about how things were going at the bank, about her friends, about her flat. She mentioned men's names sometimes, men I didn't know.

She asked about my life. Whether I'd met anyone. I told her the truth and she smiled. I'd ask after her dad, which I liked to do because when she answered I learned more about her. Her words distilled feeling in me, whittling it to raw and pure of heart, how you'd feel when, at a televised awards ceremony, a young girl with burns, skin as thin as a tambourine's, is rewarded for reentering the house to wake her sleeping mother. A medal for bravery and selflessness hung around her sore, charred neck. The audience applauds, distraught and suddenly small.

In trying to leave Mal behind, Lou had focused her love. It had gone to her dad. And in doing this, it was as though she'd given up the pursuit of convention, the hopes that she had once believed were all that could make her happy. She now understood what Mal had said that night on the beach. Why, she thought, devote herself to finding love, success, solvency—to the life she was expected to create around herself—if it could only explode so spectacularly? She needed no better an example of how a life lived a way perceived to be correct could still come to nothing than that of her own father.

The first month, Lou said, she'd spent cleaning around him. Scrubbing the smoke from the curtains, lifting the ash from the carpet fibers. Shampooing the arms of the chair where he sat, his grubby fingerprints ingrained.

The second month, circling the names of clubs, societies, groups, meetings, centers and courses in the local paper, no hiding of her desperation to enthuse him.

"But I don't like chess," he'd mumbled.

"It's not about liking chess, Dad," she'd say.

"Joining a chess club isn't about liking chess?"

"No. It's about meeting people, like-minded people."

"I can't imagine I'll meet many people who, like me, don't like chess, at a chess club."

There it is, she thought, a joke, a glimmer. He's in there, buried but alive. Dig.

"It's not just chess, you can do pretty much anything." The options held above her head like a spade, each slamming of it downward an inch closer to the target. "Archery . . ."

"Archery?"

"Yes."

"Archery?"

"Yes."

"No."

"Wine-making? Or you can learn a language. French? Spanish?"

Lou cocked an ear, how she does when she hopes you'll be pleased.

"Spanish?" her dad said. He'd not taken his eyes from the television set. "I don't like Spain. Too hot, weird portions."

"You've never been to Spain, Dad. Anyway, there are more. Model railways? No? Salsa danc—"

The volume on the television crept upward, trembling a tinny rattle in the speakers. She'd try again another time. The survivor had been located, contact made. She'd return with an industrial digger. The excavation of her dad would commence forthwith.

This, I thought, was the best type of love. The bravest type, given with no thought for oneself. It deserved medals too. She could kneel and I'd slide one over her head, nooselike, and down her smooth, elegant neck. Services to her father.

She'd update me in installments over the butchery counter. Red Ted stood behind me and listened. He never asked about her once she'd gone but he too daydreamed of her return.

The third month, the fourth and the fifth, the reintegration of her dad into society began. Lou planned routes to town for them that skirted the tree-lined streets where signs erected outside properties bore the face of the man who'd ruined his life. The estate agent, his rictus cardboard grin ever-present.

The fourth and fifth month, better and better.

The sixth month, Lou's dad went to the supermarket on his own. She cried when she told me. He brought a granary loaf and two tins of baked beans.

The seventh month. Lou took the dirty plate from the tray in his lap and carried it through to the kitchen, resting it atop the counter to be washed later on. He'd begun watching TV shows she wanted to watch, reaching out, an exploratory root pioneering a caress across dry soil in the search for water. She picked the newspaper off the table, sodden and clouded by the blue ink of her dad's doodling, florid and incessant, and opened it to the community pages.

"Boxing? No, no, not boxing. I don't want you taking up boxing."

"I'd lose my beautiful features." He laughed.

"Precisely," she said. "Floristry?"

"Flower arranging? I might as well take up midwifery."

"OK," she said, "midwifery?"

"No."

And then a bloodied, embattled hand pumped through the wreckage and debris. It clasped her at the wrist, desperate to be saved.

"Life drawing?" she asked.

He thought for a moment, twizzled the pen in his fingers, an enthused majorette.

"Yes," he said, "why not?"

She looked around her, the heavy rubble finally gone, and hugged her father. He'd survived.

The first time, the eighth month, they went together. In the church, under the lava-lamp gels pushed through the stained-glass window by the sun, a woman disrobed. Her feet were tiny and square, the balls of her cheeks fresh and pink, her hair brown, bobbed, tousled, good. She reminded Lou's dad of the wooden woman who angrily emerged from his Swiss clock twenty-four times a day, infuriated, he liked to pretend, by never having had more than an hour's sleep. The model said her name was Rebecca Mar, then lay down on the sofa provided by the vicar, naked and gentle. Lou's dad picked up his pencil and sketched, realizing quickly that he could close his eyes and still continue. He'd committed her form to memory immediately.

The ninth month, he went alone, a new and expensive packet of graphite in his pocket. He looked at Rebecca Mar's compact body, the muscle and flesh wound and pressed together beautifully as though a statuette. He traced her to the page. She curled the dressing gown around her midriff. He lingered as he packed his things. The vicar gone, they kissed by the cold stone altar.

Against the wall in the car park outside the butcher's, Lou cried, my arm around her.

"He came home a new man," she said.

"Nice that the rebirth should happen in the church." I smiled.

At her house, the wall in the spare room was festooned with sketches of a naked Rebecca Mar. This homage to her had a unique narrative arc. As it branched from left to right, the chronological order and method her dad had adopted to tack them to the wall, the change was explicit.

"You can see Dad's drawing getting better with every single picture," Lou told me, "and Rebecca gets happier in each and every one."

The twelfth month. Rebecca Mar stowed her belongings in that very same room on the day she moved in with Lou's dad, who did the vacuuming, cooked the dinner, and rewarded his daughter's saintly fervor by making her the happiest I'd ever seen her. It made me love her all the more.

"I'll come by the shop tomorrow," she says. "I've been thinking."

Sixty-One

My heart performed a pirouette when she asked me the question. It spun and it raced, refusing to slow, like no force was great enough to ever stop it. This was the feeling, I now knew, of getting close to what your heart desires.

We were standing outside the butcher's shop window, me and Lou. The display was of cutlets and steaks, minced beef and tenderloins, shaped and divided by brittle plastic grass and shiny flowers that pretend to be alive. My morning's work. I was covered in blood and white snowflake splatters where the bleach Ted used to wash his gory chopping block had splashed across the blue material of my apron. And I needed her to repeat herself, to say it again, but for me not to look so desperately like those were the words I longed with all I had to hear. I raised a fist to my mouth and coughed into the microphone head of it because it felt like my turn to make some sound.

"Pardon?" I choked.

It felt like I'd leave the ground if I didn't concentrate my entire body weight on two penny-size patches on the soles of my feet just in the center underneath the toes. They burned as I did so.

"Will you come with me?" she said again, and I could see in the tiny line that makes a fold above her exquisite chin that she meant it.

"Of course I will," I said.

I'd have hugged her if I hadn't been caked in a pale explosion of pig guts.

"That's it then. We'll go to Ohio. We'll go to visit Norma Bee. And that dead woman's cutthroat world of residential lettings and management sales can pay for it all. Dad can have the money he needs to live on. The rest is what we'll use to escape."

Lou had stayed in touch with Norma Bee ever since she first got her letter about the trailer. They wrote to each other regularly. In Norma Bee, despite her distance, Lou found a fount of advice, more friendly than motherly but maternal nonetheless—not that this would ever have occurred to Lou. Norma Bee understood things, prescient things, in Lou's life. That they'd not met made her advice all the easier to swallow, the way you listen to a teacher, not a parent, who tells you to shut up. Because of Brian Bee she understood Mal's weight. Because of Brian Bee she understood Lou's dad's dark funk.

In rescuing her father when she couldn't rescue Mal, Lou felt she had atoned. One person less had given up on life. I'd no doubt she still loved Mal but finally she was wriggling free. I'd waited for a long time, and now that her hands were untethered, I was watching her cut at the ropes binding mine.

I thought about the reason I'd never been on a plane.

"We'll go as soon as possible then," she said, and she placed a hand on my neck to pull me closer so that she could kiss me on the peppery skin of my cheek.

She knocked my butcher's hat into the breeze and the busy road. Then she turned, her hair skipping around her head behind her like a sharply cracked whip, obediently following her up the road. I watched her all the way.

Back in the shop I found Red Ted buffing meat hooks with a thick white cloth. The hot water it was soaked in condensed in the air as it touched the cold metal. He didn't even turn around, our having worked together for so long meaning our movements were synchronized, our spatial awareness of each other tuned the way ducks follow ducks in lines. It was how we avoided errant knives and raised cleavers.

"Ted," I said. "I'm leaving. I'm going to America. With Lou."

"OK," he said.

"OK."

My pardon had arrived.

Sixty-Two

I formulated a strange revenge that night in my bed, listening to Mal's stupefying snore. I decided not to tell him that soon I'd be gone with Lou. Instead I thought about how it must feel to sleep in a different room. To turn to a different face, not the ashen patty before me now. Hers. To see a different ceiling.

Over the next few days I sneaked my possessions into a suitcase that I kept underneath my bed and that I only took out when Mal was asleep, Dad was in the attic and Mum was keeping watch upon some simmering pan or other. I rooted out the passport I'd had but never used, and signed the visa papers Lou organized. Not knowing how long we'd be gone for, I carefully folded away everything I owned. Soon enough the case was fit to bulging, spilling out over the sides, tearing and stretching at the seams. I sat on it and used a stiff finger to probe the clothes inward, warding off the frustration each time the zip fell apart by imagining I was sitting astride Mal, prodding at his innards as they flapped about the carpet, sticky and collecting dust.

Weeks and weeks seared past, and by the time the Tuesday of our flight arrived I'd still not told anybody bar Red Ted about my departure. At sunrise I wrote a little note for Dad explaining that Lou and me had gone on holiday, that I wanted him to take care of Mum and Mal, if she'll let him, and I slipped it in the thin crack between the entrance to his loft and the ceiling, where it sat. Then, in a hurry to leave before Mum delivered a piping-hot English breakfast, I took my case and left quietly. Mal got a parting glance. I walked to the taxi waiting at the far end of the road, out of sight.

"You're his brother, aren't you?" the driver asked me.

"Whose?" I said.

"Malcolm Ede's."

"Yes."

Because I had that effervescent insomnia a bride has the night before her wedding, I waited restlessly until we'd picked up Lou, who was waved off by her dad and Rebecca Mar standing in their dressing gowns, and then I told the taxi driver the story of what happened the last time we went to the airport. They both laughed, reminding me that I could talk when I was in the mood. My obstacles were often my own.

Soon we were paying, the taxi driver shaking my hand. We loaded our two bags onto a misshapen metal trolley and I followed Lou's lead through the airport as we performed a routine I found both hectic and reassuring in preparation to board the plane.

Inside, the man directly across the aisle twisted in his seat and said, "Excuse me, are you . . . ?" So I turned my head, leaned over Lou's lap and looked out of the window, waiting to watch the world roll out of view.

The kick-start of the engine on the runway set my body in concrete and bound the back of my head to the seat. I didn't even notice that I was kneading Lou's cute little wrist, turning her flowery skin white. The muscles in my legs stiffened until they were both chicken-wire rickety with cramp as we moved faster and faster, with each second my body breaking new ground. Blastoff. One thousand feet. Two thousand feet. Three thousand feet further away from home than I had ever been. Climbing at six hundred miles per hour, powered by fire, breaking my orbit. I was airborne, a broken spell and a lifted curse. The machinery made noises as the wheels were stowed away. I was breaking my mooring. Leaving my dock. I was no one's brother in the middle of the sky.

I saw the white cliffs of the English coast and remembered when Dad told me why they were that color. Billions of years of bones, he said. Trillions of lives, all the skeletons of the sea, ground up by the tides and impacted by the waves. Pressure plus time making chalk. Amazing. Enough pressure for enough time will always make something new.

Sixty-Three

Day Seven Thousand Four Hundred and Eighty-Three, according to the display on the wall.

After the kerfuffle, the noise outside gradually dissipates as the people in the crowd that had gathered to watch Mal's interview with Ray Darling make their ways back home. I peek out of the newly resurrected curtain and see that a few still remain. I wonder where Lou has gone in this time before we meet.

I hear Dad, back in his attic, the clanking of metals as he powers into this latest creation with a new and proper urgency. The vibrations make the metal in my legs hum mellow notes. Bang and clatter, tinkle and clash. The panels of the ceiling rattle like he might fall through them.

"What is he doing up there?" I say, convinced that if he does fall through the roof he'll land on me, rather than the hundred-stone man handily spread across the room like a huge pink trampoline.

"I don't know," says Mal, with a slight shrug of his shoulders made nearly imperceptible by his size. I wonder, if you cut him open, what color his fat is. I decide on withered mushroom.

The familiar shuffle of Mum's slippers arrives with its cha cha cha through the door. In her hand she has a first-aid kit in a green plastic lunchbox. She sets it down on the floor by Mal's bed and, like a magician's assistant, plucks an antiseptic wipe from a little packet. With tiny forensic dabs she anoints it onto the network of bright red scratches Ray Darling's desperate hands tore into Mal's skin. He doesn't wince at the sting of the antiseptic, his nerve endings long since desensitized by the turmoil the stretching of speed weight gain inflicts on the body.

A huge thud from upstairs makes Mum jump. She channels her fright into squeezing with some force the tube of emollient cream she has in her hand, with which she'd planned to lube Mal's cadaverously colored groin. A spurt of it ejects with surprising velocity and leaves a slippery trail up Mal's gut, across his sagging glands and all the way into his mouth.

"Oh," Mum says, "what is he doing up there?"

"I don't know," I say, laughing.

I watch Mal bunch up his puny eyes. They sink backward into the thick plate of his face at the foul taste of the cream.

"Look what he's made me do!" she shouts.

I laugh some more.

"What does he think he's bloody doing?"

"I don't know," Mal and me repeat together.

I hope whatever it is saves him.

Sixty-Four

My eyes were gooey. I shuffled a slow, post-flight zombie shuffle to the endless metal snake of the carousel. The colors on the signs seemed so much brighter. The American yellow was a truer yellow, the American blue more honest and the American green clearer. Everything looked new and big and unafraid to talk to you. We were ushered through with polite instruction delivered so formulaically as to not be polite at all, and found ourselves slumbering through an automatic door that opened like wings webbed with metal. Lou held my elbow. It felt traditional, gentlemanly and good. Unsure of what I was looking for, I faked a confident stride, hoping that the people in the expectant crowd of loved ones would notice my gait before they did my eyes scanning their signage. We walked to the end of the row, where we ran out of people, the runt of our flight's litter. I watched people I recognized from the plane throw bags to the floor as arms not seen in some time were flung around them. Embraces exploded in excited squeals.

"Excuse me."

An accent, new and pleasurable to our ears, like bathing in the sound of a happy belly. Together we spun on our heels, where a sign written in blister-red lipstick on the inside of a cereal box read simply "Lou." Wrapped around it were nails in that same stop-sign red. They clung like cockles to fingers bedecked in clusters of sparkling golden rings. Discs and bands and jewels. Rings with names, rings with faces. They moved around and over each other, a busy hive of shiny wasps. Our eyes were magpies, gliding up two smooth black arms to Norma Bee. Her smile was a grand piano, her laugh a grandiloquent diva snickle. She had breakneck curves from her neck down over her huge bosoms and out in glorious rolls round her hips. She had a mayoral amount of jewelry wrapped around her and her bright blond hair shaved to curly miniature ringlets.

She took us both in her arms and laughed some more, kissing us, leaving rails of red across our faces. We curled up and wallowed in her genuine warmth.

"Lou. And Mr. Ede, I presume?" she said in the best way. "I've been expecting you. Now let's go eat."

We followed her, through more doors, to the tarmac. We came to her car and she talked at us, I caught barely half of it, not concentrating, Lou nodding, our bearings shot.

"Have a good flight?" she said. "So looking forward to your visit. I've made you some beds."

Beds. Plural. Our stay followed an explanatory letter, I thought. We were not together, not in Norma Bee's head or Lou's. Only mine.

Her car was huge. Wide and full of crisp, cold air. In the back I had room to extend my legs without them touching the door, and the leather was new and pungent. I inhaled it, clearing my sleepy head. While Lou and Norma Bee made small talk in the front, about Mal and England and tents and fat and butchery and trailers and my mum and dad, I was bombarded through my window by Ohio sunshine. Hard to think it was the same sun. The sky in America seemed so much farther away, the roads you viewed it from wider, the eyes you saw it through tinted. I saw the America me and Mal learned about on late-night television. Red fire hydrants. Hanging traffic lights. Steam. I felt smaller and smaller around each corner. More new visions in a journey than in a lifetime so far. We got faster and faster as we drove out from Cleveland, farther from the stores and billboards, bigger and bigger distances apart until soon there was little around us but road. Then the lanes multiplied, winding like a neckerchief around a new city on the horizon. The dry heat sucked wet stencils out of my back and by the time we arrived at Norma Bee's house on the outskirts of Akron, my white shirt had joker lips.

"Here we are," said Norma Bee, standing in the center of the patchy rectangle of grass where the trailer once cast its shadow. "Home sweet home."

It was a small building, a clear distance from the neighbors on either side, with wooden steps cut thick leading up to a sparse veranda and through a dirty screen door into the house. Inside a small dog yapped and bared its teeth until Norma reassured it that all was fine and it climbed into its basket, gnawing on a bone twice its size.

"Now there isn't much room, so we'll make do," Norma said.

The inside of the house had been knocked-through in part to make room for her dead husband. I found a fold-up travel bed laid out in the hall. Though it looked little more than the debris of a crash between some twisted metal springs and a pile of knitted rags, I looked forward to having my own room. I unpacked my clothes into the drawers she provided in cupboards vast and heavy. There were shirts and trousers in there with no purpose any more. Enormous and specially made, some of them the circumference of those huge Army-issue water tanks rolled out when there are floods. There were waistlines for clowns and chest sizes for bears. There were collars that would fit the Sphinx and jumpers so wide you could have hidden children in them. And I thought how odd it was that I wasn't used to the sight of gargantuan garments, because Mal was always naked.

By the time we'd finished unpacking, it was early evening and a buffet fit for a returning war hero crowned a table on the porch. We sat there all night, relaxed and calm, the sky a thunder blue but clear and quiet, disco-lit by stars and the blinking bulbs of planes far away. But for the bark of the dog at the passing of a car, there was nothing. I was cast out of the storm and it was beautiful. We ate charred roast chicken and glazed ribs and drank red wine until we slurred our words like badly controlled puppets. And then we went to bed. In it I resolved to make Lou mine here.

Sixty-Five

I woke with the dog licking my face, its tongue like a piece of ham. Its eyes were too big for its skull, two pool balls inside a melon. Horrible. Lou walked in immediately afterward wearing pink pajamas, carrying a steaming cup of coffee and looking early-morning sexy, all bedraggled and messy. Once we'd showered, we ate huge breakfasts. There were combinations of varieties of bacon and eggs and onions and potatoes. Glossy condiments in squeezy tubes like children's paint sets. There were bottomless juices, icy servings of citrus. Nothing seemed to empty. After we had eaten we headed into town to the shops to stock up on supplies, and I took the brief opportunity to call home.

"You can use my phone at home," Norma Bee said.

I considered it good manners not to do so but didn't know why.

It rang a strange ring for too long, a new beep.

Dad answered. He was out of breath, that biting wheeze that reminds you of a man's age.

"Hello," I said, like Norma's dog scolded for growling, ears down, eyes to the floor, my tail wagging.

"Hello," he replied. No telling-off. Sometimes I forgot how old I was. "I was wondering when you'd call. Where are you?"

"In Ohio. Where the trailer came from."

"Oh," he says. "Wow. That's a long way. I thought maybe you meant the seaside." He liked that one of us had escaped, I could hear it in his pant. "With Lou?"

"Yes."

"Yes? Wow."

My face turned the scarlet of an illusionist's cloak, and I caught the reflection of it in the metal coat of the telephone box. Through the glass I could see Norma Bee and Lou loading angular brown bags full of strange boxes and packaging, colors and brands into the car.

"How long are you going to stay there?" he asked.

"I don't know. Just a holiday but we'll see. It's nice here. Quiet. You'd like it, Dad, you know?"

"I don't know," he said, wistfully, "but I imagine you're right."

I detected the heartbreaking twang, how jealousy sounds in a father's voice.

"Well done, Son," he said.

I said good-bye as my time chimed to a close, and stood still there in that phone box like a Neanderthal suspended inside an ice cube.

"What's wrong?" asked Lou as I climbed into the back of the car.

"Nothing," I said.

Lou's money, all that was left of her mother's earthly residue, burned slowly here. We took Norma Bee to diners. In the evenings we drank her homemade wine and prepared vast meals together. And when we sat and spoke about Brian Bee, or about Malcolm Ede, I sensed that both Lou and Norma Bee had that same part of them that was lost. And most nights I reclined in a big wooden chair on the decking with the dog curled up in my lap. I listened to their therapeutic to-and-froing, stroking the hound's hairy head roughly how it liked it. As the pattern was sustained, the more comfortable we became.

I took a job in the local butcher's. The owner was impressed by my knife work, how clean off of the bone I could trim the cow. I told him about Red Ted a little but he never asked any questions. Instead he listened to the basketball on the radio, recounting from memory highlights in the commentary from his favorite-ever games. He called everyone by their initials. I was to call him GDF, just as everyone else did, and he told me lots of different things that it stood for. I never knew which were true.

One night we went to GDF's house for dinner, so that I might meet his family.

"You must be Mrs. Ede?" he said to Lou.

She tucked her hair behind her ear, ruffled the tip of her nose and laughed.

"I must be," she said.

GDF slapped his thigh. His wife came into the room, oven gloves making warm pillows of her hands.

"You must be Mrs. GDF?" I said.

She said that she was. Mrs. GDF worked in the local bank. She and Lou talked while GDF and I watched basketball on the television. The following Monday, Lou started work. Norma Bee said that if we liked it so much, we could stay as long as we wanted to.

"We don't want to get in the way," I said.

"I've worked around men much bigger than you," said Norma Bee, her giggle reaching every room of the house.

Weeks and months went by, each hour slower than the last but each passing anniversary coming with what felt like an ever-increasing frequency. Lou and I grew closer still, my heart fonder, the pair of us contented. Our moods and movements intertwined, and I stood a gardener watering a seed he planted long ago, watching it begin to emerge from the earth. We grew so close that Norma Bee asked us if she could paint our portrait together. We agreed, and night after night on the veranda she mapped us out on her easel, the birds fleeing from the trees around the garden every time she boomed her laugh into the black sky and it ricocheted off the moon. Lou said she thought of her dad's drawings.

Norma Bee was at her easel, shading, shaping and coloring one morning, when, as I rose from my bed, she said in her delicious brogue, "Here, I made you breakfast."

By the time Lou got to the table, she found I'd already poured her an orange juice with bits in, just how she liked it. She sat down next to me and I willed the memory of Mal to leak from her into the ground. We were lulled into a new inertia, comfortable and unmoving. I didn't want to wake us in case when I did she couldn't get back to sleep. I knew that I would easily.

Sixty-Six

Mal was turning forty, I remembered. Fifteen in-bed years. I bought him a birthday card with a monkey on it, hanging upside down in a bright cone hat. It was smoking a cigar, which it shouldn't have, and its teeth were mauve. At supper I put it on the table with a pen, its nib an oily wedge. I wrote: "Happy birthday, Mal." Norma drew two fleshy feet protruding from a bedstead and signed her name with a curve and a bounce. I walked the dog, and when I returned the envelope was sealed, the pen in its pot. Later I held it to the sun to try to read what Lou had written but the lines were sandwiched by the thick slates of card. I promised to post it the next day and considered steaming open the envelope. But I didn't. We talked about home for the rest of the evening, and what little might have changed in the four years we'd been gone. They were as suspended in time as we were.

"How is your father, Lou?" asked Norma Bee.

"Happy," she said, happy too at the notion.

"And your mum?"

"My mum?" I said, late to remember that Lou's mum was dead, so little did we talk about her.

"Yes. How is your mum?"

A wash of sorrow came upon me. I'd not thought of her as much as I should have done, not as much at all.

"Fine," I said but with only half of my heart.

"You think?" said Lou.

From her tone I gained a temper, the itch before a swelling.

"Yes."

"Stockholm syndrome fine?"

The itch reddened and boiled.

"What?"

"Hostages are happy because they've got a roof over their head and dry clothes. Doesn't mean they're fine."

"You're not really qualified to comment, Lou," I snapped.

Surprised, she flexed in her chair. I wanted to remedy this in an instant but a chant began internally that wouldn't abate, and the blame I put at her feet for being free but still not being mine squatted hot and angry on my lips.

"You didn't leave. Not that easy, is it?"

"But I did!" she said, shrill and spiked. The scream of the firework.

"Perhaps it isn't a question of geography!" The explosion in the air.

"Guys!" said Norma Bee, placation. The coos of the crowd at the flame in the sky.

Lou went quiet, her gaze intent on her knees. The relationship had always been fractious, Mum's and hers. They'd no grasp of their commonalities, twins forever at arm's length. They both loved him. So I tell Lou and Norma Bee about my mum.

My mum had lived in that bungalow her entire life, as had I until I was thirty-six. Her dad had walked out when she was young. I knew more of my grandma, frayed by senility. She was still alive when I could first form memories, just as hers began to dissipate. Her neural pathways were dug road.

Mum cared for her completely for what remained of her life. I remembered how she would kneel on the floor, Nan's feet in her lap, bathing her brittle corns in soapy water. Watching the wax of her mother's weakling candle flay to nothing. Her last words to Mum had been telling, the final hurrah of her mind. "You really have been lovely."

"She wants to care for people. I'm not sure she knows what else to do," I said.

Her and Lou didn't know how similar they were.

Lou lifted her chair from the porch and set it next to mine. She kissed my ear.

"Sorry," she said. "I hadn't meant it like that."

I twined my fingers in hers like the closing jaws of a Venus flytrap.

"It's OK," I replied.

Norma Bee watched the clouds circle. Vultures in the air.

Mum, Norma Bee and Lou were all the same to me. But one had a focus, one had lost hers and the last had yet to find it. Even though it was set right next to her and she was squeezing its hand harder still. I knew she was thinking of him. Mal was still in between us, the space between magnets. But I had knocked them farther apart.

Sixty-Seven

Then a letter arrived, for Lou, its postmark stiff and British. Inside it was a sketch of a naked Rebecca Mar. She was holding a cape of emerald silk, a corner in each hand clasped to each shoulder. But for that, naked. Hammocks of intense shade cuffed her bosoms. Lighter grays fell in triangles on her belly, giving it that boxy shape of middle age, when the muscle is reticent to tighten. She was standing in the doorway of Lou's dad's kitchen, and behind her the flowers in the garden stretched to skim the wasps.

Dear Lou, it said on the reverse, the webbed black scrawl and expanding blots of a pen meant for calligraphy.

> *It's your dad. Obviously. Hope you two are still doing well out there. I must come and visit. And say thank you to Norma for me for those recipes. Guess what! I sold a sketch that I did. Of Rebecca, naturally. Just a simple thing, a line drawing of her tending the garden. I did it about the same time I did the one I've sent you here but I can't remember which was first. And not for much money either, just a few pounds. Another guy from life drawing asked to buy it, he said it might help him (he's only just started) with perspective and things, and it's not very often we get a new guy (he's the first since I started), the rest are just old ladies. It was a bit embarrassing . . . he asked me to sign it! Couldn't really say no, could I? He's even paying Rebecca to do some private sitting for him. He must*

*have too much money I reckon, but she doesn't mind, money
is money.*
*Been past Malcolm's house a few times. Crazy. You know, your
tent is still there.*

I watched Lou read his name. She stopped on it but I couldn't
tell if it was any more than she might at a full stop or a comma.
Good.

*Anyway, love, write back. Let me know when would be a good
time to come, if Norma wouldn't mind.*
Love to you all,
Dad

"He sounds well, doesn't he?" Lou said.

GDF died later that same week, suddenly, teaching a grandson
how to play basketball on the driveway of his house. At his funeral,
his wife asked me to take over the butchery. I said yes outright,
then discussed it with Lou and Norma Bee later that night in a bar
next to the bank. I didn't tell them I'd already decided but they
agreed I should do it. This had been home for a long time, our lives
for longer still.

I called home monthly, sitting in the corner of Norma Bee's
lounge watching her and Lou from the window in the garden. And
I felt sick before and during but reprieved when I replaced the
handset back in the firm grip of the receiver. Each evening afterward I recapitulated for Lou. I made it sound as boring as possible,
as staid and as plain as a lump of unbaked dough.

I didn't mention his celebrity, that on his fortieth birthday there
was a party for him outside our house attended by some people he
didn't even know. Day Five Thousand Four Hundred and Seventy-
Five, according to the display on the wall. That he was well over
sixty-five stone these days.

I sat on my bed, telling her simply that he was still in his. That Dad was still in the attic and that Mum was still Mum. I tried to make it about us.

"Means I'll be forty in two years," I said.

She laughed, realized I wasn't too and apologized.

"Yeah, but I've been thinking. There are things I want that I don't have. And I think I'm old enough to have them."

I scratched at my chin. She softened.

"Go on . . . ," she said.

Then Norma Bee called us outside.

We found her in the yard, standing inside a large barrel and crushing ripe purple grapes with her bare, stained feet. It was dusk. All the shades of the night were a powdery version of their selves by day. Norma was at her easel, its back to us until the end result. Lou stood at the table in a long white dress, cleaning wineglasses with a small yellow cloth. I pictured her sitting with her legs wide open, running her fingers up and down the finely tuned strings of a majestic golden harp. I told Norma what I'd just told Lou of my unrest.

She was still teasing the canvas with the brush as she spoke. She drew a few deep breaths, storing energy like the dynamo on a bicycle. Then she began.

"See, Brian, my husband, God rest his soul, he had no choice. He was not a well man. The two of us, we were big. I mean, look at me. I ain't gonna win no beauty pageants. We ate well, every day, three times a day. I used to love feeding him, you see? I used to love doing things for him, all these little things, and soon I had no choice to 'cos Brian couldn't even move no more. He couldn't go to work no more, he just got too big. He used to work as a security guard. Sure, he wasn't the fastest security guard but he was a difficult man to get past all right. And then soon he was just too heavy. He couldn't walk very far. He couldn't even stand for very long without getting out of breath. And so they fired him, and he came home, and he lay on that big old bed of ours and he stayed there until the day I came through that door with his pancakes and his coffee for breakfast and I found him right where I left him, dead. That was the hand he was dealt by the Lord, and that's fine because that was the hand I was dealt too. I was put on this earth to look after Brian. To feed him and take care of him. And he was put on this earth to have me do that for him. That was why we were meant to be together until the good Lord decided it was time to take Brian away. That was the way it was meant to be. He would eat the food I made him and I would paint his picture. That was how our little family worked."

I looked at the table carpeted in food. Hot dogs and ribs. Potatoes and fried chicken. Legs, wings, breasts, sauces and carbonated drinks. But I had no appetite, my stomach felt distended and tight. And I looked through the window at the paintings of Brian that lined the wall. Each of them were exquisite. Pastel renderings of his legs, huge and segmented by fat like giant larvae. Watercolor impressions of his arms, thick as punchbags heavy with pâté. Oil daubings of his gruesome bloated paunch, flanked either side by flattened, sagging breasts like the ears of an elderly elephant. I felt nauseous.

"Lou," she said. Lou was standing, leaned against the rim of the veranda, her arms bowed, made from incredible shapes. "You aren't the same as us. You're not me. You're not Malcolm's mother. What you're doing isn't caring anymore, honey. What you're doing, and you've been doing it for fifteen years, is grieving. The problem you have is that Malcolm Ede never died. He never let you give the love you had for him to someone else." *Me*, I thought, *me*. "What are you going to do, honey? Wait here for him to die?"

Lou was weeping, a whispering horn. I gripped the dark wood of my chair, forcing soft indentations. I beamed implorations into Norma Bee's brain, a telepathic puppeteer. *Go on*, I yearned, *go on*.

"I don't mean to upset you, Lou, sweetheart," she said, her

grapey footprints padding across the floorboards, "but trust me when I say from experience that the things you want won't be there when he's gone. You need to realize that he already is."

With that, Norma Bee walked back into the home she wished more than anything she could pass down to a daughter. I could have kissed her, kissed her rubbery lips.

Lou didn't come to me, didn't put her arms around me. There was no parting of the clouds, no tractor beam of sunshine falling on me.

So I said it, even though I didn't mean it.

"Lou." She looked at me, face striped and pink. "I can't do this anymore."

I thought of Sally Bay, pretty Sally Bay, the only girlfriend I'd ever had. How I'd deserted her without a thought. And I trembled, deserting one who doesn't even belong to me but to my brother, like she always had.

"I'm leaving," I said, and I prayed it was enough.

I went to bed.

Sixty-Eight

An hour in the morning, pre the slinking of the moon, and she was looking at me, differently though, different in the details, so close up, of her face.

She leaned forward, her hand on mine on my knee, and with her lips prised just slightly apart, her hair tangled about her face and her eyes closed as if to sleep, she kissed me. It lingered awhile. Numbed, I could not move.

I lay back down and absorbed the aftermath of an immense, exhausting high. I fell asleep almost immediately.

In the morning I was woken by the dog's long nails clacking across the hallway. I realized only then that at some point in the night Lou had climbed into bed with me, this tiny single put-me-up, and was fast asleep with her arm around my waist and her face nuzzled in the cradle of my shoulder. And now she was mine, and I worried that I should ever move for fear it wouldn't last forever.

I kissed her on the forehead, my magnificent beauty, and closed my eyes again, pretending to sleep until she opened hers and kissed me back.

In that little wooden house we didn't talk about Mal again. We went about our lives as though he hadn't existed as anything other than the bitter aftertaste of a drink wrongly ordered. In a conscious effort not to end up like poor old Brian Bee, me and Lou politely declined seconds, thirds and fourths most nights. When I wasn't working, I put my mind and hands to work rebuilding the walls that Norma Bee had demolished when she moved into the trailer, and with a group of her neighbors even extended the back of her house into the yard. I took it upon myself to widen some of the smaller doorways as Norma widened herself. She remained a mother hen. Where my mum would have flapped like a scared, trapped chaffinch, Norma Bee would cluck and preen and warm her eggs.

I missed Mal and Mum and Dad but I would have swapped nothing for this. Lou. It was glorious. I could have basked in the heat of it forever.

Sixty-Nine

Walking into town, we enjoyed seeing the people. I liked it when they passed the church. They would sprinkle their face and shoulders with the angles of an imaginary cross. We stopped for milk shakes at a diner. There was plenty of space on the bench opposite but Lou always sat right next to me.

Once we'd finished, she blew bubbles with the straw in the marsh at the bottom of her glass while I paid at the counter. Then we parted at the exit, Lou to the bank and me to continue painting the walls of the extension where that morning for the first time we had made a proper bed together. It was deep and thick, with layer upon layer of heavily stuffed quilting. The pillows were plump like Brian's feet. I walked home, my pocket rattling with change. I steeled myself to make the call home. It had been a month.

Dad answered. He wasn't out of breath. He hadn't been in the attic.

"I was hoping you'd call," he said.

"I always call at this time," I replied.

But he knew that. He was clockwork, a second hand keeping perfect pace. He was the brain behind the arms pulling the levers in the engine room at the heart of all chaos. Something was wrong.

"I don't want you to worry," he said.

I started worrying.

"OK."

"Or to worry Lou."

"What is it, Dad?"

"It's Mal," he said. A release of air. "He's fine."

"What then?"

"He had a heart attack, a small one but a heart attack. They can't move him, they're treating him here."

I sank. My back slid down the varnished wood by the window until my knees sidled close to my chest. My backside landed on the dog's loose hair lining the floor. I was jammed between the wall and the floor.

"There are wires and machines everywhere from the hospital. Your mum has gone crazy, obviously, but he's fine. They've called it a warning shot. The first cannonball over the bows, if you like."

I stayed silent.

"It's been in the newspapers."

I could hear his huge, hard hands shaking. I could hear him wanting me to come home. I could feel the plug pulled from the bottom of the sea I was swimming in.

"But he's OK. He's OK. I just wanted you to know that he's OK before you read about it or heard somehow, from Lou's dad, whatever."

I asked him to describe to me what happened and I built the film of the story for playback in my thoughts. I picture it perfectly. Mum was making supper. Waffles with bacon and slippery handfuls of beans. Garlic bread slathered in mayonnaise to cool and intensify the taste. She was lining it up neatly on a tray in the trailer, push-ing open the door with her rear. She walked past the tent and the memory of Lou, through the front door, kicking off her slippers so that they land together like two kittens fighting over a milky teat. Through another door, past the dirty metal ladder that leads to the attic where Dad was making plans, failing and beginning all over again. She prodded open the door of the bedroom and Mal was there, a sheet tucked under the bureau of his gut. She rested the supper upon the side. He took a waffle dripping with the grease of its pork jacket and bit two-thirds of it away. Mulch mulch mulch, his jaw rotated, his tongue forcing the food against his teeth, eroding it until it slipped in a disgusting flume of pulp down his throat.

"And so it's just a normal evening," said Dad but I directed the scenes in my head and turned it into a picture sharp enough to shred my skin.

She was using the serrated edge of the stainless steel knife to force mouthfuls of food onto a fork for him. A lonely orange bean hung from his mouth, sliding down his chin the way the last dollop of toothpaste is forced out of the tube. And his eyes started to bulge. The veins in his neck rose. And he was gripping the tray with a force so immense the plastic cracked in his hands. His heart got faster and faster, the valves inside it clapping a computerized drum surge, dum dum dum dum dum, faster the blood pumped through his arteries so hard it scored the lining. It tried to squeeze more thick crimson through the tiny gap. Dum dum dum dum dum, faster, and she was panicking. There was a tray on the wall and mayonnaise on the curtains. A piece of garlic bread rolled to safety underneath the bed. She was screaming now, they both were, him clutching at her arm and it was wobbling and sweating and burning right up. She was crying and he couldn't breathe, hyperventilating, and it hurt, it was fear, the blood not reaching the extremities of his fingers and toes, and they were curling up in rapturous knots. He clawed at the span of his chest, pulling the hairs out of it.

I moved the hot phone to my other ear.

"But I want you to know he's OK," said Dad.

"I know," I said. "I know."

Seventy

In the extension at the back of Norma's house the tin roof was rattling as the rain landed hard upon it like bucketfuls of pins. The sound was awesome, so loud that in the brief sojourns between downpours you could still hear it. I was late. I wasted half an hour standing outside sheltering with the dog under the lip of the porch, trying to falsify the face I had on, wondering whether to tell Lou. This happiness that was finally mine, which I was now so scared of losing.

I pulled back the bedding and clambered in for the first time. It smelled sweet, like lemon and lavender. The sheets were warm with her.

"Did you get wet?" she asked, half asleep.

She didn't turn over but she wasn't angry. I pulled in tight behind her, flexing my spine until we made the same shape, slotting together like a children's toy. My hand rested on the outside of her thigh, my nose nuzzled in the crown of her hair.

"A bit."

"You're still wet, you idiot."

"I know."

She shuffled her feet to try and warm them, hiding them between my calves when it didn't work.

"Norma has finished our portrait," she said. "You haven't even noticed, have you?"

I sat up and turned, and above us on the wall was me and Lou in thick oils, solid blocks of color. We were on the porch, her in a strappy, fluid gown shaped by the air, me topless, gray trousers and no shoes. I dangled a thin, pensive finger over the line where her hair skirted the back of her neck. In the bottom right-hand corner was Norma Bee's name, signed in lipstick the violent red of a sting. It was fabulous, we both agreed.

I didn't tell her about Mal. Instead, and for the first time, we made love, underneath the picture on the wall.

Afterward, while she slept, I watched the dog frolic on the grass through the window. It rolled on its back. It twitched and jolted on the slimy surface, its little tongue hanging from the side of its mouth, its ears pricked. Its tail wagging like a windscreen wiper, kicking up moisture into the air, a trail behind a jet. I wanted to join it.

I decided then not to tell her about Mal at all. I stopped phoning home. The days got better still.

Seventy-One

I looked at my reflection. My middle hung over my bottom. My navel frowned, a droopy eyelid in the face of my trunk. My rhythm, sleeping and eating, had been settled quickly by the completing of contentment's triumvirate, love. Sleeping, eating, love. I was expanding, steel one year baked in the sunshine. I saw Lou, mirrored, sidling in behind me. She kissed me on the shoulder, licking a zigzag to the apex of my armpit, where the flesh had begun to overtake itself.

"I'm getting fat," I said.

She petted her belly, its slight gorgeous bloom.

"Me too."

"No, you're not," I said, and I pecked her just above her left ear, where a faint silver emergency flare had been shot.

Norma Bee was up and out early, the shadow of her car still cast in taupe dust on the drive. I fetched my freshened apron from the muffin-topped laundry basket and struggled, fingering its strings behind my back. Lou tied it deftly, then perched my white mesh butcher's hat on my head. Together, her writing, we made a list.

Rib-eye steak.

Lamb cutlets.

Kidney.

Sausage.

Rump, if there's any.

Chops (big bag).

Lou XX

I promised not to forget to bring it home again. Lou used the blunt end of the pen to open the envelopes with the bills inside them. We talked no more of what we'd mentioned, giggling and drunk, the night before. About the stars on strings hanging from the ceiling, or the cot, wooden and grand. Lou had beamed at the suggestion of stencils, wild animals, tigers and leopards defanged, I'd joked that I would paint on the ceiling. A fantasy inside our own.

I went to work, the list poked into my pocket. Lou, with the pen still in her hand, took a single slip of paper from the pile in the drawer on the desk. She chewed the lid, the impressions of her teeth highlighted when the saliva puddled in crescents, echoing the glow from the lamp. She thought of it all at once, smiled and wrote "Dear Mal." It was done within ten minutes.

Lou took the letter to be sent from the office close to my shop, where the queue for Wednesday's "Gut-Busting Mid-Week Meat Deal" snaked out and past the window. We had lunch together, tacos haloed with golden cheese, and she headed home to help Norma Bee prepare for dinner.

The booty sweated inside the bag as I walked it home, moistening the warm plastic. Norma Bee's car, dirty and tired, slept deeply. Two cats reclined floppily beneath it, rolling as the shade trundled. I opened the door.

Lou was on the sofa, next to a man. His skin was a pallid ivory, badly strapped to his skeleton. His gray hair was lank and dangerous cabling, fringing the broken sockets of his eyes. I'd never met him properly.

"This is my dad," Lou said.

I didn't need it confirmed that Norma Bee had collected him from the airport.

He pushed the lamb chop I'd grilled around his plate like a general in the war room shifting troops about a map of Europe, consigning them to their deaths.

Lou put him into our bed and found me outside, wet cigarette like a thermometer hanging loosely from my mouth. She told me what she'd gleaned from his sad whispers, what fool's gold was panned. The division in her attention I could see in what color was lost from her eyes. It made my being duller.

"He caught her with the man from life drawing. Went round like he said he would, drop off some stuff. A gift—he'd ordered a set of pencils and they'd delivered two. They were sleeping under the sheets that keep the paint from marking the furniture."

"Poor bastard," I said.

Norma Bee's floor creaked. The cats screeched, pleasure then agony.

I imagined his house, the wall of her portraits torn to shreds. The pieces of her body ripped into tiny pieces on the floor, his heaviest pictures among them. A murder victim drawn.

"He needs me," Lou said.

"I need you."

I was thick and selfish but my momentum unstoppable.

"I'm his family."

"I'm your family."

"You'd have me kick him out, would you?"

"No, of course not."

"What then?"

"I don't know."

"He's here for a week, that's all. He arranged it with Norma as a surprise for me."

Her dad's dismantled robot parts lay strewn around our bedroom floor, the workshop of the only mechanic who could rebuild him.

Lou went to her dad. When I poked my head around the door, she'd fallen asleep in the wicker chair I'd put next to the bed, where I would balance her breakfast when I brought it. I imagined the sound of Mal's snoring. Sounded like laughter from across the sea.

Seventy-Two

"And that's how some people are rewarded for a lifetime of being good." Norma Bee laughed. She always laughed. Even bad news had ticklish fingers.

"Poor bastard," I said again.

In the kitchen pots boiled on every surface, squeaking urgent whistles, the control room on a warship. We talked and talked and talked. Jealousy and wanting always coupled so well.

"What me and Brian had might not have been perfect but we had love. There were people in this town used to say I was a bad lady, letting him get like that. I didn't pay no heed to those people, though. Letting him get like what? Letting him get happy? Letting him get happier than them, that's what those people didn't like. Know what I figured?"

I had never really noticed before but Norma Bee spoke a lot in questions.

"What did you figure?" I said, piggybacking her tongue.

"Only the people that care about you can make you happy. So it was my job."

Norma Bee, big fat oracle.

I stirred whatever she pointed to, piled it onto plates whenever she instructed me.

"That man in there"—she nodded through the wall I built—"that's how he's been rewarded for his life of goodness. With two women who could never love him as much as he loved them. But at least they gave him the best thing he's got, right?"

"What?" I said. "Dramatic weight loss?"

"No, honey," said Norma Bee. "Lou. She's the only one who cares about him, and as long as that remains the way it is, she'll do everything . . . everything she can to make him happy. Altruism, honey. That's what love is."

I saw that she was counseling me, pulling into my vision something blatant I'd somehow stupidly missed.

"You gotta realize, love is a long line. It's all love but it has opposite ends. There's the end that's good. The one they write romantic songs about. That's the end you wanna be at. And there's the end that's bad, because love can destroy you too. And that end of the line is where most people are at. Happy as Brian and I were, I was destroying him. I can see that now. Could I see that then, when I was feeding him the delicious things I made? No. Because he was smiling when I did it. It was still love."

I crouched on the floor by the refrigerator. Its motor rumbled in my spleen.

"And my mum and Mal?" I asked.

"Don't it just make her happy?"

"Yes," I said.

"He's smiling, ain't he?"

"Yes," I said.

"Then it's love. Doesn't mean it won't destroy them both."

I could smell burning. Norma Bee spun a switch to chide the gas. I swallowed.

"And Lou?"

"Poor Lou," said Norma Bee, weaving two forks through a colorful salad. "She's watched one man she loves destroy himself. She's not gonna let another. He needs her."

"I need her too," I said.

Norma Bee struggled to her knees in front of me. Her jewelry was cold like the pavement on my cheek.

"Then you'll wait. You just gotta not get destroyed while you do."

"But I will be," I said.

When I raised my head again she was back at the stove.

"I'll look after you," she said. "Here, eat this."

Seventy-Three

Lou's dad stayed in bed through the daytime, rarely rising in the evenings but for food. A fierce depression had its jaws around him and was doing crocodile rolls around the murky riverbed. He didn't fight. It dampened the feelings he was capable of having, disconnected them from experience. That one great act of falling in love with Rebecca Mar had led him up too quickly from the depths. Now he had the bends, the bubble of oxygen in his brain a sadness. He had sunk back to the bottom, where the crocodiles had found him. Now he was never to ascend.

Lou was down there with him, trying in vain to lift her dad from the stuck mud of the floor.

She swung on the chair that was strung between two beams, the dog drawing lines with its nose on her thigh. The time was sorrow-scented, a dream you enjoy that collapses out of distance of your recall.

"I need to make him better," she said.

She rubbed the flat of her palm on the back of my head. The hair bristled.

The dog pounced, landed on a fly and killed it. It licked the busted spindles of its legs from the wood.

"I'm sorry," she said. "I can't just watch it happen again."

I could feel the pull of Mal's orbit, her dad the probe that traveled ahead to collect information before the long journey home.

"Stay here in Akron with me," I said. "Your dad too. We can buy a bigger house. We can have children."

"Why would you?" she said. "If growing old is this."

Sounded like my brother.

"You'll stay?" I asked.

Seventy-Four

I was an elevator with a snapped rope, plummeting down the deep shaft of a mine at incredible speed, only stopping with a crash and crushing everything flat. Because she was gone. All that was left of her was the portrait. Lou, two-dimensional and ten inches high.

My feet squelched with the sweat that I dripped. My shirt a saturated second skin, a thin wet shell. My hair hung in sodden strips. I searched the store, aisle by aisle, through the frozen foods and shelves of cans. She wasn't in the warm corner where the smell of fresh bread came over you like a homely malaise. The freshly made baguettes reached out from their baskets begging for coins, monkeys' arms at a hot zoo. She wasn't standing by the chilly force field of the fridges. This is where we'd linger on the days when the heat of the midafternoon sun stroked our skin with its steaming mitts. She wasn't at the till chatting happily with the shop assistants, whiling away the hours of the day, recognizing people from the bank. She was just gone.

I walked home past the butchery, raised a brief sad salute to the young man I'd trained to take over from me, a talented young guy who always remained clean, no matter what we cut, chopped or pulled apart. He'd rearranged the fixtures in the front and stood, resplendent in his whites like Hollywood teeth. I knew he'd be good for the old place and thought of a happy Mrs. GDF.

Norma Bee was standing on the porch in sweat-soaked luminous yellow Lycra. She was painting at her easel, the dog modeling for her in silly woolen booties she'd knitted.

It scattered from its basket as I stormed past, an angry black wind blowing ashore. Norma Bee leapt into the air and shrieked as I pushed her easel to the ground and the mutt-colored paint disfigured the floor. With a donkey kick I knocked the screen door off its bottom hinge so that it hung there dead and awkward, and I ran through to the back of the house.

I was crying at the foot of the bed when Norma came in and bent around my shape.

"Calm down," she said. "I'm gonna go fix you something to eat."

"Why did you take her to the airport?" I said.

"Honey, she asked me," Norma Bee said. "She knows her dad couldn't stay here. She knows exactly what is right for him. She loves him."

We have warm apple pie with lashings of cream in silence.

I wondered if the birthday card I sent sits in the mountain of black bin bags full of unopened mail Dad told me is stacked in and around Lou's tent on the lawn.

For hours I rocked in her chair on the porch, plucking caught strands of her hair from the joins in the woodwork and winding it through my fingers. The dog was still too scared to come into my vicinity. Norma Bee tried to soothe me. Soon she realized she made little headway and returned to silence, occasionally rubbing my shoulder as she passed, bringing me snacks and meals and drinks.

I went to bed.

Seventy-Five

In the middle of the nights I'd open my eyes. No more color seeped in. I thought of her next to me but she was still not there. I thought I could hear the gentle whir and click of the clock on the wall, and I dreamt I bathed in its bright green glow. As the sun rose I heard Norma Bee making my breakfast but I didn't even bother to get dressed when she brought it to me on a wide plastic tray.

Every day Norma painted me. I stopped answering the phone. It was never Lou.

I was in bed.

Norma Bee told me I could stay.

I ate and slept and grew. The trinity of pleasure that cupped me, now missing a side, had fallen over. I had tumbled to the floor.

I ate fatty American delicacies. Meals a nation was created on sated my transatlantic palate. In the daytime, when it was hot, I'd lie underneath a single sheet. In the nighttime I'd build a pillowed wall and seal myself inside it. Where she'd been was now just nothing but a space I was gradually beginning to fill.

Time began to wobble along. Great racks of lamb. Chicken, rice and peas. Tortillas with salsa and hot summer-shaded dips. Fajitas soppy with sour cream, noodles with a brown vinegary sauce and finger-sized lumps of duck. Meatballs. Lots of meatballs. Norma Bee made great meatballs. Soggy spring rolls. Cannonballs of ice cream. The days had slowed down. Now sunrise to sunset was just one long blink of nature's eye, the changing of the shade of the day interminable.

There were seven paintings of me in bed on the wall facing where I slept when clarity found me. Norma bundled through the door, a cardboard bucket of deep-fried meat twizzled in bread-crumb armor underneath one of her wings.

"Lunchtime," she sang.

She always sang meals. I thought about Mum. I knew deep within my being that it was time to return. But I had rested here now, settled, stagnated and tired.

My impetus arrived early one morning. I woke to the unpleasant nuzzle of heartburn wringing my tongue with acidic hands. The light through the window showed me to the mirror on the inside of the wardrobe door that had, for the first time and accidentally, been left open by Norma Bee. I saw myself and recognized the reflection but not as mine. The clusters of pustules jostling in sweaty patches of my face. The pale stretch marks slashing across the dirty, expanding skin. Taller and wider, not the man in the paintings but the brother I left behind. I'd turned forty in this room but the icing on the cake had been no signifier that the day was that different from any other. I had to go.

I took one portrait with me. Norma Bee missed Brian Bee with all of her colossal heart. She said I'd always be her son.

Seventy-Six

Day Seven Thousand Four Hundred and Eighty-Three, according to the display on the wall.

No one notices me pulling on my coat as the darkness arrives. I am exhausted by the day. Lou coming home. The interview. The fight. The people outside, some who remained. My legs ache, the metal pins still spearing my shins.

Mum is still applying cooling antiseptic lotion to the trails that ladder Mal's skin. He is laughing about Ray Darling, about today, but the pressure of the weight his body lays on his lungs is five baby elephants and the noise doesn't emerge at first. He is too preoccupied with it, as Mum is with his nursing, to watch me slip through the front door.

Dad is on the lawn, standing behind Lou's old empty tent. He has finished the frantic banging he'd been making in the attic and is talking to the dozen or more people still here. With them arced around him, he looks like a preacher on the mount. He gestures toward the house, to the window where Mal is lying as though in state. He makes grandiose, upward-sweeping movements with his arms.

He doesn't notice me hobble quietly down the path and onto the street. The moon is up. Its light shrouds the trailer and the cold sucks my fingertips. I walk briskly and, taking care not to slip on my crutches, retrace backward the way Red Ted used to bring me home from work every day in his little car.

As I finally round the corner where the butcher's shop sits, the nervous vise in me begins to twist its sturdy metal handle. I wait there. The chance to see and touch her is an angry needle. It wants to spike her for an apology, stab out an explanation. It tells me to turn around, to go home, to never speak to Lou again. I know that I can't obey it.

Then I am cast in light, as though I were a criminal chased along the wall of a prison from which I have just escaped. It is from a car, just arrived and now parked opposite me, its beams blinding. I maneuver myself carefully on my crutches and shamble slowly out of the glare. Putting one foot in front of the other, I make my way to the driver's-side window, which winds down to greet me.

"Hello," says Lou, older but her voice trapped in time.

"Hello," I reply.

I am a textbook full of questions with stained, maddened pages.

"What happened to your legs?" she asks.

The car smells brand-new.

Seventy-Seven

The taxi driver who drove me from the airport to my home didn't ask me about Mal. Time had erased me a little, rubbed me out. I had faded like a photograph buried under soil. I was tanned and older, weathered and experienced and fat. I was what we all become, a by-product of the torture of ourselves.

As I passed the trailer, I thought of Norma Bee on her own, about the food that must have been going to waste.

Lou's tent was unloved on the lawn, torn and faded but secure where Dad had nailed it down. I opened my suitcase, took out the painting of the two of us and placed it inside. It didn't smell of her anymore. It smelled of dust and heat and the humid summers I had missed. I wondered if I should climb in, run the zip up behind me and lie in wait, a mousetrap primed and ready, a tasty chunk of cheese set invitingly on the edge. Instead I left the portrait there propped against the side and headed into the house.

Home was always the same inside. Its exterior grew and shrunk depending upon how long I'd been away but indoors it was a precise mold. There were turns I could make in the dark, that smell of food and perfume and linen and Mal. Creams and sweat. Creaks that the walls always made, the clanking of badly tuned pipes in the cavities. Home was always the same temperature. It always had the same map. It always welcomed me in the same way.

What greeted me when I pushed open the bedroom door scooped my foundations from underneath me and I collapsed, compacted floor by floor into the carpet. Mal. Huge. The folds in his skin were blistered red eclipses. The sores that peeked from his underside shimmered with clear secretions that glossed his sodden bedsheets. In the middle of the day he was asleep. Drowning in his own fluids, a chicken slowly turning on a spit. The walls were lined with newspaper cuttings and randomly apportioned piles of his post. There was box upon packet upon plate. There was Mum, who slept in a chair in the corner. She had more color than I recalled, glowing cheeks and rosiness. There was the display on the wall.

Dizzied, I staggered backward to where Dad's ladder's black rubber feet met the carpet. Stepping aboard the first rung, I gave the hatch a tap with a pointed knuckle. There was the clatter and movement I expected and remembered, and then it opened to Dad's face, older yet more fatherly, surprised and pleased.

"Ha!" he shouted, jumping down and tossing his arms around my middle, pinning mine to my sides. "Look at you," he said, "you're home!" Then he moved away, saw that the look on my browned face didn't match his. "She didn't come back with you?" he asked.

"No."

I'd not known how much I'd missed him. His hair was a wise gray and wild, his face full of movement and his eyes wider. They glinted like underwater coins. He looked how I'd imagined Einstein did in the flesh, crackling with energy. He was charged up, new.

We woke Mum. She hugged and she kissed me, and when I was close to her it didn't feel frail as it once had but warm and soulful. A grand emotional renaissance had taken place. As separate as their lives were, happiness was upon them.

Mal opened an eye, set back on a thick cheek like a button buried in the wool of a winter jumper.

"Hello," he said.

In the furrow that indented trenches in his chubby misshapen brow, I saw that he knew I was not here through choice.

I leaned my suitcase against my bed—it was still there next to his—and with a sigh and the thick stink of malaise clouding any way out which might have existed, I resigned myself to the fact that perhaps, just perhaps, neither Mal nor I were ever supposed to leave this house.

"Do you want to talk?" he asked.

"No," I said.

"All right," he said.

I looked at him in bed and was lulled temporarily by the unspoken logic of it all. He might be right, I wondered. What life is this, giving you the wonder of a heart that beats and then smashing it to a million tiny pieces? When everything you're taught to expect comes to nothing? If this is life, then why get out of bed?

Like an old pet dog, my mattress remembered my scent and my shape and it welcomed me with indiscriminate affection. I slept for days, my great escape aborted.

Seventy-Eight

The lime-green liquid crystal morphed and maneuvered to different shapes and times, up and up and up, but the light never pierced the thick black around me. My eyes numbed once more to the sight of Mal's body as it enveloped him and he disappeared inside himself like a rolled-up sock.

I watched the sun come, then the leaves the rain and the snow. I watched the interest mount. I watched Lou's tent and Mum's arrival, with heaped fresh plates full of food. They were the only constant, the storming on of time all that differentiated one day from the next.

Mal and I were watching a film we'd seen before. It was old, so black-and-white that it glowed blue in parts, and John Wayne espoused the relative benefits of laying down your life for the good of others and the rewards it ultimately brings. Neither of us were really listening.

It was Day Six Thousand Six Hundred and Forty, according to the display on the wall, a long time since my thoughts weren't soured. Mum had finished tending Mal for the evening and so just the two of us lay there, side by side, big and small Russian dolls.

"This has to stop," he said, the pelican undercarriage of his chin jiggling.

"Turn it off then," I said. "I'm not watching it. The remote control is probably under one of your bellies."

"Not the film," he said, "this. You. You have to stop."

I pulled myself up to a sitting position.

"Me?"

"Yes, you."

"What are you talking about? You are fully aware that none of us would even be here right now if it wasn't for you."

And suddenly release, the pressure punching past. My face reddened, the hue rising up it like the mercury in a thermometer.

"But you're sitting there feeling sorry for yourself," he said. "I'm not."

He was right, I knew he was.

"You ain't got your photograph yet," he said. "I've got mine."

I got dressed in a hurry and called Dad down from the attic.

"Can I help you?" I asked.

He dusted himself off like he'd been waiting to for a very long time.

"Tomorrow," he said, "we shall go to the roof and you can see what I've been making."

Seventy-Nine

On the roof we were causing a stir. Dad was wearing an orange boiler suit salvaged from his lift-building days, topped with a scratched plastic yellow hard hat. Underneath his steel-toe-capped boots the burnt red slate crumbled and gave. I struggled to balance. Swinging my arms in continuous circles, I walked a constant trapeze, occasionally finding brief respite in stillness.

The day was bitter.

"Here," said Dad.

Kneeling, he lifted off one of the larger slates that sat over the two sides of the roof the way a tea towel is draped across the arm of a waiter, and placed it carefully to one side. We were both looking down into a hole the size of a dinner plate that led directly to the attic, a fantastic grotto when seen from above. There were shiny rods and metal cogs, materials, hooks and joints, all disparate parts to my eye, a freshly opened jigsaw. Dad grinned, a treasure hunter celebrating the accuracy of his instinct.

"Who made this hole?" I asked.

"Me," he said.

"Why?"

"Because nothing moves anywhere without a hole. Now wait here, I'll be back in a moment."

He scrambled down the ladder and I stayed squat, my skin pimpled by the freezing morning air, wondering why I didn't wear anything more substantial than an old pair of running shoes. I surveyed the surroundings of the house. The tent, Mrs. Gee's garden, the huge mound of post that had arrived for Mal, arranged into a pile.

I heard Dad climb the smaller ladder inside the house. The hatch opened and he appeared in the loft. I saw the pate of his head bobbing around below me, his baldness a pink egg in a wiry silver nest.

"Are you still up there?" he said.

"Of course I am."

"Right. Grab ahold of this."

There was movement and metallic sound and suddenly a thick silver steel pole began to emerge from the hole, almost knocking me backward and to my doom. It too had the circumference of a saucer, and it continued to rise until, with a clunk, a new pole began to emerge from inside it, and another and another telescopically until it injected the frozen sky above me. I listened to the wheel Dad was winding from inside begin to slow down and I held on to the tower that had just appeared from the top of the house like a lightning rod. It swayed a little as the wind caught it. Soon he reappeared, carrying large bags full of rods and chains and wheels, and they were cumbersome but still he managed to move around the rooftop with some unorthodox grace.

"I've been planning this for a long, long time," he said.

"What?"

"This. Ever since I built that fishing rod. And then, when I saw them bring that trailer in too, I thought to myself 'I can do that.' It's the same as lifts, you see. Weights, space and distance. It's all ratios. Technically, if you get your mathematics right, you can build something to do just about anything with the minimum of energy. It's about knowing how to amplify your exertion."

As I gripped both sides of the roof with my tired legs, he was standing, sometimes on one foot and on the tips of his toes, running ropes and chains through holes and loops, around cogs and across hooks.

"It's about doing nothing but doing something incredible at the same time," he said.

I nodded.

"Look." He pointed. "See down there."

I leaned out as far as I could. By the window between Mal and Lou's tent he had stacked a pyramid of sacks full of Mal's unopened post. It shimmered as the winter breeze blew its skin. Around it he had wrapped strips of thick material, four of them, which unfurled from each corner framing the heap of bags. They were joined tidily and securely at the top as a Christmas present is bedecked with pretty ribbon. Attached to that was a hook.

"What a great way to test it," he said.

Those bins full of misfiring equations. Those aborted attempts and flawed prototypes and scale models.

I stood precariously to help him, each new rush of wind bullying me toward a fall, and it started to rain thick droplets. Dad shimmied up the great metal mast and I grabbed the seams of the trousers of his overalls. I steadied him as he took the assembled pieces of equipment and slipped them into a slot he'd prepared at the summit of the rod. Bringing it round into position, it looked like a futuristic gallows. It was a rudimentary crane. The morning clouds seemed to gather in the distance, and I thought more about how smooth to the touch a bolt of lightning would find us.

Next Dad threaded a rope and chain through a link at the far end of the rod that extended out from the mast above the sacks of mail in the garden. He had an admirable abandon in the way he moved, the kind you'd need to dangle above a shaft that hurtled toward the darkness at the center of the earth. And then, just as easily as he had climbed up, he came back down to where I stood on the roof. My legs were bowed, the effort demanded of me to stand safely draining me like bark tapped for sap.

"Here," he said, handing me a thick silver hook attached to a sash of pea-green material so sturdy as to be impossible to rip.

"Take this and hook it to the hook on the top of the pile of post bags. I am going to put this little wheel together, wind it through the pully to the rope. If I'm right, the distance between the center, here, and the bags means that I'll be able to lift their entire weight just by turning this tiny wheel. Just how you'd flip a fish out of the water."

I loved him, seeing his enthusiasm and ecstatic that he had it.

As the rain waxed a damp slippery gloss on my skin and clothes he said, "See, much better than staying in bed, isn't it?"

And then I was not concentrating anymore. An error. I snatched the hook from his hand and stooped, bending my knees and preparing to take chicken steps on my way down from the roof.

The tile beneath my left foot crumbled in the pressure and the moisture, and the sound of lost footing cracked through the air like a scratched record. My dad shouted my name in drawn-out baritone. My back hit the surface of the roof with astonishing force and my bones moved around inside the bag of me as a supersonic slap clattered through it. My ribs tinkled like dropped chopsticks and my lungs inflated, airbags in a car against a tree. I opened my eyes and the sky moved upward past me. Sliding down the roof, I clawed at the wet slate for a hold but none came. My angle was set. I tombstoned off the roof. Midair I felt the blood trickle down my back where the skin was scraped from it like the peel of an orange. The pinkish holes it left welled with more blood. My hand dripped it. I saw I had missed the pile of soft postage bags that would have caught me in their cushioned black mass, and I closed my eyes unsure of which way up I might be as I hit the cement of the pathway in front of the glass.

I landed straight-legged, hands across my chest. A coffin. The impact of my body weight on my heels forced them up into my shins, which shattered immediately into shards of bone that concertinaed, bursting out in red explosions through the skin with sharp white fins. My kneecaps lurched to the insides of my legs, I buckled entirely, my right tibia smashing my right fibula to crumbs, my left tibia punching through the denim of my jeans.

My brain opened an emergency trapdoor of endorphins. None of this was mine. None of it was even happening. I lay quietly in a puddle, crippled and cracked.

I rocked my head back and rolled my eyes. Mal was there through the glass, he could see it all, but his screams couldn't keep me awake.

Eighty

A bed but not my own.

For the first few days I lapsed in and out of consciousness, guided by a chemical hand. When pain arrived, it beckoned me toward a light and as I entered it, it tricked me back from whence I came. Slowly everything was not so white anymore, and if I listened carefully I could hear the beeps of the equipment by my head singing to the rainbows of tubes and wires that ducked in and out of my body, giving me electric pulse and life. I wondered if I was Mal.

And then one morning I was in the hospital, able for the first time to remain awake. Mum was by my side.

"Get some rest," she said, and I heard her voice and I knew she had been here as long as I had, at my bedside. Telling me stories. Telling me that I was going to be OK.

My legs were the color of damage, quarantined in metal cages that skewered the skin. My thighs had angles and my feet were packets of broken biscuits. They hung up high in stirrups either side, and they didn't look or feel like mine but rather like I operated some enormous robot with the strength of ten men, like I could stand up right now and kick through the walls of this hospital until I was walking through the still of the countryside, destroying everything that blocked my path home.

"It hurts," I said.

"I know," she said. "Get some rest."

In my bed it became clearer and clearer over the days and weeks and months. There was a reminder every time my bolts got turned. I remembered nothing about the day I fell off the roof but for the hints left by my scars, which never forgot where I had been or what I had done. Mum fed me jelly and ice cream. The nurses acted extra-nice toward me when I was polite.

"Who is looking after Mal?" I asked her.

"Your dad," she said.

She was stroking my arm and filling my drink. She brushed hair from my eyes and winced when the doctors lifted the titanium spikes that pepper my legs like the stanchions of a famous bridge.

"Just relax," she said.

Her face said he'd gone to the attic, a tortoise back into its shell. His own recovery ruined by wet slate and my unsuitable footwear. Sabotaged by my lack of balance.

"Anyway, I am here for you."

And as I was going to speak I slept, muted.

They turned me tighter and tighter once a week. When they did it, I could hear my bones whinge. They felt like they might snap in protest. They taught me to walk. They massaged my muscles and stimulated my nerves, reset my bones and broke them again. One day as they helped me to stand straight, I bit the tip of my own tongue off. I needed eight stitches and I spoke like my mouth was full of sawdust for the rest of the month.

With my legs locked up there was too much time to think.

I watched television and had reconstructive surgery. I did puzzles while they washed me and read books as they tweaked. I had wire tentacles.

It was as Dad, listless, wheeled me home that I accepted my fate at the third attempt, that I was meant to be with Mal in that room, to ride this out to the very, very end. I went to bed.

Day Six Thousand Eight Hundred and Eighty-Eight, according to the display on the wall.

Eighty-One

"Oi. Look. Here. Oi." I lifted my head. "Would you like one of these?" asked Mal.

He had an open packet of six blueberry muffins resting on his naked chest. One toppled out and rolled down the landscape of his huge flat slab to his groin, where it jammed.

"Mmmm, yes, please, I'll have that one. What time is it?"

"Four," he said. "And no need to be funny."

His voice started so deep inside his chest that it sounded by the time it emerged as though there were a little version of Mal in there trapped inside a cave, hollering for help.

"Four in the morning?"

"Yes."

"You woke me up."

"To see if you wanted a muffin."

In what was still the fledgling hours of my first morning out of hospital, I was a seething, emaciated wretch. Expert mediation of my painkillers had ended. My legs felt hot but, unable to regulate their own body temperature, they were covered in goose pimples, little hairs standing to attention around the bases of the metal tubing where it pierced me, like pilgrims praying at a sacred rock. I looked down at Mal's enormous thighs, like pugilistic weaponry wrapped in burger meat, enough space to fit six of mine in, pins and all.

A small fly balanced on the end of his big toe, the nail of which was yellow as custard. The insect perched there on its hind legs, rubbing its front two together smugly. Mal couldn't feel it moving for the thick layer of dead skin Mum would come to grate off in shards as long as the careful shavings of a pencil.

I sighed.

"What's wrong with you?" he said.

"What do you think?"

Despite the blue light from the television and the green light from the display on the wall coloring me with cheap neon, in the dark I fell asleep again quickly, perversely aided by the rasped metronome of Mal's continual struggle for breath.

I woke again three hours later when Mum brought a jittery tray full of china heavy with globules of ketchup and mustard. She opened the curtains and gave me the sunlight. It prevented me from one final doze, and I watched as she rubbed lotion into the brittle brown toughness of the scabs on his sides. She removed and replaced tubes, emptied and filled bags, wiped with cotton wool inside the many little folds.

Then she tended to me, dabbing at the wounds where the steel met the skin with antiseptic that stung the inside of my nose. She lifted me and I leaned on her. She placed my heavy legs inside the two slings Dad had designed, made especially and hung from the ceiling, and she handed me a cup of tea so hot the mug ringed the wood on the bedside table.

She was hands out and ropes attached. I imagined her pretending to be a master puppeteer in a small French theater, making her two most popular characters dance in perfect unison with the careful and practiced manipulation of the strings that moved our arms and legs. She cared for us. I'd always known it was for this that Mum was made.

Sometimes I turned my head to find he'd fallen asleep, a dewdrop of drool linking his mouth to his pillow. Morning. Snoring. Ceiling. Breakfast. Cleaning. The monotony tapped at my head, threatening to cave it in like a woodpecker's first burst through the stiff outer cloak of a tree. If I'd had the energy, I would have exploded through the walls.

I didn't know how many days had passed. It was more than steps I had taken. A solitary bead of sweat helter-skeltered around the thick girth of Mal's naked arm until it dropped from his chubby red finger and landed on the grubby plate beside him.

I burned angry bile in my chest like fossil fuels. Using all the power I could muster in my thighs, I swung my legs in their slings until they clacked hard together, smacked teeth on the road. The three feet between us was a canyon, the little gap a lifetime. I wanted to get to him. To scratch, bite and kick him. I thrashed in the air and my fists pounded the bed, a fish from its bowl to the shallow puddle on the kitchen floor. I flailed with my remaining drive, pulling the slings from the ceiling in a hail of plaster and fell, exhausted, into the space between our beds, facedown, my metal leg scaffolds tearing the cheap material that my bed was made from and jamming me in.

"Are you OK?" he asked.

I waited for Mum to come and help me back to my bed, and I thought about the end.

Eighty-Two

Day Seven Thousand Four Hundred and Eighty-Three, according to the display on the wall.

Easing my legs into Lou's car is simple because it is big and American, imported, the front and backseats two long, continuous surfaces like benches with slippery leather coats. They have the smooth hides of sharks to the touch. I lower my bottom in and then rotate myself around, my legs unable to bend more or straighten accordingly. I am awkward.

It is hushed in the car park by Red Ted's Quality Meats. The steady fall of the rain makes the windscreen of the car move and wriggle like bacteria under a microscope. The light shifts as it drops from the lampposts.

"You didn't come back," I say.

The ecstasy of seeing her versus the agony of losing her, a million births and a million deaths.

"You left me," I say, and I shake so that the crutches rattle.

"I know what I did," she replies.

I can't ignore that her face is still such a pleasure to behold but I summon resolve and give her my shrift.

"I think you should talk," I say.

I think she is crying. I briefly see tears illuminated in passing headlights on the road but so briefly that I could have pretended they were there because the tears on my own cheeks catch the glow in tiny prisms of water.

Lou drives.

"I've spent my life watching your brother give up, waiting to die. I couldn't watch my dad do the same."

"What about me?"

"I knew you'd never give up."

Her eyes are washing her face away, her vision is as blurred as the glass it bores through. When I finally speak my voice fluctuates rabidly, like the needle drawing on the paper measuring the shifting of the plates that hold the planet together. She looks into her lap, meshes her fingers into a cradle by the steering wheel and wrings the skin on them together until they squeak.

"I heard about the interview. I thought today might be the day he ends it all."

"Us?" I say.

She nods.

"I thought he might have read the letter I wrote to him."

"It would have got lost, you know how much he gets. They barely opened any of it after we left."

"Shame."

"What did it say?"

"I asked him to end it. For you."

"Why for me? If you'd have cared about me, you'd never have left Akron."

"I knew I'd be back for you."

"What, now?"

"Now."

"And your dad?" I ask.

"I've saved my dad," she says.

"How?"

"I got him another love. One that will always love him back. I got him a grandson." I put my hands on my lap and I squeeze. "Well, technically, you kind of got him one too."

We pull into my street. There is shouting and arms reaching

for the freshness of the air. They point at the roof of the bungalow, where Dad systematically removes the slates and hands them
down to the small, soaked crowd.

I take Lou's hand, still damp with her eyes dried on the back of
it, lift the metal bumpers protruding from my legs and step out of
the car. When people see who I am, and when people see who I am
with, they move.

Eighty-Three

By the time me and Lou have reached the front door, I am sick and dizzy and elated, flustered by the surrounds and the busy factory of my thoughts. A child, I think. Faceless, unreal. I float for a time.

One by one Dad is pulling the slates from the roof and handing them down a chain of people to the concrete that spurned my soft bones. Lou's tent is underfoot, forced into the freshly churned mud. There are people pressed tight against the glass of the window to the bedroom, so firmly that it looks as though it will crack and implode, showering Mal in glass swords and invisible splinters. Every time he takes another slate away, or pulls free a piece of roof, there is a cheer, raised hands and fists. There are cries of "Mal Mal Mal." A fire engine arrives on Day Seven Thousand Four Hundred and Eighty-Three, according to the display on the wall.

The roof is coming off. The urgency of a coup, Dad at the helm.

"Dad!" I shout but he can't hear me. "Dad!"

I rummage in my pocket for the keys to the front door, find them quickly and push Lou inside, following her, closing it behind me, breathing so deeply the clockwork of my heart shifts through a multitude of cogs.

Mum is at the foot of Dad's ladder, her head rested on her hands. But she isn't crying as I expect. Inside the noise from outside sounds like thunder underfoot. She looks up at me, at us, sees Lou and smiles.

"It's ending, isn't it?" she says. "Malcolm told us when you left, he told us this was the end."

Without a prompting, Lou walks over, drops to her knees and places a thin, slender arm around Mum's shoulders. In turn Mum buries her nose in the nape of Lou's neck. She looks so old. Thin as a scroll and a cobweb, tiny like a model made of matchsticks.

"Stay here," I say, and I turn slowly, painfully, my bones' architecture complaining.

And I open the door to the bedroom, and I wobble and I flounder, but I slowly move inside. I can't hear my headache for the shouting at the glass. This fire of grand denouement, this burning of momentum.

I can't believe what I see when I enter the room. All of that noise disappears to a muffle. All I hear is him. Mal.

"Hello," he says.

"Hello."

We sound the same.

Great sashes of thick, sturdy material emerge from underneath each corner of his mattress, meeting at a huge metal hook at the ceiling to form a pyramid around his body that flows and spills from the sides, his fat hanging off of him like lumps on a badly iced cake. He looks up, and where my eyes meet his line of vision I see that the hook is attached to a chain that disappears through a freshly punched hole in the ceiling, into the attic. But the attic now has no top, and we see the sky and Dad, his hands frantically moving, clearing the roof of tiles and pulling apart the floor underneath his feet. We can see metal tubing wrapped around the internal workings of the house, threaded through the floorboards like a skeleton. A life's work. All that noise he made. We watch from underneath as he wrenches up one board after another, and the flecks of plaster and wood fall slowly downward, landing and settling on Mal's massive plateau of dry, purple skin like dirty snow.

I slump to the floor. The house shakes around us as the ceiling slowly disappears and the volume grows to an eruption. I take Mal's hand in mine and he does all he can to bend his fat fingers around my wrist but there is no give in them, just an arthritic murmur. The thickness that sleeves his arms brushes mine. The four great swathes of material tighten and slacken as the hook toys with their strength. I can almost hear the dum dum dum of his heart quicken. His breath chug-chug-chugs like an old coal engine, a machine long since exhausted.

I notice that he is crying. I lay my head on the sweeping bed of his chest. He shakes and it ripples through a hundred stone of fat like a child trapped inside a monster.

We hear the tearing of plaster until all that separates us from the sky is a structure made from metal and chains and pulleys and pipes and rods and cogs and hooks and Dad, peeling away his attic from around him. A feat of modern engineering. The crowd outside make electricity with their voices. They bring the house down.

He grips me as hard as he can. The green light from the display on the wall bouncing off the great metal spider above allows me to see his petrified face.

"Why?" I whisper in his ear.

He does all he can to hold me tighter. A tear drops from my face to his, turning to steam, and I lean in so close I rest my cold ear on his hot, panting mouth until I feel his wet lips lap at it.

"You had Lou," I say.

"Who you loved."

I squeeze his hand harder. The putty of his flesh forms sausages between my fingers. His skin boils, his eyes round and running away.

"Don't pretend you did this for me," I whisper, and lower my ear still closer to his sticky mouth.

The sobbing is the only noise above the commotion, the hole in the roof, the shouting of our dad and the buzz of the crowd. All

I can hear is Malcolm Ede. He speaks to me. I smell the hot acid of his panicked breath.

"I couldn't sit back and be content with a life of *ings*. Saving. Paying. Breeding. Working. But never living."

I hear his deathly rattle.

"This isn't living," I say. "For any of us. You've made Mum a slave. You've made Dad a recluse. Lou is all I've ever wanted, and I couldn't have her because of you."

The tightening of his grip.

The mattress, a sodden red and brown, jolts as the hooks and chains tug at it. Dad takes the handle and turns the wheel above us. The howls and the cheers and the screaming.

I put my mouth to his ear.

"You destroyed this family," I say.

"No," he says. "I saved it."

I rest my forehead on his.

He says, "When emperor penguins huddle together for warmth in the freezing winter storms, they adopt the same positions as Roman legionnaires. They take it in turns to change position. The penguins on the outside move back inside to shelter from the cold and the warmed penguins on the inside take their place, like bikers temporarily taking the lead of a convoy. They do it because it's best for their family."

The mattress rises, levitates just slightly. Mal's heart goes ba ba ba. He raises a pudgy hand up his chest, as close to the center of it as it will go, his fat fingers massaging the mottled skin like he might pluck the beating instrument out.

"I gave Mum twenty years of loving someone. I kept her alive."

"And Dad?" I say.

"Look at him," he says.

I do, turning the cogs of his crane. He is joy. "A new photograph."

"I gave you Lou," he says.

I don't move.

"When?" I say.

"Now," he says.

I close my eyes.

"You?" I say.

"Think what my life would have been. Normal. Now look around you," he says. "You're in my picture."

I feel his pursed lips on my cheek. I wrap an arm around the stump of his neck, lay across his hot flesh, feel the gradual winching upward of Dad's invention taking his son from the house. The display on the wall ticks over. Day Seven Thousand Four Hundred and Eighty-Four. Outside is pandemonium.

"I'm scared," he says.

"Don't be," I say, and the strain welds pained wrinkles in his face. "You're an uncle," I say.

I kiss him on the wet tip of his nose, step slowly down from the mattress that hovers now two three four feet in the air, and look up at Dad. He is turning the handle of the huge wheel that triggers the complex mechanism that lifts the hundred-stone man up inside such a small space, and he is smiling and he is alive and he is done, he is there to be cared for once more. I think of how well Mum will do it and how happy it will make her. All she ever wanted.

I leave as the bed rises slowly through the roof.

Taking Lou's hand, I leave through the front door. My legs stop hurting. I don't see Mal leave the house, and as we walk back to the car together the beeps of the machinery protract to one long one.

Eighty-Four

Me and Lou, we don't hear Mal's name so much anymore. It is there all the time but turned down quietly in the background, soft, like the trundle of the trains on the track behind your house.

I meet my son on the beach, where his granddad, Lou's dad, has him in his arms. I walk with him into the ocean. Neither of us has been into the sea before.

Acknowledgments

I am in scary amounts of debt to the priceless patience, advice and friendship of my agent Cathryn Summerhayes and my editors Francis Bickmore at Canongate and Paul Whitlatch at Scribner.

Thank you to Becky Thomas and Eugenie Furniss at WME, Jamie Byng and everyone at Canongate and everyone at Scribner.

Thank you to the clever people from To Hell With Publishing, Laurence Johns, Lucy Owen, Dean Ricketts and Emma Young, and their judges, India Knight, Greg Eden and Kwame Kwei-Armah.

Thank you to *Narrative* magazine for publishing an early piece from the book.

Thank you to my family, Mum, Dad, Alison, Glenn, Darren, Alex and the ones who can't read yet, William, Oliver, Thomas and Anna.

Thank you to all of my mates.

My Baby's Got an Atom Bomb

A New Story by David Whitehouse

1941

Just because Vern was the only plumber in Wendover, it didn't mean he had to spend all his time elbow deep in other people's shit. Quite the contrary. One day in mid-August he was sitting in his car outside Mary Beth Horton's house, drumming his fingers on the steering wheel.

That was the first time he ever saw a military vehicle. A dusty green truck was driving toward him east down Wendover Boulevard. As it approached, his windscreen began to rattle. Vern busied himself rolling a cigarette, avoiding eye contact with the two soldiers sitting in the front. Strands of tobacco danced on the paper as they passed. When the truck drove on, quiet descended on the street. There was no wind and the flags hung lank. Then a chubby hand rapped on his window and Vern jumped.

"Son, is my house flooded?" said Howard Horton. Mary Beth's father had square shoulders, and comb lines made his head look like a cube.

"No, sir. At least, I don't think so," said Vern.

"Is my toilet blocked?" Mr. Horton's breath made misty blooms on the glass.

"No, sir. Well, I mean, I haven't checked."

"Then why in God's name are you sitting outside my house?"

Vern worried that the old man's eyeballs would burst. He was sure Mr. Horton knew the answers to the questions he was asking. He must. All assholes who asked questions like that did.

Mary Beth watched the men from her bedroom window, willing Vern to drive away with her mind. At school his dogged pursuit of her had been charming, or at least never short of amusing. Since school had let out for the summer Vern's attempts to woo her had continued, but with no one around to observe them, it had become embarrassing, like a joke oft repeated but with no one new to hear it. Poor Vern would be in Wendover forever. Her fate would be different. The move to Salt Lake City was all planned out. She would go to teach the children of Mormons and miners how to add and subtract. All the bright sparks were headed the same place to burn. "The Crossroads of the West."

What was her father doing there still talking to Vern? What if Dean Marlo drove by? If he saw Vernon Lunt he might think he was there in a romantic capacity. Or, God forbid, he'd see her father kicking Vern through the flower beds. Mary Beth and Dean had only exchanged the briefest of pleasantries at the store, him in his uniform and new to the area, but she had blushed for the rest of the day. In a town of one hundred people, he was the only man worth a second glance. Handsome. Wild. Smile that opened up like an accordion. What terrible luck, that she should be looking to leave just as he arrived. There were a handful of other attractive girls from her school who were not going anywhere, and they would be sure to try to catch his eye while she was away. How could they resist him? His good looks. Him serving his country. Men like Vern the only competition. And though she hated to entertain it, she knew what soldiers were like. She could only hope that Dean Marlo was different. He certainly seemed it to her.

Mary Beth wished that the pipes in the bathroom would suddenly burst, and that a great wave of dirty water would come through the front door, cascade down the steps and wash both her father and her admirer away. She watched as Vern twisted the keys in the ignition and drove home.

Within a year Vern was seeing military vehicles every day and would stare down their drivers for kicks. Wendover, Utah, was a perfect location to build an air force base. Though the town was remote, the Western Pacific Railroad ran right through it, and the land around them was virtually uninhabited. They enjoyed excellent flying weather for most of the year.

Vern's mother, Bettina May, worried that the war would come to Wendover. Vern showed her where Britain, Germany and France were on a large wall map his father had left to him. Thirteen inches, she said, was "not far enough." Besides, it was the Japanese she was worried about. Who knew what they had invented for winning wars, what dastardly tricks they might pull.

"Mom," said Vern, "there ain't nothing worth bombing in Wendover."

"If those apes keep buildin' here there might well be soon enough. I swear by almighty God they're not just coming to Wendover for flying practice, y'know. You can go anywhere with the sky for that, and last I heard everywhere has the sky, at least in America."

For Vern the building of the air force base was exciting. More people in the town meant more houses. More houses meant more work. More work meant more money. Vern had been saving to buy a pickup truck of his own. The weight of the tools in the trunk of his car had ruined the rear suspension, and no woman was going to go home with him in a clapped-out old tin can like that. Especially Mary Beth Horton. He needed a vehicle that would impress her and her father. The truck would have his name on it, *Vernon Lunt Plumbing Services*. It couldn't fail.

One Friday afternoon in July Vern finished work a little early. He thought he'd be at Mrs. Burrell's house all day, but her blockage was a standard-size hair ball, nothing more. Finding it was a blessed relief. Her cat, Franklin, had been missing for a week. Vern half expected to find it in the pipe, its stinking carcass spongy with bloat. But Franklin was elsewhere. This was just a hair ball the shape of an egg, and Vern had seen bigger. Once, he'd pulled a hair ball the size of a boxing glove from underneath a bathtub in West Wendover, just over the border in Nevada. The women in West Wendover molted like dogs.

Vern drove into town. Even in the shade the day's heat stultified, kneading your pores open, squeezing your lungs. He pulled up beside Joe's Bar and undid his overalls to the waist—they made him look less skinny than he was—then forced his greasy mop of hair underneath his cap. A week's worth of stubble made him look like he hadn't slept since he'd last shaved.

Joe had known Vern since he was a boy. Vern's dad would drink in the bar most Saturdays and Vern would pass the time by rolling marbles around the floor and teasing the dog. Joe gave him lemonade that made his face pucker. Years later Vern would have his first taste of alcohol at Joe's—also homemade. He spent that night spraying purple vomit all over his mother's porch, retching until there was nothing left to pass but his stomach lining, which emerged as a twisted black string. Nothing in the bar could be described as decorative. Joe was famed locally for his cheap liquor, not his qualities as an aesthete. Seven plain stools lined the bar. When Vern walked in, four were taken. Joe had a beer lined up for him before he had even reached his seat.

"That one's taken," said a guy with busted teeth, a row of bombed houses. Vern hesitated. The rest of them laughed.

"Funny," said Vern. He sat down. He hadn't seen these men before. They were bigger than he was, and drunk, a combination that made him feel like a dog in the company of wolves—a feeling he had experienced with regularity since the war started. He quietly spun coins on the bar until they finished their drinks and left. Joe was wiping the counter with what looked like an old pair of underpants.

"Who're those pricks?" he said.

"Competition."

"Women ain't all about muscles, Joe. Look at you, you've been happily married since the Bible was written, and when you take your shirt off you look like a seahorse."

"Not talkin' about women."

"What you talking about, then?" Joe slung the underpants over his shoulder and made his way down the bar until they were facing each other. He had a wiry black moustache with the occasional red hair in it, a rusting awning over his lips. His vest was damp with sweat and booze.

"They're all plumbers."

"What?"

"It's true. They're plumbers up at the base. Training them up there for the army or something. Heard all about it, before they got so drunk they couldn't speak."

"Joe, you're a real asshole sometimes."

"Then don't believe me," said Joe. He spat onto a glass and began polishing it.

"You're kidding me?"

"Them soldiers gotta shit, too." Vern didn't like it when people talked about his trade in such course vernacular. Plumbing was a basic and substantial part of every modern economy. Nobody mocked the bowel surgeon. He too worked with poop. They both fought disease. They both fixed dirty things for the good of humanity. Toilets saved more lives than bowel surgeons. Vern was pretty sure that was a fact.

"Damn," said Vern. Joe plucked the cap off another bottle. Vern took a swig. The square outside was busier than he'd ever seen it. People were practically lined up to get into the general store. Two men lay shirtless on the grass. They had matching tattoos of a buxom woman holding a deck of cards on their forearms.

Suddenly Mary Beth Horton drifted into view. Rarely did a day pass that Vern didn't see something of her life. Her father yelling at the mechanic. Her mother buying fish. Today she was standing on the opposite side of the square with a silhouette Vern would happily have had inked on his skin. He watched her through the window, sipping on his beer, wishing that he didn't have a rotten wooden leg.

Mary Beth had spent the entire week preparing for this moment. The corset she'd chosen crushed her ribs. She hated that looking good had so much in common with being swallowed by a python, but the corset, under a white blouse and with a maroon skirt that ended just below the knee, best created the effect she was trying to achieve. Her father would have died if he'd seen her. Once, she had argued that had she actually gone to Salt Lake City, he would never have known what she wore each day. It had done nothing to placate him. That was why she had gotten ready in the public lavatory by the park this afternoon.

It had taken a long time and much effort to secure a date with Dean Marlo. Being constantly cast beneath her father's beady eye had not helped. Neither had the fact that like most of the soldiers, Dean chose to spend his precious downtime in the company of his squadron, drinking until they poured him into the transport home.

One Sunday night a few months earlier, in her bedroom and sick with an indefatigable longing, Mary Beth had decided to secretly write to him and make him realize she was "the one." She bought a new pen, expensive notepaper and some perfume to spray on it. It took seven attempts staggered over three nights, but the end result was magnificent. Each individual letter was exquisitely realized with a smooth flourish of ink so black it could have been squeezed straight from the squid onto the page. At no point did she make plain how attracted she was to him, but the greasy lipstick kiss with which she sealed the envelope made it perfectly clear. She had heard that this would drive a man crazy, and it worked. He replied in a letter adorned with a military postmark a week later. It read, simply, *Let's do something*. Mary Beth had hoped for more, but guys didn't like to write, so this would do. She hadn't slept properly since. All of her subsequent letters were crafted just as meticulously. One was the product of fourteen aborted attempts. That was her record.

Now she was nervous. Dean pulled up to their appointed meeting place in a gleaming red 1940 Mercedes-Benz 170v borrowed from a friendly corporal he had stood up for once back in Texas. He leaned over and popped open the door, leaving his upturned open hand on the seat, a dead crab, so that Mary Beth would sit on it. Both of them knew it was no accident. She pretended it hadn't shocked her, rode out the sense of violation—a passage made easier by her not having experienced it before. But this was as futile as ignoring her shadow. It still went with her. Dean, a little drunk, pulled out into the oncoming traffic and sped off toward the railroad.

Vern watched from his stool, so jealous he thought his piss might boil.

"Horton's girl?" said Joe, rubbing his underpants up and down the brass door handle like he was pumping water from a flooded hull.

"Yeah."

"Forget about her. No way you can have a pop that big an asshole and fall far enough from the tree. I mean, shit, she'd need a hurricane to carry her into the next field."

"Hurricanes happen." Vern had a few more beers, and in time got up to leave. Joe didn't charge for the drinks. Pockets didn't come any emptier and he knew it. Vern drove home with his head hanging out of the window like a dog, trying to sober up. The noise of his engine outside her bedroom window didn't wake his mother. Worrying about her son all evening had exhausted her.

Wendover's roads grew wider. A new baseball field was built. New houses sprung up as if they'd been planted and watered. A big one went up on the plot next door to Vern's. Men in uniform would come down to check on its progress every week.

"Those are some expensive-looking pipes they're putting in that place," Vern said one day to Bettina, who was making his breakfast while he watched from the window. This was the first time she could remember not having eggs in the morning. The store had sold out. Vern ate his toast with bacon. His mother took care of him and he was grateful, but he wished that he could show it more. When he'd finished eating he rolled up the left leg of his overalls and strapped on his prosthetic limb. It was made from hickory, which was harder and more shock resistant than most other wood. That was why they used it for baseball bats. He pulled the two leather straps at the top of it tightly around his knee, being careful not to twist his foot out of line, lined up the holes and threaded the silver buckle through. But for his limp, which few ever remarked upon, a passerby would not have been able to tell that one of Vern's legs wasn't made from flesh and bone. Once dressed he searched for his keys, which were, as always, on the hook his father had made for him on the wall by the front door.

Bettina watched him scrambling through the laundry basket and wished she could go back in time. Then she saw all those local boys sucked in by the black hole of the draft and wondered whether she would if she could. At least Vern was alive. At least Vern wasn't being tortured in a POW camp somewhere, a man screaming in a foreign language, pushing nails through his wrists, which is what Mrs. Herman had told her was happening when she had sat next to her at church. Ever since Bert's death, Mrs. Herman had been one of the few ladies who still talked to her about anything, so Bettina was inclined to listen.

On Vern's eighth birthday, he and his father had gone on a hike to Beaver Dam Wash. A few hours in, they rested by a barrel cactus, chasing away lizards with flame. Bert Lunt was an amateur cartographer and had instilled in his boy a love of the outdoors that wouldn't make it to adulthood. Bert broke some bread and watched Vern eat it. He saw equal parts of Bettina and himself in the boy's face. His brow, flat and broad. Her nose, the shape of a teardrop. They had made a single shared, unsullied footprint. A rustle in the yuccas drew his attention.

"Shhhhh," he said, bringing a finger to his lips. Vern stopped moving his jaw. The bread turned to a pulpy slug on his tongue. Two bighorn sheep stood motionless fifteen feet away, their horns as thick as fence posts, curling backward from their heads like on old drawings of Beelzebub. Bert opened his bag and took out his rifle. He wasn't given to hunting—the gun with which he'd one day take his own life was just for emergencies—but the day had been without trophy, and the majestic head of a desert bighorn would look fine on Vern's wall with the maps and the diagrams. "Don't move," he whispered, and rose up onto a knee. Both sheep lifted their heads proudly. Bert slowly pushed a bullet into the chamber, and, as quietly as he could, closed the barrel. It shut with a click much louder than he had expected.

"Daddy!" screamed Vern. The valley had curved the gun's sound, made it sourceless and infinite. Rattled, the sheep were bolting straight toward them, the frightening percussion of hooves beating the ground. Bert, panicked and flailing, squeezed the trigger. The bang scattered the sheep in different directions. The echo meant that every beast in Beaver Dam Wash had only a vague idea of where Bert Lunt was when he accidentally blasted off his young son's left foot.

1943

Vern loaded his tools into the trunk of the car. Expecting another bracing day—the first flushes of winter were proving cold—he put a bomber jacket on over his overalls and hit the road.

It was custom to let the soldiers' convoy pass, but Vern had sat at the junction by Wendover Fields for fifteen minutes the week before, penned in by a convoy that stretched back as far as he could see. Today he let a couple of jeeps cross, then dashed out in the space before a huge truck. On the back of it, bound in thick industrial rope, was a black steel tube. It could have been a silo, but it was twice as big as any Vern had ever seen. The driver, all dressed in green, let the cigar in his mouth slope toward Vern like an accusatory finger. "Fuck you," mouthed Vern. He knew those army boys were never going to stop. They were free of individual thought. Vern wouldn't have to piss just one off, he'd have to piss them all off. Joe had told him there were more than 17,500 military personnel at Wendover Air Force Base now. The truth was they were all too busy being pissed off at Japan to stop the parade and hand out a beating to Vern.

Rosie Summers was new to Wendover. Her house, just a few weeks old, had sprouted in a row of twenty-five others on the fields behind the school. For a short time she'd have a splendid view of the hills that made a hammock for the sunset, at least until plans to build a picture house in the way came to fruition.

"Come in," she said in a Southern drawl to which Vern's ears were unaccustomed. She had white-blond hair that hung in bulbous tumbles like a strange flower. The hallway behind her was full of boxes, furniture scant. Rosie had managed to hang a few pictures, trying to make a new house a home using memories of places far away. In one she was the winner of a child beauty pageant, in the next a bride. She looked unchanged. Her husband, himself only twenty-two, had married in full military regalia when Rosie was just seventeen. Vern perused the pictures while Rosie fetched him a glass of lemonade. He had to admit her husband looked very smart, and already had an impressive selection of medals on his chest for one so young, but if you looked into his eyes they were as blank as a cat's. He wondered what came first, the posture or the uniform. He guessed the latter, on the grounds that he had neither. He was soon on his knees, his head and arms inside the cupboard underneath the kitchen sink.

"That's the problem with a lot of these new houses," he said, his voice amplified by the confines of the space. "They're just sling-ing them up so fast. No attention paid to the details. Don't worry though, ma'am, I'll get it fixed." For the previous three days, Rosie had been forced to hose down dirty plates in the yard. On two occasions she had done this in her nightdress, to the delight of the builders finishing the veranda on the house beside hers.

"Thank you," she said. "I guess it's just an air bubble. Something like that. I certainly haven't been washing my hair in the kitchen sink." Vern laughed.

"So your husband is in the army, huh?" Externalized, the words assumed the vulgar qualities of an illicit proposition. Rosie Summers was a married lady. Vern winced. Rosie didn't notice. Men always asked her this question. She figured it was because of her legs, though her eyes were nice too, a blue that under bright lights glinted silver.

"Kinda."

"What do you mean, 'kinda'?" She ran a finger over her collarbone like she was making a wineglass sing.

"Well, he works at the base, but he's just a plumber." Vern banged his head on the sink's metal belly. The clang echoed around the kitchen. "Are you OK?" Rosie kneeled down next to him. Her skirt was short and the cold tiles against her knees gave her goose bumps up the back of her thighs to her buttocks. Vern twisted his neck, freed his head from the cupboard and faced her. Her lips were sticky and red. They looked delicious, a fresh, sumptuous apple.

"But he's in uniform in the wedding photograph," Vern said.

"They all have uniforms up there, it's the air force," Rosie said. "I know they train a lot of people in that stuff. The dirty work, he calls it. I'm sure if the day comes they'll swap his wrench for a rifle. I'd rather they didn't."

"Well, in that case, he could have fixed this for you. Anyway, all done. Just an air block, like you said."

"Oh, thank you. He told me to call somebody. I guess if you do it all day, it's the last thing you want to do when you get home to your wife. And they make him work all hours." Vern wished Rosie was his wife. He'd do his own home repairs no matter how bad a day he was having.

On the last Saturday night of 1943, Joe's was heaving with people. A second bar had opened up close to the train station, catering exclusively to men from the forces, and that was full, too. The windows on both bars wept with condensation. Vern had started working for Joe at weekends. It boosted his savings, edged him closer to that pickup, and helped Joe deal with the influx of drunken soldiers and civil engineers. His sales had more than quadrupled in six months. They could really drink, and they could really make a noise. Joe had warned Vern not to let them annoy him.

On this night, a particularly drunken man sat at the end of the bar. He was young and muscular, dressed in fatigues with a long black jacket. Vern watched his head sway, oblivious to the bustle of his colleagues around him. He nudged Joe. When they weren't fighting, the drunks were pretty funny.

"You OK there, buddy?" said Joe, tapping the guy's arm. He slowly lifted his head.

"What?" Vern recognized him instantly as the soldier he had seen with Mary Beth.

"You're falling asleep. Here," Joe opened another beer and put it in front of him. He was already on the ropes. The drink was Joe's uppercut. "So how's it going up there?"

"Where?"

"The base. I drove by a few weeks back. Looks like you guys have been busy. Used to be a couple of cattle sheds. Barely room for runways now." The guy took a slug of beer. The backwash formed a shifting brown web of bubbles in the glass and he perked up a little. "Oh, yeah. We got a whole town up there now. Swimming pool. Hospital. Bowling alley. Girls. You name it."

"Wow," said Joe. "And what you do there?" His friends shut up, as though someone had opened an airlock and sucked the sound from their mouths.

"Me," said the guy, "I'm a plumber." The space around him swilled with talk again. That's what Joe had thought he'd say.

"Yeah, like fuck you are," said Vern.

"What's that, asshole?"

"You heard me." Joe stood between the two men, his arms outstretched to divide them. Dean stepped down from his stool. Vern took a deep breath and began to walk to the other end of the bar.

"Must be tough, huh, asshole? Spending your time handing out beer to men like us, then hobbling home like a pirate." Vern stopped dead. Everyone in the room had turned their heads to him. "Wanna know what we're really doing up there, pirate? We're working to save your fuckin' lives, that's what." The bar fell quiet again. A large man stepped out from the crowd behind him and placed both hands on his shoulders.

"Come on, Marlo," he said, "time to go." Dean jerked free of the guy's hold before two men, somehow even bigger than the first, grabbed his arms and legs. The three of them carried him outside and slammed his floppy body against the door as it closed behind them, his shouting muffled by flesh.

Vern was glad to see him go. After taking a moment to compose himself he began serving two men smartly dressed in shirts and ties. He had no doubt that they were military too, though they were clearly of some higher echelon.

"A plumber. These dicks, thinking we're stupid. Whatever you guys are doing up there, it's sure to be bigger than something you shit in." The first man didn't react. The second raised an eyebrow.

"Don't be talking like that, friend," he said.

"Yeah, why not?"

"Hey," said the first man. He hadn't taken his sunglasses off all night. "Let's all shut up, huh?" The second guy concentrated on his bottle.

Vern took their cash and put it in the register. He figured that he would have enough for a new pickup truck by next autumn.

Dean Marlo smoothed down his jacket and fingered the tear that had opened on his trousers just below his left knee. On his second attempt he managed to clamber over the fence at the back of Joe's Bar and landed on his backside in a puddle that had begun to freeze over. The back door was unlocked. He opened it and found his way to the bathroom unnoticed.

He splashed some cold water on his face to soothe the swelling around his right eye. It was already turning purple. A cut half an inch across made the shape of a bloody smile in the mound. The man who punched him had been wearing a wedding ring. He flushed out the wound. It filled again instantly. Fumbling with the zip of his jeans, he held his breath. The bathroom in Joe's stank so strongly of piss he could feel it in his lungs. He walked back into the rear of the bar with his head down, stopping to complete a triangle of three men by the jukebox. It was a loud spot, and the man next to Dean had to shout to be heard. Hot spittle landed inside his ear.

"I thought I told you not to come back," he said. Dean tightened his grip on the neck of the bottle in his hand, smashed it against the jukebox and drove what remained into the man's face like a sword. The flesh on his cheek fell away. When the glass jarred on the man's jawbone, Dean dragged it left across his mouth, slicing half an inch from the end of his tongue. The man's friend punched Dean so hard in the back of the head that he wasn't sure if the blood he landed in was his own or not. Before falling unconscious, the last thing he felt was the full force of a kick to his chest, the metal toe cap breaking four of his ribs like they were breadsticks. Vern had to lie across him to prevent him from being torn to pieces, though he had never felt more reluctant to do anything.

1944

September was hot. "Good weather for moving house," said Bettina over the fence to the smart-looking woman unloading boxes from the trunk of a car. "Sure is," said the woman. Bettina was relieved. The local newspaper had reported that the barracks at the base were full to capacity. Surplus soldiers were being housed in Wendover. She didn't want to live next to a house full of young killing machines. Vern didn't get on with them. The worry and the noise would do nothing for her insomnia. Seeing this delightful young woman unpacking made her tired in a good way.

It took Bettina three days of looking out through the kitchen window to spot the lady again. She was in the front yard watering flowers. Bettina dashed outside with an apple pie she had baked to welcome them to the neighborhood.

"Thank you very much," said the woman. "I'm Lucy Tibbets. Nice to meet you." Two children sat behind her, playing on the lawn.

"How do you do," said Bettina. "It's nice to finally have some neighbors inside this big old place." As they spoke, a B-29 flew overhead, its shadow swallowing and then vomiting up entire plots as it descended for landing at the air base. The volume of the engines tightened Bettina's chest. She felt asthmatic for the first time in sixty years. The children began to cry. Lucy took them in her arms and shushed them.

"Don't be scared," she said. "That might be Daddy." Lucy smiled. They calmed down. "He's a pilot. Due back from New Mexico today."

"How marvelous," said Bettina, who immediately hoped she would never have to console Lucy on the news of her husband's death.

That morning Vern had pressed a crisp white shirt and put on a neat red tie—the first time he'd worn one since his mother had stopped forcing him to attend church on a Sunday. They had eaten breakfast together, the smell of the apple pie making him hungrier than usual. Bettina May was so proud of how smart he looked and how excited he was. Vern took a second serving of eggs over easy, strapped on his leg and left the house, waving to the lady watering the flowers next door.

Vern stopped off at the barbershop on Wendover Hill and got himself a respectable short back and sides, then he walked another mile and a half, a purpose in his stride easily mistaken for that of a man who had made up his mind to kill. He had paid for the pickup truck a fortnight previously, but had resisted the urge to flaunt it around town until the paint job he had specified was complete. Today was the day it became fully his. He wouldn't need to tell people he was the only real plumber in Wendover anymore. They would see his truck and they would know.

An hour later, Vern drove his new prize into town and sat in busy traffic on the north side of the square, a cigarette hanging out the window. It was a beautiful machine and could carry significant weight in the back. The cab was light and airy. Compared to his old car the dashboard was positively futuristic. He nudged the knot of his tie up and watched three young soldiers sitting on a bench, passing time as they waited for the shuttle bus that took them to and from the air base.

None of the soldiers noticed the woman pushing a stroller along the sidewalk toward them. If they had seen her, they certainly hadn't paid any heed. Vern was too busy admiring the cream leather upholstery on the seats that creaked when he moved his buttocks to spot her in his wing mirror. She wore an ankle-length navy blue dress that she liked because it hid her hips. Underneath it was a petticoat that made her legs sweat. Her mother's hat, with its wide floppy brim, saved her the time and effort it took to do her hair these days. Time she no longer had. Vern didn't recognize Mary Beth Horton until she crossed the road right in front of him. And she certainly didn't recognize Vernon Lunt, all dapper in his new wagon, until he pulled over to the sidewalk as she pushed her stroller past the new butcher's shop.

"Mary Beth," said Vern. He leaned over and popped open the door.

"Vernon Lunt? Is that you?"

"Yeah." He hesitated. "It's just a haircut."

"Certainly is."

"Are you going to your mom and pop's?"

"Home, yes," she said. She wasn't looking at Vern anymore.

He could tell she was admiring his truck, its attractive calligraphic livery. He had a hunch—one which he chose to promote to a belief—that the soldiers on the bench behind him were doing the same thing.

"May I offer you a lift?"

Mary Beth took the baby from the stroller and Vern lifted it into the back of the pickup truck. It was heavier than he had expected. He closed the doors and climbed back into the driver's side. Mary Beth held the child in her lap. He didn't need directions to her house, and that made Mary Beth smile.

"I heard where they sent Dean. I don't doubt that he deserves it, but that is some prison they chose. What is it like at Sugar House?" said Vern. He had been interested in Sugar House State Prison since he read about the execution of the murderer John Deering in 1938. Deering, a death row inmate there, volunteered to have himself hooked up to an electrocardiogram while he was shot by a firing squad so that scientists would learn what effect a shooting would have on a body. They found that his heart stopped beating after about fifteen seconds, but that his other bodily functions registered as active for a surprising amount of time after. Sometimes Vern felt like he was the breathing that continued after the death. The pointlessness of the thing left behind.

"Oh, I don't visit him," said Mary Beth.

"You don't need to sound so apologetic. It's not you in there." She kissed the baby's forehead. "Hey, at least that asshole got the hell out of Wendover." Mary Beth smiled. She loved the smell of new leather. She looked at Vern in his shirt and tie, clean-shaven with a cutthroat razor, and wondered if she would always associate it with him. "Do you mind if I stop at my house on the way?" he said. "I just need to collect my tools."

"Not at all. You must be pretty busy these days I guess, with all these new houses and all."

"There is that. It's important, y'know." A soldier transport drove past them in the opposite direction. "I'm trained to save lives. Not take them. But we all deal in shit." Mary Beth laughed.

Commanding Officer Paul Tibbets had been holding both of his children since he walked in. His wife, Lucy, was unpacking boxes by the fireplace as he stood in the window and watched the truck pull up outside the house next door, a smartly dressed young man and a pretty woman with a baby in the front. Lucy stood behind him.

"That must be her son," she said as they watched Vern get out and limp toward the house. "She mentioned he was picking up a new truck today. That must be it. He's another plumber. Can you believe it?" Sometimes he forgot that his wife, the one person he loved and trusted more than any other, had been fed the same cover stories as everyone else. But the Project demanded that level of secrecy. Hell, most of the engineers telling people that they were up on that air base training in sanitation didn't know what they were working on themselves. Anyone caught speaking out of turn was shipped out of Wendover immediately, some redeployed as far away as Alaska. No soldier wanted to end up in Alaska, and so he'd heard that they had taken to policing their peers themselves. If one guy shot his mouth off in a bar, not stopping him made another just as guilty. That was the unwritten rule on the base.

Tibbets had even introduced his friend Alan van Dyke to his wife as a "sanitation engineer." The man had a master's degree in physics and a doctorate in applied mathematics, was working under Oppenheimer and Szilard themselves. He had their phone numbers, and when he called they answered. With the exception of Tibbets, there weren't many people they did that for. On the rare opportunities the two men got to relax over a beer they would laugh at the thought of van Dyke handling one of Tibbet's wife's hair balls.

He read the pickup truck's livery aloud.

"'Bettina May Plumbing Services.'"

"Ha," said Lucy. "He must have named it after his mother. How sweet."

"Yes," agreed Paul, wondering how his own mother, Enola Gay Tibbets, would feel about such a dubious honor.